BREEZE

DAKOTA KYLE

"Windy, not everybody can get along. Believe me. I know. I long for a day when we can all live together in peace, where nobody betrays one another, especially for love. You don't need to sow suffering to others who have no concern over the matter. But you can make yourself better from it."

O

The Desert of Turmoil was an unforgiving place on the Quinta continent, the heat deadly to other Communities. If you carelessly ventured into the vast desert in raw daylight, you'd become nothing more than the lifeless sand that burned beneath your feet. But if you were to venture out during the night, the sand became nothing more than snow's cousin. The frigid air bit at your skin, threatening a frozen death.

But this wasn't the case for the Viper Community. The Vipers lived their lives unaffected by the desert's heat or cold. The Community was located to the southeast of Quinta, with the Peacekeepers and Splinters as its only neighboring Communities. The Vipers were always busy bustling around, attending to their responsibilities. Some Vipers collected water at the oasis that surrounded their Community, some worked at the trade facility organizing materials based on Community needs, and others simply lived their lives stealing.

To others' eyes, such activities would be heinous and unfit for a reputable Community. To the Vipers, this was a life they desired, feeling no shame or guilt for their crimes.

Meanwhile, there was unrest at the Viper trade facility between a Viper and an unusual visitor. Not only did the visitor appear unusual amongst the Viper population, but her survival from the journey to the Community was unusual. It was a feat to navigate the Desert of Turmoil alive, and this woman took on such a remarkable risk.

"Your Community is responsible for delivering resources within the Quinta continent, correct?" the woman snapped at a Viper in front of the trade facility. She had long brown hair streaked with red. If you looked closely, you could even see traces of gray hair, likely a result of aging. She wore a mix of red, white, black, and yellow.

The patterns and colors were woven beautifully, a personal taste. Skybirds gave their apparel in respect to their Community foliage. Her clothes were only one more thing to add to her person, who seemed out of place in the heat. It was unheard of to see anybody wearing sweatpants and a padded dress to a place where the temperature was your only enemy.

She is from the Skybird Community, a Community that lives in the mountains. Unlike the Vipers, they were unaffected by the frigid cold and thin oxygen from the mountain peaks.

"I told you, miss. We are very short-staffed," the Viper told the woman, unbothered. The Viper looked tired, giving his partial attention to the customer.

"Give me another excuse. You already used that one when I placed the order! I received the confirmation letter a week after I mailed it. Your organizers told me the same excuse, giving me an estimated delivery date of two weeks. It's been a month!"

The Viper knew not to argue with the woman. Her head was hard, but it wasn't worth the fight, especially in their conditions. The Viper turned around, looking over at the Peacekeeper resources lazily. "What did you order, miss?"

"Three bottles of honey. Large. Do not give me small." It was as if she knew what the Viper was intending to sneak out with her.

The Viper stepped over to the Peacekeeper resources, his hand reaching for the bottles of honey. The Peacekeeper resources consisted of materials that the Peacekeepers traded, including honey, wood, sap, animal hides, and many other resources native to the Peacekeepers. The Viper walked with a tired step; his energy drained. He searched through the stock, sorting the bottles into their categories.

When he found the honey, he made sure to collect three large bottles as the Skybird ordered. With the bottles in hand, he wrapped them up in a silk bag to hand over to the Skybird. When he returned to the dissatisfied Skybird, he couldn't completely extend his arm before the Skybird snatched the bag and turned around to leave without another word.

As the Skybird walked through the crowd, she refused to look at any Viper as if they were all walking grudges. Every Community looked down upon them, as their crimes were well known to others.

Stay smart, many were told regarding the Community, should they live to see it. If you weren't paying attention or acted foolishly, you would get your money scammed out of your pockets. Pick-pocketing was uncommon, but not rare. You would have to check your pockets every few minutes to ensure you still had your belongings. If you did notice something was lost, it was gone for good, as the Vipers could blend into the casual crowd in an instant. Their acting skills sharpened over the years, but that seemed unnecessary, given how few people ever came to their Community.

When the Skybird neared the exit, she noticed the Vipers avoiding a particular spot in the sand, even giving each other questioning looks as they heard the crying sound coming from the sand. She ran toward the sound, pushing through the crowd. She kneeled, brushing the sand from the unknown yet loud object. The Skybird gasped when she uncovered the buried mystery.

It was an infant. It didn't seem old at all. If she had to guess, it appeared to be at least two months old. It was a little girl, too.

Without a second thought, the Skybird took the infant out of the sand and carried her over to the covered oasis outside the Community grounds. The shade provided minimal protection from the heat, but it was better than being completely exposed to the sun. She sat down with the infant, carefully pouring water onto its hot body. The water wasn't cold, but it wasn't as hot as the blazing sun.

How long was she out here for?

It seemed like abuse to just leave a helpless child dying in the sand inside a Community that cared about nobody but themselves.

She held the infant close to her after it received a light application of water. If this infant had been found a moment later, then it surely would have died. The Skybird couldn't leave it here. She had to take it to a better home for its well-being.

The Skybird rummaged through her bag, pulling out a near-empty jar. It was what she carried for the water supply through the desert. She twisted the lid open and refilled the jar, ensuring it had fresh water for the returning journey to the Skybird Community.

SKYBIRD COMMUNITY

I

The Skybird Community is a mountain-dwelling Community to the north of the Quinta continent adorned in its natural colors seen as beautiful to everyone. Residents live amongst the Winged Beasts, large, winged, and hooved feline creatures with vibrant red feathers, black markings, and golden horns. Rarely did the domesticated native species see a setting outside their homes. The frigid temperature may seem deadly to outsiders, but it was home for the Skybirds.

The Skybird that carried the child in her arms strolled into the Skybird Village from the mountain trail with her head held high. The Skybirds, who were outside at the time, paused to stare at the unusual infant in the returning Skybird's arms. Her relentless steps stopped at no Skybird as they surrounded her with their gaze. The eyes of the staring Skybirds followed her every move, dumbfounded at the thing.

"That thing isn't supposed to be here."

A taller Skybird intercepted her, planting his armored feet in front of her as he stared down the child. "What's that you got with you, Rose?" He was a burly Skybird with blue-tipped hair. His armored aerial clothing choice and build let others know that he's one of the Skybird warriors.

She held the child closer, staring deep into his eyes. "Let me pass, Jay. It's nothing you should be concerned about. I'm taking her home with me."

"I can't let you walk through this Community with something you stole from the Viper Community. Or should I say someone you stole?" Jay tossed his head high, sizing up the smaller Skybird.

Skybirds began to gather with slow steps and looked out their windows, listening to every word in wonder.

"I didn't steal her. I found her in need. She was left to die in the sand. What else could I have done?" She pleaded against the monstrous Skybird.

"Look at her!" Jay motioned toward the child. "She is a Viper. She is made for the sand."

"There's something different about this one." Rose looked at the child, scrutinizing her. "If she were a Viper, why would she be overheated? Why would the Community ignore her?"

"Because those are the Vipers. It would be concerning if someone from the Peacekeepers were to neglect their daughter. But this Community is the complete opposite of the Peacekeepers. They only care for themselves."

Rose shuffled her feet, finding an opening beside Jay. "I am taking her in, whether the Community likes it or not. Nobody can dictate my actions. If I feel like helping someone in need, regardless of the Community, I will do so."

"That thing is an outsider. Who knows what it could do to our Community? We have been neutral and happily at peace for generations." Jay mirrored her steps, stubborn but testing.

The crowd shifted away from the unhealthy noise, their feet scrambling away from the tension as quickly as they could. To the Skybirds, disagreements were either resolved privately or never started in the first place.

"You have no idea what she could do in her life. She could make a change and be just what this Community needs, and we don't know it. Now, once again, please let me pass."

Jay shifted his weight to the side, and Rose took that as a sign he was done talking, so she could walk past him. She didn't mind the crowd that had gathered. It was none of their business, anyway. She held the child close to her and looked at no one, focusing on her walk home.

Ceramic pots in Rose's home were scattered along the shelves and on the floor—some empty, and some had plants growing in them. The planted pots contained flowers native to the Skybird Community, in colors white, baby blue, and even a milky yellow hue. She had few decorations, those only being large, red feathers draped along the walls like murals. These feathers were plucked from the wings of Winged Beasts. Such powerful recreational creatures were so large that they were often used as decorations within homes and shops.

On the floor was a large bed that seemed fit for a large pet of some kind. With the child placed in the bed, the bundle of innocence looked at the brightly colored feathers, their colors standing out against the rest of the cerulean-colored bed. Her hands began reaching for the colors, a curious mind developing so young.

Rose stood over the child, her face twisted in thought.

"How could anybody leave you to die?" she said to herself. "If you are going to be my daughter in my Community, I should call you as such."

Rose thoughtfully sat on the ground, inspecting the young girl. Her mind spiraled through Skybird names that could fit her: Cirrus, Arrokoth, Vivian, Cardinal, or Wikoni. Names that offered freedom, peace, and life.

As Rose stared at the child against the blue of the bed, an idea came to mind. She knew how to name this child correctly to fit with the Community. The blue contrasted with her skin in a way that truly showed a girl who would be free under the sky and run with the wind, free of care from judgment.

Windy.

My only hope for you is to be free like the wind.

2

Windy has never been outside since she was brought to the Skybird Community. During her five years of seclusion, Rose prioritized all care for Windy to help her develop the skills needed to thrive in such an environmental Community such as the Skybirds. She had certainly developed quickly, an unusual feat for someone of her age. She had also grown just as fast, nearing Rose's shorter height at the age of five.

But while Windy grew in seclusion, the Skybirds steadily spread concerns through their comments and conversations. Though she was "out of sight, out of mind," the Community's buzzing chatter was often carried with the wind, all words travelling like a delivery service.

"She couldn't be what we think she is. That Community died years and years ago. Don't you know we are a four-Community country?" said Storm, a short leather-armed Skybird carrying a lightweight paper bag. Her body relaxed against a shady pear tree, her toned arms wrapped around a paper bag.

"Then what is she? Please tell us all if you know everything," snapped a taller, more burly Skybird. Bobcat's unkempt hairstyle that grew down to his beard gave an impression he was maned to the naked eye.

"Behave yourself, Bobcat. I will not have you continue talking to women like that. Anyhow, I don't know everything. I am only assuming from the history that our Community stopped teaching children."

"But weren't you the top of your classes when it came to history?" he asked dangerously as his lips creeped up.

"Doesn't mean I know everything! I don't know why that thing is here. All I know is that we need to keep our eyes on her. Whatever she is, we need to be careful. Skybirds through and through, after all."

"Yes. Our Community must be protected. And our children. Let's go. Speaking of children, Oakley and Aspen need this almond milk. They have been begging for days, and I'm done with it."

"Kids. Yeah, let's go," Bobcat grumbled as he treaded gracefully, an unusual action for his size.

As Bobcat and Storm's footsteps trailed down the gravel path of the cold Community, Skybirds' eyes followed their footsteps, bodies shifting in their direction. But though the outside Community housed discord, the walls within Windy's home contained a contrasting energy.

"Mom! I'm good. I'm a good Windy! Can I please go explore the Community?" Windy begged Rose, her adoptive mother.

Within the worn, vintage walls of the house that contained the Community anomaly, a wave of excitement flooded the house, particularly for the one who sought freedom.

"I trust you, Windy. But I don't trust the Skybirds. It's dangerous out there, and I don't want anybody hurting you." Rose's head tilted down at Windy as she walked toward her. Unlike her firm, protective speech, a trembling hand gripped Windy's shoulder. Her fingers lightly brushed the fabric of her clothes as if it could promise safety and peace within the Community.

"Everyone will like me! I want to see other people and help them. Please let me go out! Please, please, please, I promise nothing will happen!" Windy's ears perked up, and her feathers spread out like a frill. For a child of the mountains, she had darker hair and a tan lean body that accented her white red-tipped feathers. One could safely refer her as a beautiful mutation.

But she was desperately excited to see the new world.

It was natural to be excited at such a young age. After Jay confronted Rose about bringing Windy into the Community, she received harsh comments from the other Skybirds, and their fear of outsiders in the Community lingered ever since that day. Skybirds have always been Skybirds. That's how they obtained their neutrality. Nobody could hurt them while they stayed out of Community conflicts.

Growing up, Windy was taught that she couldn't run into life right away. She needed time to develop so that she could be ready to face life. Although that would generally be the case, children of her age were encouraged to explore life by playing with other children and developing their curiosity about the world around them. But these children of her age all came from the same Community and looked alike. There wasn't a trace of difference between such people, so there wasn't much room to criticize one another or fear danger.

To Rose, Windy was being protected from the comments the Skybirds would make about her. There was too much room for such unnecessary criticism. The way her dark skin contrasted with the other lighter-colored Skybirds. The way her feathers grew on her body was unlike normal body hair. Even the way her brows were naturally furrowed gave her an unhappy impression. Never have the Skybirds seen such a sight. A beauty left unseen by an anxious Community.

The comments never ceased throughout her life, even when she wasn't to be seen in the Community. There was always a comment made here and there. But if Windy could grow without such criticism, she would be safer from the Community. At least, that's what Rose believed.

"It's dangerous out there, Windy. Skybirds aren't the nicest to others who aren't of their descent."

"Descent?"

"Skybirds aren't the nicest to people who don't look like them, I mean." Rose's fingers trailed up to the feathers sprouting from her bushy dark hair.

"But I am a Skybird! Look at me, I have this pretty dress like all the other girls!" She puffed her chest, her confidence radiating through the traditional Skybird dress the women wear. Their clothing choices reflected their bright, cold surroundings. Padded but beautiful.

"They don't care about the clothes they wear. They think you're someone else. That's not true, but it's because of how you look."

Windy's pointed ears drooped, her feathers fanning into her hair. "That's mean! Why are they so mean? Maybe I can show them they are bad! They are bad to be mean to other people."

"Windy. Please promise me something." Rose adjusted Windy's feathers. "Do not believe anything other people say if it hurts you. Only believe the things they say if it makes you feel happy."

"Okay! So, can I go out now? Please, please, please?!" Windy shook her caretaker. Even though she was five years old, she was as strong as a young teenager.

Rose turned her shaky head towards the door, where children freely roamed the Community. Children of Windy's age who knew little of their world so far. "Yes, Windy. You're little, after all. Please come back home when the sun starts to go down." She placed a gentle hand on her shoulder.

"Okay! Bye!" Windy spun around, happily running to the door. She swung the door open, stepping into the life she had been sheltered from for so long.

Windy gasped. The Community seemed so bright to her. The various colors of the Community bled from every direction—from plants, buildings, people, and the Winged Beasts walking alongside their owners. Windy journeyed through the Community, unsure of where to start first. What was there to do here for someone like her? There seemed to be so many things to do and places to go. While her presence was screaming at the Skybirds, they would acknowledge the tall bundle of immaturity, taking no care to put their day on hold.

Why was she behaving like that?

How old is she?

Where is Rose?

Windy was avoided like a plague. Whenever Windy smiled at others, they would look away. Whenever she waved, they would pretend they didn't see her. When she was out of earshot, they would gossip about her appearance, behavior, and her potential worth in the Community. After all, how could that thing possibly do good in this Community?

Skybirds gathered in huddled groups, partnerships, or even by themselves, the mountainous people's days unbothered by conflict. Each of their brown, golden, or blue eyes trailed down to the large child stomping through the otherwise silent Community. Particularly, their criticizing eyes were focused on the particular direction the bundle of overwhelming joy bounded to.

Poor Skybird.

As Windy continued exploring the newer Community in her life, a sympathetic sight crossed her path. A girl had her legs crossed, her face in her hands. Her short tan hair covered her neck like a mane as she hunched over. There was a small Winged Beast kit bundled beside her. Concerned, Windy walked up to the girl, kneeling before her.

"Hello! Are you okay?"

The crying girl looked up at her. She covered her face as if she were blinded by the sun. "What are you? Don't look at me. You look weird."

"I am a Skybird, just like you. Why are you crying? Are you okay?"

"Yeah. I'm okay." The girl made a snotty sniffle. The blonde child with copper eyes appeared just barely older than Windy.

"You don't sound okay. If you were okay, you wouldn't be crying. Why are you sad?"

The young Skybird hesitantly lifted her head to meet Windy's eyes. She slowly wiped her sadness on her pants, her shoulders appearing heavy. It took her a moment to speak, the duration of her sobs trapping her ability to speak. "My Winged Beast got hurt."

Windy looked at the kit, now understanding why it was bundled up like a loaf of bread. "Where did it get hurt?"

"The leg."

Windy carefully held her hand out to the kit. It was as if the girl's sadness was a virus, because Windy had definitely caught it. "Can I see it?"

"I'm telling mommy and daddy if you hurt it!"

Windy stayed quiet as she gently picked up the kit, the creature squeaking in pain.

"Shhh, it's okay. I'm here to help." Windy gently stroked the kit's head, its eyes closing in comfort.

Windy looked at its left front foreleg. As she had said, her leg was indeed hurt. It didn't look firm like the other legs. It hung down her hand like it were dead. It must be broken. Windy stared at the leg, wondering what she could do to help it. It had to heal somehow. She needed to put it in a state that would allow it to heal efficiently.

Her mind reeled with solutions, the thoughts making her head sore. If Windy hurt her leg, she wouldn't want to walk on it. There must be some kind of binding to keep it firm and free from pain, like the rest of the legs.

She spontaneously took two feathers off her shoulder, squeaking. The feathers left two large holes in their place where the quills had been set in her body.

While holding the Winged Beast's limp leg, she began to create a makeshift splint, her eyes rarely blinking. Her hands moved effortlessly around the broken leg, Windy's process entrusted by the fragile nature of the creature.

For someone of Windy's age, this process would have been impossible. The little girl stared with sparkling eyes as Windy gently put the Winged Beast down, the small creature limping over to its owner. The gracious Skybird gently cradled her pet to her chest, the hug equivalent to a mother returning to her child after years of disappearance.

"What's your name? How many years old are you?" She looked at Windy, her eyes shining with gratitude toward the stranger. "I am Oakley."

"My name is Windy! I'm five!"

3

Rose held Windy's hand as they walked through the gossip, their steps focused on the cold, rocky road. Earlier in the day, Rose found they were running low on food at home, which was not a surprise. Windy had been eating according to her growing size, resulting in Rose's frequent trips to buy food. She often stocked a variety of prepared meals, desserts, and small snacks, many of which Windy could enjoy at her age.

Windy's attitude was never short of active whenever she ventured outside to explore her newer surroundings, especially with her mom. The bright outside world was far more exciting than being trapped indoors in the dark. But this time, Rose decided to invite her along on her afternoon errands.

During their focused walk, Windy's eyes raced around everything, asking Rose questions a secluded child like her would ask: "Why are the birds so loud?"

"Why is it so hard to breathe sometimes?"

But especially: "Why do people always look at me?"

Wherever Windy stepped, Skybirds looked at her as if she were a walking artifact never meant to be discovered. Through their disapproving nature, Rose paid no attention to what others were doing to Windy. She knew they had to teach themselves to allow another kind of human into the Community, regardless of appearance.

If they had no leader to govern them, they needed to do it themselves. But even within a Community full of exclusion, she only smiled and waved at everyone, displaying the nature that Skybirds failed to understand.

In the shop, Windy's eyes shot in every direction in the new environment, her head twisting and turning like a snake. Various goods were stacked on shelves, racks, and even in buckets filled with snow to keep certain foods cold.

"Mom, do we just take whatever we want?" Windy gasped.

"No, Windy. That is called stealing."

"Stealing?"

"Yes. We don't take things that aren't ours." Rose looked at her. "You can look, but don't take anything without telling me."

"Okay!"

Windy walked around the shop, looking at the various foods, Winged Beast tack, house decor, and many other things the Skybirds traded and hand-created. Many were things Windy wanted, even if she didn't quite know the purpose of them. Her hand was drawn to each item on display, taking in their appearance and guessing what their use might be.

While looking at one of the Winged Beast beak bits in the section for such large animals, an elderly Skybird, Fern, who was carrying purchased goods like food and toys, was shuffling past some people. Every step resulted in an *Excuse me*, but most only glanced towards her before going on their way. They continued to search for what they needed to buy, thinking of her as nothing more than a public nuisance. While Fern was trying to get through the crowds, her bags fell from her arms, her legs collapsing over the mess on the floor.

While she gained attention from the Skybirds, none rushed to help. Instead, the Skybirds around her groaned, her accident a disruption to their shopping visit.

"She's 83. She'll be gone soon."

But aside from the Community's rudeness, Windy approached the Skybird, her hands instinctually reaching for the goods sprawled across the floor. "Are you okay?"

"Yes, I am. Thank you, young lady," said Fern as her stiff arms aided Windy.

"Can I help you go back home? I promise I won't take anything." Windy smiled at the Skybird, her working hands pausing at the fallen goods.

"Oh, that would be lovely, young lady." Fern returned the smile.

"Let me ask my mom if I can go!"

Windy spun around as she searched for Rose, peering over shorter Skybirds and racks. As Windy loudly searched, shoppers cringed from all directions, muttering under their breaths at the adult-looking child. Through the weaving and shouting, Windy found Rose inspecting various prepared meals on shelves, her head moving back and forth through the variety.

"Mom! Mom! There's an old person who needs help. Can I go help her?"

Rose looked at her, her eyes just as furrowed as Windy's. Many things could go wrong, if the Community resented Windy for so long. But if Windy could continue to prove herself, an elderly lady surely couldn't be of harm. "Yes." Rose hesitated. "Please stay safe."

"I will be!" Windy weaved through different sections of the shop once again. Only this time, it was less noisy.

By the time Windy returned, Fern had her goods placed on a table by the entrance of the store, patiently resting on a chair. Her brows were creased on her wrinkled face, her mind heavy. She didn't look up from staring at the floor until Windy returned, indicating her presence with her lively voice.

"Hello again, dear. I assume your mother let you help?" Fern asked with a newfound smile on her face.

"She sure did!" She puffed her chest out, her feathers frayed in confidence.

"You may follow me. My house is down the road." The two began to carry what their individual strength could withstand. For someone of Windy's age, she was strong. She had the strength of a teenager.

"You're strong, little Skybird." Fern's frail gaze glanced up at the tall child.

"I am? I think I am."

"How old are you?"

"Five."

"Ah, that is indeed incredible. Incredible. I have heard of a people with your power. But I do not know if they continue to live. I have not known about our outside Communities for years and years."

"What were they called? I want to know about people who aren't like us!"

"I do not remember, little child. However, I do know of the Communities that walk our land."

"Who are they?"

"Ah, well. Seems like you have little knowledge of our world. Let me help. As I can remember, there are four Communities that walk this land. There was once five, but I cannot remember the name. My memory ages as I do. Our current Communities are the Skybirds, Splinters, Peacekeepers, and Vipers.

"The Splinters are far from us. Unlike us mountain people, they are mages that live in forests, which they call the Tree Kingdom. But beware. They have been known to be horrible. A horrible Community. Imagine a splinter on your finger. Once it bites you, it's hard to get out. When they fool you with their lies, it's hard to run away from.

"But luckily, there is a much kinder Community. The Peacekeepers are also forest dwellers, but far unlike the Splinters. They are one with life instead of altering nature. People look unusual, such as yourself, but that is what they value. Like our Community, they prefer neutrality but solve conflicts through words and not blood.

"And finally, the poor Viper Community. Oh, what an unfortunate Community they are. You have probably seen them around, with their silk-white robes and tanned skin, such as yours. They are the delivery service of our Community. They operate a trade facility where we all send orders and offer goods. But oh, they have been torn up by their former allies: the Splinters. Know who you trust, little one."

"That's bad! They're just as bad as how people see me." Windy's shoulders slumped as she carried the groceries, her ears steadily drooping along the side of her head.

"No need to worry. I can assure you our Community is far greater than the Splinters. Patience. That's all you need."

As they focused on the Skybird trail, they looked no different, except for age and height. They walked in silence for no more than a few minutes until Windy started talking. "That makes me think. Why are people here so mean?"

"They don't mean to act that way. They see you as someone different, and they are unsure whether to trust you. That is what happens when trust isn't fully given to someone. I have certainly heard the rumors."

"But I have helped people."

"You have the heart to do it. But nobody here leads us, so nobody can say for us all if you're safe or not, so we all go off on our feelings."

"Why does someone need to say it?"

"Because when nobody leads a group of people, it's a hard world. To live, you need trust and authority from those around you. If not, you might end up being left out or not living."

"So, I need to show everyone that they can trust me?" Windy's eyes sparkled with ideas.

"Yes, indeed."

As she stepped over stones and adjusted the Skybird's bags, her mind swirled with ideas, those that pushed her to become determined to change her life within the stagnant Community. She had to prove herself. If the Community saw her as a threat, she needed to show them she wasn't a threat. Windy already dedicated herself to service, but to the Community, it wasn't enough.

At the elderly Skybird's home, the Community's utilitarian atmosphere disappeared from the first step taken on the worn-in placemat. The Skybird guided her toward the back of her home, where a small kitchen was located. Sitting on a small round table in the corner was Osprey, a young girl with a single streak of white down her flat hair. She noticed the stranger as she unpacked the food from her grandmother's bags.

"Who is that? Why did you bring a weird thing here?"

Fern's eyes poked toward the child, disapproving of such behavior. "Remember. We don't judge other people."

"But she looks weird!"

"This kind young lady offered to help with my groceries. I am thankful someone offered to help if you didn't want to come with me, and you should be thankful too."

Windy glanced over at the girl, who was now slumped in her chair.

"Who is that?" asked Windy.

"That is my lovely granddaughter, Osprey. Please excuse her. She needs to learn how to treat others."

Windy's brown eyes sat on Osprey for a moment longer before returning to her gracious work. The room fell silent, an awkward air within the kitchen. Once groceries were placed, only various toys remained, including stuffed animals and small wooden games. Fern shuffled for a stuffed goat from the bag, turning to Windy with a smile.

"Here. Because you were so kind, I would like to give this to you."

Windy looked at the goat, her eyes wide with fascination. "Do I need to pay for it?"

"Pay for it? Not at all, young lady. I am giving this to you. It is yours now."

Windy relished the goat, smiling brighter than the snow. It's soft, plush imitation mimicked that of such a creature. "Thank you so much, miss!"

"Hey! That's supposed to be mine!" Osprey demanded sourly, standing up from her chair.

"A kind person such as she should be rewarded. Please, don't be rude," Fern said without looking at Osprey.

"Thank you! Goodbye!" Windy waved as she left the vintage home, holding the stuffed goat close to her chest. The cold felt warm with the sense of belonging she received, even if it was little. Though the Skybirds endlessly stared at her, Windy found herself ignoring all the eyes that were attracted to her. It wasn't hard to be good to other people, so why did others find it so hard to treat Windy the same?

In the Community, it was no longer unusual to see a tall five-year-old jogging around, learning about her outside surroundings. She would walk up to Skybirds, asking them questions like, "What's that?" or "Why are you doing that?" or, especially, "Can I help?" unlike what the Community assumed about her. An innocent child like her wasn't capable of being a threat to the Community, especially one with kind morals. But to the Skybirds, such a fact was unbelievable.

Windy rested on an armchair near a window, gazing out at the lively Community. The Skybirds interacted with bright smiles, their sense of comfort apparent to those who looked like them.

But Windy was like them, at least, to her morals.

"Mom, why does everyone love other people but me?" Windy asked, her eyes never leaving the scene in front of her.

"I'm sure they do appreciate you, Windy. They just don't know what to say to someone who looks like you." Rose explained, her voice projecting across the room. She was cleaning the dusty red feathers along the wall.

Windy's ears drooped, her weight following as she turned around. "So, they don't like me?"

"No, Windy. That's not what that means at all. They haven't ever seen someone like you, so naturally, they don't know what to think. If someone asked you something confusing, would you understand it?"

"No. But does that make me confusing?"

"To other people. But once they get to know you, you won't be so confusing."

Windy sprang from the armchair, running up to her mother with determined strides. "So, they need to know me? And learn about me?"

Rose turned around, looking at Windy. "Knowing a person takes time. You can't walk up to someone and expect them to instantly like you. But you're still young. You have more than enough time to show everyone who you are."

"But why am I not supposed to go outside all the time? All the other kids do it." Windy crossed her arms, her patience running thin towards her mother.

"Because of what I told you. People don't know you completely, so they can't trust your actions. I don't want anybody hurting you while I can't do anything to help."

"But I want people to know me!"

Rose turned back around, her hands returning to the dusty feathers on the wall. "And they will. You just need to be patient."

Windy stepped back, her face darkening to frustration. She heaved her disappointment into her room, her steps growing heavier as she neared the comfort of her bed.

Her body fell onto the bed, the softness of the mattress making the weight of her feelings feel lighter. The silence of the room gave way to thoughts. Thoughts that Windy couldn't help but think about.

Why couldn't she be like the other kids and play freely? They didn't seem to discriminate against one another, even though they all looked just as different as her. How could she ever prove herself if other people couldn't see what she's like?

What could she do?

As her eyes began to get heavy with emotional exhaustion, her ears perked up. The house seemed too silent. She knew her mom was cleaning, but her thoughts cleared, giving way to more silence.

Windy slowly walked out of her room, looking around at the interior of the house. She couldn't track where her mother was. It appeared to be only Windy in the cozy Skybird home.

Her body itched for freedom, something that could get her what she wanted. Her eyes looked at the scene behind her, but her feet padded toward the door just ahead of her. Her hand reached for the doorknob, her body shivering in fear. First her hands, then her arms, then her whole body.

Her hand turned the doorknob, her senses on high alert for Rose. When the door opened without a sound, Windy slipped out like a mouse, closing the door just as quietly.

Outside, she could feel the very thing she desired nip her body in welcome.

The winds of freedom.

Windy sat with her legs sprawled in front of her under a tree that cold afternoon, eating a goat leg wrapped in a large maple leaf. Such was the diet of the Skybird Community. They were omnivorous, after all. They hunted prey animals in their region, such as goats and crows, and cooked their meat until it was rare. The Skybirds needed the iron in the meat to sustain themselves in low-oxygen environments. Whenever they weren't hunting, they were scavenging for plants and herbs found in shrubs or trees that were suitable for consumption and even healing.

While Windy was savoring the lunch she provided for herself, a young familiar Skybird sat next to her.

"Hello, Windy! I want to say thank you for helping my friend."

It was Oakley, the Skybird child that owned the Winged Beast that Windy saved. The growing red creature in the girl's arms no longer had its splint, and it fought stubbornly to wiggle out of its owner's grip, wanting to see the strange girl who had helped it.

Windy smiled, patting the eager kit's head. "I don't know what I did."

"You helped my friend!"

"But I don't know how."

"You should know how. My mommy and daddy have been talking about it."

"What did they say?"

"They don't believe you. They think kids shouldn't know what you do."

Windy's eyes shifted focus from the kit to her feet; her head hung low. "I don't know a lot about me, too. I feel like something told me to do it, but it wasn't a person telling me. I don't know how my body could tell me. That seems funny."

Oakley noticed her mental conflict. "Do you have one of these?" the girl asked, the radiating smile diverting Windy's attention away from her dysphoria.

"No, but my mom has one."

Windy exclaimed as the Winged Beast kit found freedom in Windy's lap, purring and chirping as he tried to climb up her body.

"What's his name?" Windy asked as she grabbed the kit.

"Ruby."

"Ruby," Windy repeated, trying out the name with her own mouth. "What's yours?"

"Oakley."

"Hello, Ruby and Oakley," Windy said as she gently hugged Ruby. The more Windy bonded with the growing Winged Beast kit, the more she found peace with the Community that cast her out of their minds. The kit was soft, like the petals of the Community's native flowers. His golden horns had the sheen of the silk flags posted around the Community. His feathers, if looked at a specific angle, glowed with the snow, as if the sun and anything pure were the same. This Winged Beast was precious to her; precious to the Community.

"I love Winged Beasts," Windy remarked after bonding with Ruby, a revelation only discovered after interacting with the real creature. Goats, rabbits, wolves, and deer were present throughout the Community territory, but nothing like the domestic Winged

Beasts.

"I love them too!" Oakley reached over to pet his head. But as the girls were playing with the creature, a taller Skybird approached them, his footsteps like thunder on the grass.

Windy turned towards the adult, leaning back as his form sent waves of discomfort throughout Windy

"Oakley. I have been calling your name for ages. Why did you run off?" Aspen, Oakley's brother, bent over as he glared into Oakley's eyes.

"I was thanking my friend for helping Ruby." Oakley's body shrank into her arms. "I'm sorry, Aspen."

"Mom wants us home. She's preparing dinner. You know her."

"Okay." Oakley slumped. "Can I have Ruby back, Windy?"

While Windy was handing the squirming bundle of feathers over to his owner, a gasp escaped Aspen. "Windy? You're that thing! Why are you with my sister?"

"She's my friend." Windy frowned, the aggression hitting her like a clean blow to the gut.

"No sister of mine will talk with some anomaly. "

"I'm not whatever that word means. I am one of you. I helped your sister." Windy grabbed Ruby, holding the squirming bundle up to him.

Aspen snatched the kit from her hands, the innocent creature squeaking frantically. "You had no business helping her. Freaks like you should mind your own business and find people your own size. Smaller than us."

"Hey! Be careful with Ruby, he's getting better." Oakley

desperately reached for her Winged Beast, only to be snatched by her brother.

"Let's go, Oakley." Aspen's hand locked on her arm, pulling her up to her feet and dragging her away. Oakley knew not to say a word when it came to her big brother. It was apparent from the way she looked at the ground, never looking up to see where she was going.

Windy was left alone once again, watching her new friend shrink into the distance. While she sat in isolated silence, she focused on her Community. The herds of brown and red painting the cerulean sky, the groups of Skybird warriors laughing as they hop from shop to shop, the various individuals bustling around the village, and then finally to herself. What was so wrong with her? Someone saw her for her talent of Winged Beast care, so why couldn't others see her as such?

But then Windy glanced at the Skybird warriors again. Something about them was special. They looked barbarous. So did she. Why did they get acceptance but not her? Was it the way they were equipped to be naturally awesome? Did they hold a certain pride Windy couldn't grasp? Or was it the fact that they could do things no regular Skybird citizen could do? Whatever the case, Windy needed to be more than them, if not like them. If she could show people she is more than them, she could get more attention. The good kind.

Yes, that's a great idea!

That night at dinner, Windy and Rose relaxed on wooden chairs by the fireplace as they ate morsels of prime meat and oats.

"Mom, what do those tough-looking Skybirds do?"

Rose glanced at Windy, gently placing her carved plate on her lap.

"Do you mean the Skybird warriors? They protect our Community in case anything bad happens to us."

"Will anything bad happen?"

"No, Windy. Our Community is the safest. But there's a saying: better safe than sorry."

"But Mom, why are they so special? Why do people like them?"

"Well, often they're admired for how strong they are and how they can bond with Winged Beasts. They're good at fighting and flying. Do you want to be one?" Her last words faltered, her speech weakened.

"I want to be more than one!" Windy said, quickly biting into a piece of meat and hungrily eating her oats. "I want to do something no cool Skybird can do."

"Windy. Those are very good goals to have, but you're too young. You could hurt yourself while doing it."

"No, I won't. I will be safe. I pinky promise!" Windy reached her hand out, the innocence radiating off every fiber of her being.

Rose sighed. Wrinkles of doubt covered her face as she looked at Windy. She hesitated, making no move to the child's remark. "Windy. Understand that if you get yourself hurt, I won't be happy. I know you want to make it through here, but maybe I should go with you this time. The Skybirds don't seem to understand who you are."

Windy pushed her hand closer to Rose, ignoring her warnings. "Pinky promise."

Rose latched her finger onto Windy's, heaving a sigh that seemed to have been held in for eternity. "Remember what I said. That's my pinky promise too."

Windy eagerly navigated her day, her dedicated strides pushing her forward with each step. She began to wander. Wandering farther and farther away from the village. Wandering into places she had never encountered. The mountain trail was adorned with blue and white flags, each featuring the Skybird emblem or white streaks. As the flags waved in the wind, their silk shone like a gem, no different from what the Community presents to its people.

Windy struggled to breathe the farther up she went, her young chest tightening with each step. The wind became stronger, and the temperature dropped, all oxygen following the disappearing comfort. But Windy's determination allowed nothing to stop her on her journey.

Adrenaline was her best friend.

The snowier the peak became, the harder it was to navigate. What was this place? Why did it differ so much from the Skybird Community? As Windy marveled at the metallic foam, her feathers ruffled. Almost instinctively, Windy scanned the area, her eyes focusing on every inch of the area, even through the falling snow.

It seemed as if divine intervention was involved when a flying butterfly landed on a white heap, quickly flying off when the heap moved. Windy had just enough time to grab one of the flags up ahead, using all the adrenaline provided for her to break the thin wooden pole off its post and drag it on the ground. Whatever was up there was a threat.

Windy stayed put, refraining from whimpering out of fear. Though every cell in her body screamed to run, she stayed put, her muscles preparing her to fight.

But how does she fight?

She's only five years old.

What does she do?

Her hands shook through the colder temperatures as she carefully lifted her makeshift flag. Her chilled ears were pinned flat against her head, teeth chattering.

The white mound began charging after her, revealing itself to be a snow wolf. The mangy beast growled with each stride it took, its hunger the main threat. As if it were a torch, Windy began waving the flag, shouting her fear at the animal. The wolf looked at the vivid silk, growling. It saw both of these moving things as prey, and it needed to pick one.

Windy slowly stepped back, continuing to shout at the beat and waving her flag as violently as she could. As the wolf stalked closer, each step of its paws demanded death. Demanding red upon the white.

Windy shouted again, this time swinging the flag in front of her, hitting the beast's muzzle. The splinters from the worn wood bit at the beast's nose, stunning it. The wolf only lunged; the next thing Windy saw were its teeth and claws. While the wolf made its killing attempt, Windy ducked down, her twisted body positioning the broken end of the flag toward its throat, as if it knew what to do.

The wolf strained a yelp as the flag's sharp wooden splints dug into its fur, its body missing Windy's now disfigured, scrambling-for-life flesh. Though its teeth missed her in the stabbing collision, its claws made contact with her shoulder—the closest it could get to survival, and the closest Windy could get to death.

Windy continued her barbaric movements, fear providing any sense of safety.

But neither threat would give up.

Windy shielded her young form with her weakened flag, but its teeth and claws snapped at her face and scratched at her arms. Flames of pain radiated throughout her arm, her mouth throwing itself wide with painful shrills. The wolf was bigger than her, stronger than her. Windy was no match. But while the wolf snapped at its prey, a gust of wind blew against the hunters, and against the flag's silk, especially. The silk found itself in the wolf's snapping jaws, the beast stepping back as it got twisted in the fabric.

Windy allowed the wind to propel her toward the distracted beast, the silk flying free from the wooden rod. Windy gained the speed to thrust the wood into the wolf's upper body.

Again.

Again.

And again.

Until the wood tore through the wolf's mangy pelt and sank into the flesh.

The wolf yelped as it ripped the fabric out of its mouth. Its bloody body snapped toward Windy, its teeth demanding victory. Her eyes fell on the color that contrasted the beast's white pelt, a color unlike what she had seen in the Community.

Her stomach churned uncomfortably as her throat became queasy. Windy's eyes closed hard enough to see only darkness.

Her muscles tore the wooden pole out of its body and thrust it into its neck, the wolf weakly yelping as Windy flailed the wooden pole around as it dug deeper inside its flesh. Blood coated them both. What was prey became the hunter, an equal fight.

As the wolf began to weaken, Windy ripped the wooden pole out of its throat once again, raising the wood to slam its face, the impact causing the wolf's head to be tossed to the side like a sock.

A snap tore through the snowy battlefield.

It wasn't just the pole that broke.

Windy stood over the wolf's body, catching all the breath she had lost. She gripped her left arm as the fabric of her dress was torn away, replaced by a dark red. As Windy's adrenaline wore off, she regained consciousness of the world around her.

The wolf had fallen limp.

Did I kill the poor thing!?

Windy gasped, putting her safe hand over her mouth. How could she have committed such a vile act? Windy took no care of the fact that she had saved her own life.

What did I do? Did I really need to do this?

Windy stood over the limp beast, body ignoring the frigid snow sprinkling across her body. A killer.

She was now a killer.

"No. Please, no. I'm sorry!" Windy weakly stepped back, her feet softly padding on the snow.

As she stood distanced with weak legs, a crow flew overhead.

The Skybirds ate crows. The Skybirds killed innocent crows to save their own lives by providing themselves with food.

Windy watched the crow fly overhead, cooing as if it were praising her for her kill.

If Skybirds killed innocent animals to provide for their Community, Windy will provide for her Community as well.

Windy took the wolf with her good arm, dragging it along the snow. Her injured arm draped lazily along the side of her body, its mobility hindered by the growing pain. The struggle that had suddenly overwhelmed her was nothing like what she had done. What was a struggle when there was strength and determination?

Windy was determined to show the Community what she had done.

5

S he was the talk of the town. Not like before. Her looks weren't the only thing to talk about amongst Skybirds. Her unknown origins were no longer the focus. What people needed to know was how.

How could someone her age kill such a deadly threat?

Who is she?

"Mom, I'm home." Windy had said as she didn't have her usual excitement coming home, which was strongly noticeable by Rose.

"Windy! What happened to you? What is that? It's making a mess all over!" Rose's hand hovered over Windy's left arm.

"I did something." She stepped to the side, exposing more of the wolf's carcass. "I'm sorry, Mom."

Rose looked at Windy, anger threatening to escape. However, her softened face showed no anger, only relief. Rose hugged Windy in an unforgettable embrace.

"Let's get you cleaned up."

Windy wore different clothes today. It had shades of blue and white on the torso with a red, white, and black skirt. The sleeves were baby blue with warm white cuffs, like clouds. Even the neckpiece resembled that of a cloud. A yellow belt was clipped around her waist.

Windy was with Rose as they sat outside, selling the wolf's meat and pelt Windy had killed. Windy had a leaf sling tied across her body, her arm resting in the pouch.

The injury from the wolf fight left Windy's arm steadily growing numb, its mobility hindered as it struggled to recover. She handed chopped meat to Skybirds with her right arm, the only arm she could use without experiencing sensations of pain.

Windy sat beside Rose, barely looking up unless she needed to. She couldn't bear looking at her mother after what she had done. She knew better. She knew not to worry her mother the way she had done and then return in an injured state. Any sense of pride she previously felt toward her worth was now replaced by guilt. Such an ugly feeling of guilt flowing like sap through her veins.

Even Rose's face never looked down at Windy. Her lips were tense whenever Skybirds weren't around, and they softened, welcoming her customers as if nothing were on her mind. Rose hadn't experienced a scare like that, and she focused on never letting it happen again.

As people bought the fresh food, they all focused their gazes upon Windy. She didn't notice them. Her head was heavy with guilt. While purchasing, Skybirds paid less than the advertised price for their items.

"I'm not paying this much for something killed by that thing. It could have been a fake kill for all I know."

Windy didn't flinch, but she felt like the dead wolf being sold of its remails. The only thing she could think about was that she had done something bad. She began to tune out her surroundings, lost in her own thoughts. She wanted to be seen, but not in the form of a killer.

Or fake.

Inside their home, Windy focused on going nowhere but her small room.

"Windy."

Windy heard Rose call for her before she could step inside.

"Yes, Mom?" Windy replied, her body hunched over, uncertainty flooding her mind.

"Come here, please."

Windy turned around and slowly walked over to where her mom was sitting in the kitchen. Rose was putting a small amount of coins of various colors and sheens into a leather satchel. There weren't that many left on the table.

"I want you to have these," Rose said, sliding the remaining coins to Windy when she entered the kitchen. "You deserve them."

Windy looked at them as if they had fallen out of the sky. "What do I do with them?"

"Whatever you want. Save them, use them; they're yours."

Windy took the coins, holding the delicacies. "Thank you so much, Mom."

Rose smiled. "If nobody will believe you, I will, my little warrior."

Windy's composure brightened. Any guilt or insecurity was replaced by the unimaginable situation. She was just as good as the people everyone couldn't help but love. Windy took the coins and continued to her room.

Windy sat down on the small bed carved out of wood, staring at the coins. She didn't know how much these were worth, but they were worth using. But how to spend them? What to spend them on? Windy sat staring at the coins, her mind racing through thought after thought.

She could take a visit to the shop, revisiting the various products it has. Maybe she could find something there that she likes. Or, she could keep the coins, treasuring them as keepsakes from her struggle. Whatever the use, Windy grabbed them and placed them on the small table in the corner of her room. She carefully lay down on her bed, having nothing to do for the rest of the day. This was often the case. If Windy had nothing to do—no exploring, nowhere to go with Rose, or nothing to help with—Windy slept. Her growing body needed the sleep, after all.

Windy was woken up by Rose, who gently shook her shoulder.

"Windy, some of the Skybirds want to talk to you." Rose said softly, a smile brightening her older features.

Windy's hair was matted, and her feathers were ruffled. She was in no condition for conversation, especially with the Skybirds. "Why? When?"

"Now."

Windy blinked and rubbed her eyes free from the dryness that came with sleep. She sat up, combing through her hair with her fingers and cleaning her feathers like a cat, licking her fingers and running them through the plumes.

While she fixed herself, Rose stood outside the room, hunched against the doorframe. Her eyes gazed off into the distance, a frown on her face. Windy got out of bed once she appeared presentable, walking with Rose to the door with slow steps.

At the door, there was a group of Skybirds waiting for Windy. Some looked like they were casual citizens, and some were warriors. The crowd led her to the center of the village, where Rose was walking with Windy. As they walked, the crowd moved aside, making room for them to travel. Windy looked around, taking in the crowd's energy. They all looked at her as if she committed a crime.

What did they want her for?

When they arrived at their designated spot, there were Skybirds holding notepads and pencils. There were no more than six. Rose stepped back as one of the reporter Skybirds walked up to Windy.

"Good day, young lady." He had to look up to her. "We would like to ask you a few questions and have you talk about some things. First, your name is Windy, correct?"

Windy looked back at Rose, silently asking if she should answer. Rose gave her a slight nod, but never smiling.

"Um," Windy started, "yes. You can talk to me."

"Wonderful! First of all, we are all curious about where you come from. Do you know people of the different Communities?"

Windy blinked. "Different Communities? I only know Skybirds."

The Skybirds with the notepads started writing, some holding up their pads to shield their mouths. Some chuckled, scribbling with a more determined energy.

"That's okay. We've just noticed you're not like us, as you have probably noticed. You have probably lived a normal Skybird life, am I correct?"

"Yes. I don't know why you all hate me. I live here, like all of you." Windy quickly glanced at the writers, catching their gossiping.

The crowd froze, soon buzzing with guilt as they dropped their notes. They stared at Windy, disbelief exposed in their doings right from the words of a child.

"We don't mean it." A writer began talking louder when the reporter stated. "We are just wary of people who don't look like us."

"What does that mean?" Windy asked, innocent.

"Specifically, we tend to get a little scared when people who don't look like us are in our Community."

Windy's head spun around to Rose.

"But anyhow, we truly see that you are nothing like us. That was shown when you dragged that wolf's body home. Many of us saw that, and we are itching for answers!"

Windy shifted her focus back on the reporter.

"Don't worry, just talk. We will ask accordingly. How did you do it? Why did you do it? Where did you go?"

Windy looked down, her ears pinning back as her face slowly turned pale. The Skybird was talking to her like she was an adult.

"Um. Well, I killed it. I wanted to show people that I shouldn't be picked on, so I went to the mountains. Up that way." She pointed toward the mountain peak, and the crowd looked in that direction.

"I wanted to do something cool, like all the other cool people here. But while I was walking, there was a lot of snow. A lot of it! I have never seen so much snow!"

What a kid.

"But in the snow, something told me that I was in trouble. I didn't know what was going to happen, but I took one of the flags on the way up and used it to fight the wolf."

The writers reluctantly continued writing the truth in notebooks.

"It was scary. I thought I was going to die. But I used the flag to beat it up. Then it died. I felt so bad."

The reporter allowed a few seconds for the Skybirds to write. "No, don't feel bad. How old are you, again?"

"I'm five."

The crowd began talking, gasping amongst the chatter.

"An unbelievable task, that is. If you are able to perform such a task at your age, we know you are going to go places. Big places. Do you know what you want to be when you grow up?"

"I want to help people."

The crowd silenced themselves. Even the reporter took a moment of silence after hearing that, choosing his next words carefully.

"That is a great future to look toward. With your bravery, you will help so many people, even protect them."

"I would like to do that, too." Windy nodded.

"Now, enough about this. How did it feel to slay such a beast with something as simple as a flag?"

"Scary." Windy looked down. "But even though it was scary, it felt fun. It was like dancing!" Windy felt like she had solved a world mystery. "Yes, just like dancing! I think the wolf didn't kill me because it thought my dance-fighting was so cool, it didn't know what to do."

The reporter laughed. "Probably so. But your reactions to these answers really tell me that you're a brave person, but are still very young. However, your age has nothing to do with what you demonstrated for us. Please keep showing us all the dedication and bravery every Skybird should have."

The spectating Skybirds all focused on the reporter, their faces twisted with disgust. He was on Windy's side. It was clear to the Community he didn't believe what they all did. Backs of Skybirds turned as chatter began to rise amongst the crowd. Whispers vibrated the crowd, judgmental eyes suddenly blinking with guilt.

Guilt.

Concern.

All for this child.

Windy's confident smile radiated through her veins as the crowd slowly began to disperse across the Community, their time well spent listening to the unusual child, yet not a word about her appearance was ever spoken.

Windy spun around to face Rose, her confidence overwhelming. Rose looked at her daughter with eyes that sparked trust and a proud smile at her growing daughter.

This was Windy's time that she earned. The dependence she no longer needed.

6

Windy was standing in the Skybird shop, inspecting the different items for sale. Today is her fourteenth birthday, and Rose gave her extra coins to spend on something special. They were enough for her to buy something worthwhile for herself. Windy was particularly interested in the fabrics. The way the different materials drew her in with their texture and sheens. Silk. She was drawn to the silk. It was the same material used on the flag Windy used to kill the wolf years ago. Regardless of her personal sentiment, she liked how it shone in the sun and how lightweight it was.

But there were so many colors. So, so many colors. Deciding on a color made her head hurt.

"Need help, miss?"

A Skybird walked up to her. He seemed like the owner of the shop, with the way he had his hair pulled back into a bun and wore professional clothes. A name tag clipped on his flannel shirt read

MOSSY. Though he was an adult, he had to look up to her. Windy finished growing to a height of six feet, surpassing all the adults in the Community.

"A little. I was thinking of buying some fabric." Windy pointed at the silk fabric with her scarred thumb. "But I'm not sure what color to get."

"What do you need it for?"

"A flag."

"A flag?"

Ever since Windy killed the wolf using the Skybird flag on the trail, she was oddly drawn to the Community flags, the way they freely waved in the wind. An unusual subject for Windy, but they seemed to live lives Windy could not live. Free. Happy. Ever changing.

"Yes. I was thinking about making one, but I'm not sure what color to get."

Mossy scanned her, his face twisting in deep thought.

"I think you should get this blue color," he said, grabbing a deep sky blue color. It gleamed like polished sapphires. "It would match your personality."

Windy looked intrigued. "That's good. I'll buy that then."

"How much do you need?"

How much fabric did she need? Windy stood with her mouth agape and eyes wide, her answer crumbling in her head.

"I'm not sure, mister."

"We have the dimensions of our Community flags if you would like them to be cut to that size."

"Yes, that would be great!" Windy smiled, clasping her hands together. "Thank you."

Mossy escorted Windy to the checkout, waiting for one of the shop workers to return with her fabric. Twenty coins. Windy had forty-eight coins—ten saved from years ago and thirty-eight from what Rose gave her for her birthday.

Windy sorted her coins, eyes focused on the chips.

"May I buy some string with that?"

"Absolutely, miss," Mossy called out to the Skybirds, cutting the fabric, requesting an addition of a spool of string.

At the Community outskirts, Windy carefully placed her items under a tree, scaling the trunk with skillful hands. As she grew, her climbing skills greatly improved despite her weakened but healed left arm. Windy often spent her free time learning how to build strength to climb, finding inspiration from the warriors. Now she could scale trees and hide in them, startling passing Skybirds.

Climbing was not a skill Skybirds needed. If they needed to go somewhere high, they used the Winged Beasts. Windy did not act like a normal fourteen-year-old, given the way her body was developed and the unique skills she had. Skybirds watched them, their eyes shot with horror every time they watched such a girl display such strength. It was just impossible.

In the tree, Windy searched for branches suitable for a flagpole, similar to the flags along the mountain trail. She tested branches to assess their durability. The tree shook furiously as Windy meddled, the leaves hurrying off their homes.

Windy found a burly yet weak branch and chose it as her victim. She gripped the branch with both hands, her fingers becoming numb from the strain. She jumped off the tree, the momentum and weight of her body causing the tree branch to snap. The large stick was almost as tall as her, but it was thin enough that she could put all of her fingers around it comfortably. She began dragging the weighted stick along the stone road, shaving down the broken end so it would be as clean as the other end.

After polishing, Windy took the silk flag and began cutting holes along the edge of the material with a stick she found on the ground. Precise. Focused.

Once the end of the silk was smothered with messy holes, Windy began weaving the string through the silk onto the stick. Her fingers navigated the string swiftly, catching each hole after the other. Her eyes were nailed to the materials, crafting with an instinctual skill.

That was another thing that baffled the Skybird Community. Windy had an otherworldly instinct for skillfully crafting and performing unusual tasks that no one her age could fathom. The Skybirds hadn't taught her such skills, nor had she acquired them from her surroundings. But if nobody taught her such skills, where did they come from? It was as if she carried these survival skills through her blood.

Windy held her new makeshift flag with pride, holding her head up as she inspected her learning form. She positioned her hands at either end of the stick, the left hand at the upper end of the pole, gripping under the stick, while the right hand was at the lower end of the pole, gripping over the stick. The silk flag waved in the wind, matching the way her hair flowed in the wind.

Windy looked down at such a hand placement, getting used to

the comfort. The flag felt special to her, something that made her feel more like a Skybird. Though the Skybirds placed Community flags throughout their territory, none of the Skybirds possessed flags of their own to use for recreational purposes or for self-defense, as Windy has done.

7

The Skybird Community silently stared at the movement before their eyes. Such a prodigy could never be seen in the Community. They were all simple—hunt, gather, fly. That's all that could possibly happen in their Community. But the wonder that was moving synchronized in front of them gave the Community a variety they were never used to.

Windy was practicing her flagmanship, getting used to hand placements and movements to become one with the flag. She stood facing away from the crowd, focusing on herself rather than the other Skybirds.

As the flag was thrown into the air, its stick spun smoothly, the silk creating a beating noise that sounded like wind colliding with anything that stood in its way. Whenever she missed a catch or dropped the flag from such complex movements, they stood in silence. Such a talent was far greater than any other thing the Community could do. Though they had watched her skills develop over the years, her talent was proven to Skybirds that she shouldn't be interfered. Why criticize when they couldn't do it themselves?

"Look at her go."

"She's weird, but that's cool."

"I feel bad for the things I said about her."

"I wish I could do that."

Not only were Skybirds invested, but even creatures such as the Winged Beasts. The massive monsters watched Windy warily, chirping out of uncertainty. Whenever they saw the silk flag move in front of their eyes, they flinched back, seeing the harmless object as a threat. Their eyes were stuck on the sight of the unusual Skybird, never exposed to such a fast, loud thing.

Windy's feet moved in perfect rhythm, almost like a dance. This wasn't the first day she had been practicing, but it seemed as if she had been doing this for years, and nobody had ever known about it. Aside from her feet moving at the perfect pace, so did the rest of her body. Her body was like boned mud with the way her supported body flowed so perfectly. Windy worked tirelessly. She only stopped when she told herself to stop. She pushed herself to her limits, determined to be at her best to showcase her capabilities.

Admirable.

When she turned around at the end of her practice, her slouched body collected itself, stacking itself to stand up straight as her eyes, ears, and feathers seemed to lift at the same time. She wasn't expecting such a crowd. Not as big as this one. She was just practicing.

"Hi, everyone," Windy said awkwardly, forcing a smile.

Everyone began speaking all at once, expressing their awe at the unintentional performance. She quickly glanced at each one, her body tingling with stimulation.

What's up with them?

"What else can you do?" A Skybird called out from the crowd, soon enticing the people to ask noisy questions all at once.

"Settle down, everyone! One at a time." Windy projected her voice, but was kind about it. "To answer your question first, I don't know what else I can do."

"Can you kill more wolves for us?"

"I can."

"Could you swim across the coast?"

"I've never tried, but I think I can."

Windy gripped the flag harder, her eyes tracking each Skybird's question. Her lips parted slightly, as if anticipating each question with a direct answer.

"Can you do archery?"

"I could if I tried."

"Have you tamed a Winged Beast?"

That question made Windy go silent.

Taming a Winged Beast. Owning a Winged Beast was essential in the Community lifestyle. Everyone knew how to tame one and had a special connection with each of their pets. Windy loved the native animals. She never asked for one because she had free access to them in the Community. But to own one now? Windy sat on the question. It wasn't a bad idea; she should try. Compared to swimming the coast, that seemed like a better, safer option. To her, at least. If Winged Beasts were already tamed, surely she could just pluck a wild one for herself.

That is, to her.

She looked at everyone and walked off, holding her flag in one hand. She continued walking. Walk home. Windy opened the door that welcomed her home, the comfort of such a familiar place invigorating. She threw her sweaty body onto the sofa, catching her breath.

Rose welcomed the girl with a hug. "How did it go?"

"Good." Windy said with little emotion.

"You look tired. Do you need me to get something for you?"

She smiled. "Water would be great. Thank you."

Rose stepped away to get what Windy needed. Windy was grateful to have a mom like Rose. Anything Windy needed, Rose provided.

Windy took the wooden cup from her mother's hand, inhaling the water.

"Don't drink too fast."

But by the time Rose warned her, Windy was done.

"I'm very proud of you, Windy. I hate to see you grow up so fast, though." Rose's eyes landed on Windy's bad arm, her lips molding into a frown.

"Mom, can I ask you something?"

"What is it?"

"Do you know where there's wild Winged Beasts?"

Rose sighed. Whenever Windy asked a specific question such as that, it usually meant she was going to run off and do something dangerous.

And she was.

"They're usually not around the Skybird village. You would need to go a little bit out of town to find some." Rose's voice lowered as she gently lifted her hand to her mouth. "Don't tell me you're going to do what I think you're going to do."

"I want a Winged Beast."

8

S tep by step. Each step was planted with uncertainty, but was lifted with determination. The ground beneath her was uneven, with stones scattered as they pleased. The grass provided a soft, reassuring touch beneath her boots, as if to tell her she had a place to fall, should she need it.

Windy trekked the Community territory, scanning every bit of her surroundings for any patches of brown or red. Aside from the usual colorings of green, white, and a stony blue, no Winged Beasts were in sight.

Yet.

As Windy walked, she stood her ground, prepared for anything that could happen. She didn't know if there were predators around, or if she did find the Winged Beast herds, how hostile wild Winged Beasts were, if they were in the first place. She didn't know if she was looking in the right area of the Community. She held her flag close to herself as if she were hunting to kill. But she was hunting to befriend.

Her steps steadily grew heavy. Each step became a call for defeat. She stood in the mountain valley, staring out into the distance. Her arms fell to her sides, and her flag hit the floor with the same heaviness as her determination. She didn't know what she was looking for now. She was staring out into the distance, her mind blank. She propped her flag up, holding it as she leaned on it so it could carry her weight.

Tomorrow. It's always a new day. Windy's assuming thoughts told her that there could be no herds in this area today, or at all. If she tried again at a later date, she could have better luck. So, Windy listened to her conscience. The voice in her head that seemed to know everything from right to wrong, from good to bad, from following or rejecting decisions. She listened to such a voice and turned back, dragging her flag along the ground. She carried herself on tired feet, each step getting closer to home.

During her descent, Windy's guard was cut off, paying no attention to the familiar yet unfamiliar surroundings. She wanted to go home. But Windy regained her focus when she found herself on the ground, blinded by a sudden burst of red.

Woah!

Windy had no idea what had hit her, but she needed to act fast. She moved her fingers, grabbing something that wasn't in her hand. Windy reached for the loose flag that was on the ground, avoiding the growing pressure of the unknown attacker on top of her.

Hurry, Windy...

She reached as far as her arm could stretch, using her free hand to protect herself from the attacker.

The red color felt soft.

Windy strained herself to reach for her flag, fighting for her life. But at the peak of her strength, her third finger reached the flag, and she scrambled to roll it toward her. After playing around with the wood rod, she rolled the flag toward herself, quickly grabbing the base and shoving it beneath the attacker's neck, pushing the stick up to free herself and see who was attacking her.

A Winged Beast.

Windy choked on the chilly air, the sight almost dreamy.

When it's supposedly easy prey slipped from its reach, it hissed in her face, the sound louder than anything Windy had ever heard, especially from her sensitive ears. She now attained more information about such creatures: Wild Winged Beasts are hostile. Windy recalled her defensive tactics and her confrontation with the wolf. Now that she was using a stronger flag, she could more easily fight off the threat.

But It's a Winged Beast.

It's just a Winged Beast.

Do something with it!

Windy gasped, jumping out of the way when the Winged Beast snapped at her, lunging forward with its deadly golden claws. The flag spun quickly in her hand, the beating noise cracking amidst the tension. The sound, to the Winged Beast, was threatening, making Windy seem bigger than she really was to such a creature. The Winged Beast stepped back, chirping in fear as its tail curled up against its side and its wings flailed in panic.

The method, to Windy, seemed less harsh than attacking the Winged Beast like the wolf, so she spun the flag, distracting the animal. She lured it to a higher part of the valley, close enough to a dead end where a rock wall met the ground.

At the last second, she flipped the flag in the air, jumping onto the rock wall and scaling it as fast as she could, despite her muscles burning. The Winged Beast hissed at the flag, snapping at it and attacking it like a cat hunting its toys.

While the Winged Beast was occupied, Windy was shifting her focus between the Winged Beast and the climb. When Windy's height was above the Winged Beast, she adjusted her footing and grip, prepared to propel herself onto the Winged Beast. So, she prepared her body, her muscles aching with anticipation.

Then, she jumped.

She grabbed its black mane, adjusting her body to fit onto the beast. She knew the animal would want a stranger off of itself, so she did well to prepare for any fight she needed to protect herself from while on its back. She had little time for such a preparation, because the Winged Beast reared up as soon as it felt Windy's body plant down on its back.

The animal jumped around, feathers flying off its back in a flurry of red and black. Windy's body was a twisted mess of skin, unable to match her balance to the beat of the jumps. Her legs burned with a new soreness she had never experienced in her years. In fact, adrenaline was masking the fact her whole body burned with the strength to stay atop the beast.

If Windy fell off, she'd be dead.

But if she were to tame the Winged Beast, she needed to gain its trust and show it she wasn't a threat. While the Winged Beast was jumping around, she placed her hand on its shoulder, feeling the muscles tighten and relax while her own were tense and aching.

"Hey, it's okay. I'm not bad," she gently soothed as she stroked its feathers.

But the beast would not give up.

Windy became nervous. Her muscles were getting fatigued. She couldn't last much longer. As Windy continued to soothe the animal, she noticed it, too, was tiring out. It was now a fight to see who would last the longest. Her hand kept stroking its shoulder, creating a sweaty patch of feathers in its path.

"You're okay. I won't hurt you."

The Winged Beast tripped on its own tired legs, ceasing its fight. It panted, its feathers damp from its own sweat as well as Windy's. While the Winged Beast crouched down, unable to put up a fight, Windy took the time to sit in silence, avoiding anything that could provoke the Winged Beast's trust. In the newfound silence, the only sounds around them were the wind and their gasping pants as they struggled to catch their breath.

Windy hesitantly stroked the Winged Beast again, gentle and tender. "You're safe with me."

Windy slid off its back, showing herself to the animal that thought it could devour her. The Winged Beast growled. It wasn't sure why it was playing with its food. Windy smiled, making her presence and emotions as welcoming as possible. They maintained eye contact, as if they were conflicted about who should look away first. But after the gentle silence, the Winged Beast lowered its head at Windy, staring directly into her eyes at her level. Windy maintained her calm composure, knowing this could be her last day alive. She reached her hand toward its face—slow, friendly, open. The Winged Beast thought for a moment, as if contemplating whether she was worth killing.

But the Winged Beast placed its large face in her small hand, accepting her. Windy beamed, beginning to stroke its face. She scratched it, talking to it as if it were a baby.

"You're good! Look at you; you don't have to be a big meanie. I know you're nice. I always knew it."

Windy patted the Winged Beast's head as she walked off to collect the flag she had thrown during the fight. She rolled the silk up in order to prevent the Winged Beast from spooking. It looked like she was holding a stick now. She hugged the Winged Beast, letting it know that she was grateful it hadn't killed her. After her quick bonding time, she walked over to the side of the beast, climbing onto its body.

The Winged Beast was not as large as the others, so it was easier for Windy to mount. She stroked its shoulder again, continuing to assure it that it was safe with Windy. While seated on the Winged Beast with her flag on her lap, she inspected its body, unsure.

How would she command it to fly?

Windy sat on the Winged Beast, recalling how other owners command their Winged Beasts to fly. They use commands.

"Fly."

The Winged Beast stood still.

Windy sighed. She had to get it to fly somehow. Teach it to know the command, if anything. She reached for its mane, repositioning herself on its back. She lifted her legs to either side of herself, kicking the Winged Beast and shouting a word. "Fly!"

The beast tensed, chirped before scrambling to run, beating its wings to propel itself. The launch whiplashed Windy, unaware of how strong it would be. Regaining balance, she steadied herself on the Winged Beast's back, staying still, collected, and calm. Wherever her hands went, that's where the Winged Beast flew. So, her hands reached toward the direction of home, the wind in her face kissing her after a long day.

9

Windy stood with the younger Skybirds, pointing at her Winged Beast as she lectured the young crowd. Three years ago, Windy battled a Winged Beast, dominating its aggressive nature and earning its trust. Now, Windy was trusted with teaching younger Skybirds basic Winged Beast care and information.

"Just like you and me, no Winged Beast is exactly the same. Girls and boys have different colors, and each Winged Beast has its own unique patterns. Girl Winged Beasts have brown feathers, but their beak and horn colors are the same. Boys like Nodin are a vivid red color.

Nodin is the name of Windy's Winged Beast.

A girl around Windy's age raised her hand. "I never understood what the different colors were for."

"Well, let's think about this, Osprey. Would you want to marry someone who looked boring or who looked exciting? The same concept goes for Winged Beasts. Boys look exciting so they can find the perfect girl for them." Windy smiled. "Girls are picky."

The young crowd giggled.

"But though they have separate color patterns, no Winged Beast is the same. As you can see, Nodin has a unique blue color to him." She lowered her hand so Nodin could sniff it. "His horns, instead of gold, are blue. So are his feet and belly. Winged Beasts can be different, like any other person. It's how they're born sometimes, and they can't help it. But such differences are rare. Like our identities, no two Winged Beasts have the same patterns.

Windy lifted Nodin's paw to show them the uneven black sock pattern.

"Love your Winged Beasts, everyone. Now, when it comes to caring for them—"

"But don't they eat people?" Oakley interrupted.

"Yes, but that is why you need to earn its trust before anything. If it knows you won't hurt it, it won't bother to hurt you. I know for a fact you have, Oakley. Now, as I was saying, Winged Beast care is easy, but essential to provide your friend a happy life..."

Windy's lesson continued throughout the afternoon, the kids and young teenagers listening and engaging with questions, some of which made Windy laugh or couldn't answer. Such universal teachings created a new sense of peace and belonging in the Community. Everyone walked with a sense of acceptance of each other. All was well. But after Windy's course for the young Skybirds, she walked by a group of Skybirds that caught her attention.

"Grass isn't usually gray, Gloria. Do you see any gray grass around here?"

"I know what I saw! Come here, come here!"

"Someone could have spilled dye, and you don't know it."

Skybird women used plants from the mountains to make a paste that served as a dye, applying it to their fabrics or hair.

"Please, let me show you all! I'm not lying. Please, Gale. Please, Nimbus."

The three Skybirds rushed off with Gloria, following her with annoyance.

Windy watched them rush off. Gray was an unusual color to be found in a colorful Community such as the Skybirds. As she continued to walk, she scanned the area for anything unusual or out of place.

As far as she could see, the Community seemed normal. It was just a normal day. Windy's steps took her home, where she stood with Nodin outside. She inspected her surroundings in the Community, double-checking for anything that might be off-putting. But the Community was the same. Normal. Colorful.

"Stay." Windy pointed at Nodin as she walked off.

Windy wanted to check whether the Skybirds' talk was something she should have minded her own business about or if it was serious. Windy ran through the Community, looking around at the foliage around her. She checked the plants, trees, and sprouts that were immediately visible. But as far as she could tell, nothing was different. Windy stood by a Skybird shop, her face twisted with thought.

But her thoughts were interrupted when a Skybird came up to her, calling her name.

"Windy! Windy! Thank goodness you're here." The Skybird, Raine, crouched, panting in distress.

"Oh, hello! Is everything okay?"

"Well, if I'm being honest, no." Raine threw his head side to side, running his hand through his hair.

"What's the matter?"

"It's"—he hesitated, unsure whether he should say any more—"my Winged Beast."

"Your Winged Beast? What's wrong with it? Is it okay?"

"Well, I was hoping you could take a look at it for me."

"Of course I can!"

Windy followed close behind Raine, her steps just as urgent as the Skybird in front of her. As their steps grew steadily slower, Windy's ears focused upon the sight in front of her, uncertain.

"Is that one yours?" Windy pointed at the lying Winged Beast.

"Yes. But please be careful. I'm scared to go over there."

Windy kept her eyes on the animal as she cautiously approached it, anticipating any response it could give toward the stranger. The Winged Beast was copper-colored with red accents. Female.

While the Winged Beast was motionless against the stony ground, seemingly harmless, its ears shifted toward the sound of Windy's footsteps, acknowledging her presence. Her eyes fixated on the tall figure, unsure whether to trust the stranger.

Windy's lips curved into a gentle smile, hoping to show the

Winged Beast she wasn't a threat as her hand drew toward the copper feathers.

"What's wrong, big girl?" Windy said as she bent over to look at the animal.

As Windy lowered her upper body toward the supposedly calm animal, the Winged Beast's peaceful demeanor shifted, hissing while she swiped her golden claws in Windy's direction.

"Woah!" Windy flinched back, her hair like a wave from the movement. "Has she always been this way?" Her eyes tracked Raine.

"No, only recently."

Windy focused back on the Winged Beast, forcing a relaxed body. "Hey, I won't hurt you. You don't need to be scared."

The Winged Beast hissed again, assuming a threat. Windy quickly stepped to the Winged Beast's side, testing if she would allow her to climb on. Before Windy could go into the climbing movement to mount, the Winged Beast sharply turned in Windy's direction, snapping at her. Windy quickly stepped back, her reflexes sharp against the savage Winged Beast.

"I want to check if she's hurt anywhere, but I don't think I could check her without getting attacked. But even so, injured Winged Beasts aren't aggressive like this. They hide their pain calmly." Windy stepped back to a tense Raine, her naturally upset face emphasizing her sorrow for the Winged Beast owner.

"So, what do I do? I love my Winged Beast so much." The Skybird bit his fingers, eyes focused on the gravel beneath their feet.

"Don't kill it," Windy said with underlying hesitation. "I would say to leave her alone so you can keep yourself safe." She paused briefly, finding words. "It could probably be something she learned somehow, but this aggression isn't out of fear. It's dangerous aggression."

"Do I get rid of her?"

"At least try to avoid her until she fixes herself. I really don't know the reason for her aggression." Windy looked down, guilty that she couldn't help the distressed Skybird.

"It's okay. I know it's unusual. I don't think anybody could know what's happening. Thanks, anyway."

"Of course. Stay safe." Windy walked off, leaving the owner by himself. Back on the road, her disappointment weighed heavily on her physically and emotionally. Windy wanted to help. It hurt her knowing that a Winged Beast owner was hurting. Windy's eyes were heavy with defeat.

As Windy made the somber walk home, the ground beneath her steadily became crunchy, as if the rocks were grated into dry sand. Confused at the sudden change in grounding, Windy looked down, checking her feet. She was walking on grass, but the grass wasn't soft, like how it should be.

Instead, the grass was a steel blue, and any plants growing in that color were dying. Windy stopped walking. She couldn't go any further when there was a phenomenon such as this. Windy looked around, perplexed. The foliage was a dappled mix of healthy life and sickly life. Trees were rotting, flowers were wilted, and the grass was crunchy. Windy couldn't be sure if it was her mind playing tricks on her currently confused mindset, but she saw a dark mist in the area, as if the discoloration was causing a small patch of fog.

This was not behavior seen in the Skybird territory.

10

Windy stood at the center of the Skybird village, standing in front of a Skybird crowd she had gathered. "Everyone! Settle down!"

"What is happening to our Community?"

"Who did this?"

Windy's hands shook anxiously, her eyes darting around the loud, overwhelmed crowd.

"Our Winged Beasts are getting dangerous!"

"Our Community is ugly!"

Windy's ears pinned back, her feathers flaring out like a frill.

"It was probably those no-good—"

"Settle down!" Windy raised her voice out of stress and overstimulation, leaning toward the crowd. The crowd silenced themselves, unaware that a gentle Skybird like Windy could make such a noise. Windy's eyes widened, her feathers flattening and her ears perking up. She stood up straight, shaking her head clear of the stimulation she had just experienced.

"I'm sorry, everyone. But you won't be able to hear what I have to say if you all keep talking over one another, especially me."

Windy paused, making sure the silence was unbroken.

"Have any of you noticed anything unusual about the Community?" Windy noticed the Skybird from the friend group, Gloria, and Raine. They were hidden in the crowd, but after seeing them so recently, she recognized them. She assumed they would be the first ones to speak up.

"I've seen some weird things happen with my ladies' group."

Windy had never heard of a "ladies' group," let alone known the Skybirds had one.

The female Skybird in the crowd continued, "We've been discussing some recent disappearances with our Winged Beasts. We were going to go out on an evening flight the other day, but, well, we were in short supply." She hadn't sounded confident with her answer, but the flurries of confusion from the Community masked any genuine emotions.

"My Winged Beast has been acting aggressively lately. My back door is now my front door." Raine intended a joke, but the negative emotions surrounding the Community left no room for laughter.

The younger Skybird, Gloria, spoke next: "Hey! I found some weirdly colored grass a few days ago. Me and my friends checked it out, and it's real!"

Windy took a moment to think amongst herself, drowning out any other noise or comments that were made from the crowd. After a moment of thinking, Windy spoke up. "Everyone! You all know that I don't exactly know much about the Community, but can any older generations tell me if this has happened before or if it looks familiar?"

The crowd went silent. Either they were thinking or hiding something from her.

"Anybody?" Windy asked sheepishly.

The crowd continued to silence themselves.

Windy sighed. Maybe they didn't know. "Okay, everyone. Um, moving forward, I want you all to steer clear of any unusual animals or coloring in the Community. I don't know if it's safe, but keep your instincts sharp. Don't go outside at night to prevent anything from happening without anybody else knowing. Does that sound like a plan, everyone?"

Everyone began talking, some Skybirds whistling, and some nodding their heads. The indirect agreement allowed Windy to relax. But as the crowd dispersed, a Skybird approached her.

"Stay out of our Community's business, anomaly. Leave the big-girl decisions to the real Skybirds."

Skybirds turned their heads to catch a hint of the confrontation.

"What makes you think I'm not a real Skybird? Just because I don't look like you doesn't mean I'm not one."

"Look at you, bird! You look like the very discrimination of our Community!" Jay thrust his hand at her bodily feathers.

"I was born with those."

"And you come here. What a coincidence!"

"Jay. That's enough." Fern limped over with a cane to the fighting citizens, her presence sending a calm aura to the surrounding

Skybirds.

Windy recognized the Skybird. It was the grandmother she had helped as a child. The years were catching up to her, and it was apparent she still had a few drops of life left.

"Don't tell me what to do, old lady. Don't tell me you believe this thing is actually real."

Fern nodded slowly as if moving too quickly would drain her energy further. "I believe in her. I have seen it years ago. She has no evil bone in her body."

"How do we know that? She could be trying to soften us up even more!"

Windy stepped back, unwilling to take part in the rough conversation.

"If she had evil intentions, she would have done something to prove so. But think about it. She has done nothing but work for our love."

"You know she's a killer."

"Aren't we all? The food you need to survive comes from animals torn from their lives. If you didn't believe that, you would be dead by now."

"Coming from a grandma!"

"Who might outlive you?"

Jay's face snapped into an offensive rage. He walked off, but Windy kept her comments to herself. She watched Jay storm off, but looked at the elderly Skybird with a calm demeanor.

"Thank you."

Fern smiled warmly, a smile that could heal hurt souls. "I should thank you for staying true to yourself. More people need to see that for themselves. I know you will be the one to fix things that no common person can fix."

The sudden lightning strike woke everyone up. Windy scrambled for her bedsheets, squeaking while her ears and feathers perked up. She had celebrated her fifteenth birthday a few months prior to tonight, maturing as she further helped the Skybirds with their territorial distress.

While awake and easing into awareness, Windy noticed rain tapping her window. Rain was uncommon, so it was nothing to worry over. But through the rain, there were screams and screeching amidst the rain pattering. Windy jumped out of her warm bed, looking out the window. The sight before her made her tanned face go pale.

Windy sprinted to the corner of her room where her makeshift flag was perched and snatched it as she turned the corner, quickly adjusting her hand placement on the slanted flag.

"Mom! Stay inside!" Windy shouted, assuming Rose was awake.

When Windy opened the door, the sight was heartbreaking, especially with her own eyes and inside her own Community.

The sky was nightmarish, the atmosphere an unnatural-looking dark purple. Around her were Skybird warriors fighting against grotesque anomalies as well as citizens of their own Community. Taking a closer look at the creatures, they were black figures, each with a different colored skull. They seemed like mutants of some kind with the way they moved and carried themselves.

The sights were overwhelming, Windy unable to process all that was happening at once. Her mouth was agape out of disbelief, and she lowered her flag, creating a thumping sound against the stone ground.

Windy called for her Winged Beast, frantically looking around for his presence. When her Winged Beast ran over to her, she quickly mounted the animal, holding the mane with one hand and holding her flag with the other.

"Run! Go!" Windy commanded.

The Winged Beast ran, its tail creating a trail behind it and its back hooves creating cracking sounds against the rock. As she ran with the animal, Windy saw Skybird citizens go outside to see the destruction.

"Everyone! Stay inside! Don't come out until we tell you!" Windy panted, her chest growing tight at the impending threat within her Community.

Skybird spectators hurried inside without hesitation, locking their doors. Now the Community was free of innocents, leaving the battlefield to the warriors and enemies. Windy ran across the battlefield, aiding the warriors in their fight as she beat down enemies as a distraction so the warriors could finish their jobs. Her vision seemed to look at multiple things at once, her pulse racing through her chest.

Windy charged toward one of the beasts, lifting her flag in preparation. Before she could attempt the swinging motion of the flag, she found herself collapsed on the floor while her Winged Beast continued to run.

She sat up, looking around in a panic to find her attacker. In front of her, a creature stood, growling, its red eyes glowing from its horned, dark purple skull, and slimy saliva dripping from its mouth. Its black body was slender, ribs exposed, and spikes poking from its limbs. Its tail lashed behind it as it flexed its claws, ready to attack.

Windy took no time to think and responded by thrusting her flag forward, distracting the beast long enough so she had time to stand up. When Windy stood up, she spun her flag around, beating it around like a bat. The silk drew attention to herself, and other smaller beats joined in the assault on Windy.

Windy began pounding the disgusting creatures, stunning them long enough for backup to close in. Occasionally, Windy's force would be strong enough to snap their disheveled bodies, killing them. The attention she drew attracted Skybird warriors who were already fighting, based on years of experience. Windy's defense seemed like a toy compared to the warriors.

"Stay back! This is no job for you!" a warrior shouted beside her.

"I will defend the Community that has given me a home!" Windy shouted back at them, her voice nothing but defensive. As she turned her head, the wendigo beast charged at her, its jaws half the size of Windy.

Windy exclaimed, swinging her flag inside its mouth, the wendigo clamping down sturdily. Windy's muscles tightened as she fought the wendigo for possession of the flag.

As the beast flailed its head around, Windy matched its

movements, increasing the momentum of the wendigo's head. When the force captured enough speed, its head turned just too far, causing a chilling snap across the noise of the disturbance.

Windy pulled her flag free, taking no care of the limp wendigo body. Spinning around, Windy thrust forward, sprinting through the battlefield as she swung her flag around in a flurry, hitting their enemies upon contact.

More killing.

Her own hands once again invited death.

As she approached the Community entrance where the enemies were seen arriving, she slipped on a puddle formed by the rain. Gasping, she crashed down on her shoulder, sliding as she lost possession of her flag.

The puddle of the unusual substance seeped into her exposed skin effortlessly, as if Windy were a human sponge. As the liquid mixed with her blood, Windy grew tired, as if out of nowhere. She struggled to stand, her body suddenly feeling heavy. She groaned and pushed, using all of her strength to haul herself to her feet.

With each shaky step she took, she was closer and closer to standing up straight once again.

What just happened? What was that?

The accomplishment gave her an adrenaline boost, enough to make her jump to her free flag and grab it off the wet ground.

As she reached down, a force kicked her from behind, her initial struggle to prove itself meaningless. As Windy quickly turned herself over to see who the next attacker was, she gasped, all blood escaping from her face.

What stood above Windy looked like Windy, but it gave an uncanny image to the Skybird, its glowing red eyes showing no reflection of its human twin. She was dressed as Windy, but her clothes were in a different color palette—those of what seemed to be the atmosphere. Any white was replaced with a gray dark enough to be storm clouds.

The feral version of Windy sneered, throwing herself onto the real Windy to trap her on the ground with a metal pole. Windy grabbed the pole, her toned arms straining to lift the weight off her.

As she fought for freedom, she realized something. This was a flag similar to hers, but it wasn't cheaply made. It was made of seemingly expensive, hardier materials, such as metal and thicker silk. Such a flag was much more complex than Windy's.

It seemed as if this clone knew what Windy would do, meeting her attacks with better ones. Her mind struggled to keep up with the imposter, her moves just barely delayed.

Windy could feel her air flow cut off as the clone pressed down with gradual force, its smile basking in the pleasure of Windy's approaching death. Though cut off from any larger movements, Windy looked around, inspecting her surroundings carefully.

She noticed the weapons shop not too far from the entrance of the Community, where Windy was pinned. Windy reached for her flag, her hands fumbling for the stick. As her fingers wrapped around the weak pole, she pushed it under her, thrusting the flag upward as if she were slicing through her freedom. The clone screeched, its hands pressing against its stomach where it was blown off its wind. Windy scrambled to her feet, rushing to the weapons shop.

But she needed something else to take down this clone. Something it didn't know she could do.

Windy broke the shop's window, stepping through the glass. Some shards tore through her warm, padded clothes, cutting them swiftly.

She planted each foot on the wooden ground of the weapons shop, quickly scanning her surroundings. Her chest heaved with exhaust and her head pounded with anxiety. She didn't hesitate to sprint toward the weapon racks, where the bows and spears were placed. Windy mindlessly reached for a bow, unaware of her selection.

Looking at what she held in her hand, she reached for a pre-loaded quiver stuffed with arrows. She slung the quiver across her body, took an arrow, and inspected it. She had never used arrows, especially a bow.

Firing a practice shot, the arrow hit a sign above the iron blade sharpeners. Less than decent. It had to work. Windy crouched beneath the window, hiding herself from the commotion. The feral clone of Windy looked around the area, desperately trying to find her prey. Windy closed her eyes, taking a moment to allow her frantic breaths to even out.

Then, with calm hands, she focused on Feral. She didn't close one eye, as most archers would do, especially the warriors. Windy kept both eyes open, assuming the approximate point of contact.

Windy released the string. The arrow hit the clone, but not where Windy anticipated. The clone grabbed her leg, shouting like a roar. She jerked her head in Windy's direction, grinning with her teeth.

Windy carefully got out of the window. Her hesitation allowed the clone to catch up to Windy, its flag raised and ready to knock her out at any given moment. By the time Windy had stepped out, the clone was steps away from her. Windy quickly reacted, jolting to the side and sprinting toward the ledge where the mountain dropped beside the entrance of the Community.

Windy's feet slid as she neared a stop, moments before she could fall off the ledge.

She couldn't be scared. This clone feeds off fear.

She turned around, staring the clone dead in the eyes. As she stalked after her prey, she raised her flag. Windy closed her eyes. Before the copy could get to her, Windy leaned back, falling off the ledge backward, headfirst. Not a single shout was made. The clone gasped, sprinting toward the ledge and looking down at the fog, worried as if it had lost a precious heirloom. She paced back and forth, looking for any sign of Windy.

Then, just as suddenly as Windy fell off the cliff, the clone jumped back, falling to the ground. A flurry of red blinded her, the shock pushing her to the ground. Large wings spanned as the color soared up, a long tail following its path.

Windy clung to her Winged Beast's mane, clutching on his back with her legs as the Winged Beast turned upside down, Windy directing him toward the clone. Through a pressed body atop feathers, her heart beat furiously as she struggled to breathe, fear clogging her throat. Her eyes refocused on the clone, not daring to look away.

While the Winged Beast leveled himself out, Windy nocked

an arrow to the bow she found, aiming it toward the clone. Spontaneously, she closed one eye. She focused on her target, time seeming to slow down with each second she focused.

When the Winged Beast switched its path of travel, Windy fired the arrow, sniping the clone from above. She quickly put the bow across her body, snatching the Winged Beast's mane and guiding it to land.

Well, that worked!

"Down!"

The Winged Beast dived toward the stone, focusing on the surface as if it could fly through the solid material. Windy anticipated the closing distance and prepared to jump. When the distance closed in to a dangerous level, Windy pushed her hands forward, guiding the Winged Beast to soar up while she jumped off, reaching for an arrow as she fell.

Upon reaching the ground, she crouched down, restraining the shock put on her body from falling at such a distance. She used her crouching form to spring up toward the clone, shouting as she leaped at her. She reached her free hand toward the clone, grabbing her as she made contact while in the air.

The speed caused them to crash to the ground, and Windy shoved the bullet point of the arrow through the clone's neck, finishing the fight. She stood over the familiar body, teeth gritted as she panted fiercely.

Like the rest of the strange creatures, she disappeared into a cloud of mist as if she were a hallucination, a game to Windy's mind. Windy stood up, taking heavy breaths as she struggled to regain the air she lost during the fight. Recollecting herself as the adrenaline faded away, Windy stared at where the body had been killed, closing her eyes as if to escape a nightmare. She brought her hands up to her wet face, rubbing it as if she could wake up.

A nightmare that brought blood, sweat, and tears to all around her.

A nightmare that left a deadly footprint wherever it stalked.

A nightmare that brought forth entropy.

II

S he stood beside a Winged Beast in the center of the newly led
 Community, serious-faced and determined. Her hands gripped
a white flag while it waved freely in the wind.

The wind.

The Skybirds were never an established Community with a
designated leader. Decisions were made upon agreement from the
Skybirds themselves.

"You're old enough! This color will look great on you. Be one of us."

She closed her eyes.

*The Skybirds stood in unison, cheering as they accepted what had
once been rejected: Leadership.*

She reached her hand to find solace in the texture of the Winged
Beast.

*The new, revealing dress felt uncomfortable, her left arm exposed.
The lifelong supporter she held close to her heart handed her an
intricately crafted leather harness, connected with buckles and straps.*

She crossed the harness across her body, buckling it comfortably to the
side. She placed her blue-and-white flag and bow on the back.

"You look beautiful. You're ready for this."

She opened her eyes as she felt the wind hug her face.

The wind.

She is the Daughter of the Wind.

"Everyone, this is an important trip I must make." Windy lifted
her hands, trying to settle the nervous crowd as they talked over one
another. "I know you all are worried, but please trust me when I say
that I will find out what is happening to our Community."

The crowd continued to talk amongst themselves, some even
looking at Windy in attempts to speak to her.

Windy sighed, her fingers gripping Nodin's fur anxiously. The
texture settled her feelings, clearing her racing mind of the noise. She
clasped her hands together, smiling at the Skybirds as she spoke out
once again.

"You all have given me some very great leads. I thank you all for
that. I have prepared for the departure to the Splinter Community,
sending messengers to inform the leader of my arrival."

The Skybird crowd hushed, looking at Windy worriedly. They all
nodded, clapping for Windy. Through the crowd, some Skybirds
wished her safe travels, while some thanked her for her leadership.
Windy looked at the crowd, still smiling. She felt accomplished.

As the crowd diminished, Rose stepped through, her eyes focused
on Windy. When Windy saw her mother, she took her hands,
excited.

"How was that? Was that good?" Windy asked, bouncing up and

down with childish excitement. Despite her age, she carried herself with an innocent energy.

"That was wonderful, Windy. I am so proud of you. Here, I want to give you something before you leave." Rose reached into her fur hide satchel, taking out a good-conditioned but slightly worn map. "Here is the layout of the Quinta continent, where all the Communities are. See." Rose pointed at the map. "We are here, to the north. The Splinters are over here, to the southwest. The Peacekeepers are to the east, and the Vipers are to the southeast. Right here in the middle is safe land. Nobody claims it, so likely you won't find any disputes right there. Travel through there for safety. Don't travel through Communities."

Windy studied the map, focused. She nodded as Rose spoke to her, retaining such information. She took the map and read it for herself. Then, she looked up at Rose, folding the map again. "Thank you, Mom."

Rose hugged Windy, gradually tightening the hold. "Stay safe."

The outside land was new to both Windy and the smaller Nodin, the duo looking around in different directions as they studied their surroundings. The sun was past midday, the heat pressing down on their cold-accustomed bodies as they ventured through the true land of Quinta.

The vast emptiness of the fields brought a peace unlike that of the mountains. It was quiet, less occupied with precipitation. A calm that the Communities on the surface experienced.

Occasionally, Windy would check her map to ensure they were staying to the southwest. According to the map, the Splinter Forest, labeled Tree Kingdom, appeared hazy and dark purple. Windy assumed that if she were to find such a color, she found the forest.

Nodin panted, his flight becoming weakened and trippy. Windy noticed his condition, not hesitating to reach safety on the land for her Winged Beast.

"Down. It's okay. I'm sorry, big boy."

Nodin dove recklessly, both determined to land and fatigued from the flight.

"Easy, easy. It's okay; don't hurt yourself." Windy stroked his neck as she softly calmed Nodin. Nodin slowed his pace as he dove, his dive seeming more like a glide now. As he approached the ground, he braced himself for the landing, engaging his muscles to bring himself to a halt. But as he landed, he tripped, trotting forward with his head low as he stumbled each paw after hoof.

Windy continued to stroke him, making shushing noises to encourage steadiness. Once Nodin found his footing, Windy promptly took her feet out of the stirrups, sliding off his back. Once the pressure was off Nodin's back, he collapsed on the ground, panting. He rolled onto his stomach, finding some cool air for his bare stomach.

Windy steadily walked toward the large animal sitting next to him. Nodin turned his head toward her and rolled onto his side, his back facing Windy. She leaned forward, the top half of her body resting on the sweaty animal. As Windy's eyes grew heavy, she thought back on the beginning of her leadership duties.

"This color looks familiar, but I don't want to shift the blame onto anybody."

"What do you mean?"

"Have you learned about the outside world yet?"

"Back when I was younger. After that, not so much."

Windy recalled the conversation with a concerned Skybird.

"If you were to see the Splinter Community, you would notice that this coloring is too similar to theirs, not to mention the chaos that followed. And what's worse, they are known for their weird magic skills, or whatever they do."

What could the Splinters, a Community Windy had no business with before, have to do with the pollution that was spreading through the Skybird Community?

SPLINTER COMMUNITY

12

Nodin's trot was slow and wary, the atmosphere concerning him. He looked around, chirping nervously and flinching at every sound.

Windy completed the rest of her journey on land, relying on Nodin's running and trotting. They had now approached a forest border, where the grass beneath them went from green to steel blue, and the healthiness was dying. With an atmosphere such as that, there was no doubt Windy had found the Splinter Forest, which the Splinters established as the Tree Kingdom. Windy scanned the haunting sight ahead. There was nothing to be seen beyond the dark fog of the forest.

Nodin backed up nervously, chirping while his tail swayed back and forth. Windy, noticing his fear, patted his neck.

"Hey, it's okay. There's nothing to be scared of. At least, I think."

Windy looked around, her pats against his neck increasingly slower.

What does he know that I don't?

Nodin only backed up faster, threatening to turn around and run. Windy dismounted the trembling Winged Beast, grabbing its halter and pulling back to make it stop panicking.

"Nodin! Easy!"

Nodin looked down at her, chirping and shivering. He kept looking back to the forest and at Windy, unsure. Windy hugged him, softly caressing his feathers. She stepped back, looking at him.

"Stay. I will be back."

Nodin's frame perked up, understanding the command.

Windy turned around, taking her first steps into the forest. As she traveled along the barely legible path, she realized this Community wasn't easy to find. The fog blinded her, only able to see her hand if she reached out. Though it was late afternoon, the darkness gave an eternal night for the Community. If there were people around, she wouldn't know.

But her surroundings were chilling, not because of the darkness, but because the Skybirds were right. The Community's colorings were too similar to the Skybird tragedy three years ago. There were dying plants, the ground beneath her was crunchy, and there was an unsettling feeling of discord around her.

As time and time slipped away, Windy could hear voices. Unsettled, she tried to ground herself by clutching the hem of her dress, unsure if it was real or if she was losing her sense of reality, being lost in the darkness. She grew steadily worried, feeling unsafe in the dangerous environment.

"Hello?"

"Lost?"

Windy gasped, turning around. She reached behind her for her flag, holding it in front of her, ready to defend herself should she need to.

"Who was that?"

Silence.

But out of the silence came footsteps. The same crunchy footsteps Windy took. Then, from the footsteps, yellow markings appeared, and finally, a man could be seen a few feet in front of her, thanks to the glowing patterns on his body. He was tall, but not as tall as Windy. He had disheveled white hair, but of a decent length. His slitted eyes were the same yellow color as his bodily patterns. Such distinct patterns helped carry a sense of attractiveness to his friendly demeanor.

Was he a guide for lost travelers like Windy?

Windy lowered her flag, letting her guard settle ever so slightly. She stood up straight, presenting herself with higher authority than the man.

"Yes. Unfortunately, I am. I am looking for the Splinter Community. More specifically, I'm looking for their leader, um." Windy paused, thinking. She bit her thumb, trying to catch a thought. "I don't remember his name, but he's the Splinter leader."

"Ah. You must be looking for Shambor. Lucky for you, I'm a Splinter. I know where to find him. You're pretty far out from the Community. I don't assume you've been walking in circles?"

Windy's ears drooped, and her face warmed to a red color. She looked down as she mounted her flag back behind her, avoiding contact with him as if it would make her melt where she stood.

Embarrassment wiped away her serious delivery; she now felt smaller than the man. The man noticed her vulnerability and smiled, chuckling with delight.

"No need to get frustrated. It's common for outsiders to get lost in our forest. Or killed."

Windy's body froze at an instant.

The Splinter laughed, her response an amusement to him. "If you were sent for Shambor, I can get you back on track to the Splinter Community. You're not that turned around. Promise."

Windy's ears perked up, and she looked back at the man. She smiled, bright energy radiating from her excitement.

"That would be so nice of you to help. Thank you."

The man pointed in the direction they needed to go, allowing Windy to walk first. He followed Windy, staying close by and alert. They took only a few steps in silence before the man spoke up.

"You seem, well, important. Am I right?" he asked.

Windy giggled. "Right. I am the Daughter of the Wind. But you can just call me Windy."

He gasped, his serpentine eyes widening like an owl's. His hand darted to his mouth, covering his exclamation. He stumbled, staring at her like she had announced herself as a divine being.

"Is everything okay?" Windy asked, hesitant.

"You're Windy? Like, Skybird leader Windy?"

Windy was unsure of his behavior. "Yes. Is there a problem?"

"I thought that was you, but I wasn't too sure. Wow." He lowered his hand from his face, a mix of disappointment and awe on his handsome face. Then, suddenly, he grabbed her hand as they kept walking, shaking it hurriedly but respectfully. "My name is Orion, Windy. It would have been disrespectful for me not to introduce myself to such a new leader."

Windy smiled. "Thank you, Orion."

The Tree Kingdom lived up to its name. The Community grounds seemed barren to the naked eye, but there were tree huts, shops, and recreational reserves around the dimly lit civilization. The Splinter's homes were both built in trees and on land, but the structures varied depending on location to achieve the most efficient camouflage within the forest.

There were many tunnels, including those that were indicated by cyan torches. Civilians crawled in and out of tunnels, climbed up and down trees, and navigated their surroundings as if they were in broad daylight.

Each Splinter had its own distinctive luminous yellow markings that could be used to identify individuals. Their hair was silver, they had glowing yellow serpentine eyes, and they all wore dark, mystical clothes that matched the forest's atmosphere.

While Orion guided her through the Community, passing Splinters would gasp at Windy, staring at her in disbelief. Windy was focused on Orion, so she didn't notice the reactions of her surroundings, but they were similar to how the Skybirds reacted toward Windy during her earlier years.

"Orion! Who is this?" Two girls walked up to him. A confident, fanged girl narrowed her eyes at Windy. "Why have you brought this thing into our Community?"

"Relax, Elise. This is..." Orion paused, giving a smug,

accomplished look to Elise. "Windy. The Skybird leader."

The girl beside Elise gasped. "Windy? The Skybird leader? The one Shambor was looking—" She was cut off by Elise, covering her mouth, punching her in the shoulder.

Windy focused on the women, ears twitching in discomfort.

What was that about?

"Haste, you dense son of a frog," Elise practically hissed at Haste, her words overflowing with venom.

Windy continued staring, confused. Haste looked at Elise worriedly, elbowing her.

Elise sighed. "Windy is obviously the one Shambor was expecting, remember?"

Haste nodded. Though she was still silenced, her face spoke a thousand words of her fear. Orion chuckled nervously, looking at Windy.

"Please don't mind those two. Those are my sisters, Haste and Elise. Haste can be a little strange sometimes. Her head is a little too far in the trees."

Elise wore old-looking clothes, as if she either didn't care about her personal image or if there was some underlying reason as a Splinter. Her eyes were full of scorn, and her very presence could kill on sight. She was the shortest, but she carried herself with a dangerous power. Haste wore an entirely different clothing choice than Elise, her personality like night and day. She wore comfortable, exposed clothes that made her soft features resemble the violet flower in her hair. Unlike Elise, Haste had soft eyes that seemed they would let anybody in for a friend. It was hard to believe these three were siblings.

"Windy, I think you should take a look around yourself. Surely you'd need somewhere to stay?" Orion put his attention on Windy once again, his voice continuing to be ever so friendly.

"I was planning on staying here until my business is done," Windy replied, not noticing her hands pinched at the fabric of her skirt.

"You've had a long trip. It would be my pleasure to accommodate you so your stay here is to die for." Orion smiled.

Windy became bashful, her body becoming light. She shuffled her feet, at a loss for words.

"Please. Take a look around. I'll find you in just a moment."

"Thank you." Windy stepped back, nodding her head respectfully.

When Windy was gone, Orion redirected his attention to his sisters. His friendly demeanor was wiped off his face like wind blowing away leaves. "Come. We need to talk."

The Splinter siblings maneuvered through the darkness, leaving the Community grounds to find solitude. Farther out from the Community grounds, the trees became thicker, the darkness welcoming its familiar faces. However, the darkness was their friend. They were one with the lightless forest. As they walked the path, Orion led them astray, their feet approaching a patch of bramble.

"Here."

The siblings stopped walking. They stood in a small circle,

looking at each other. Elise's face darted toward Orion, her mouth snarling to expose her teeth. "So, that's who he wanted to see?"

"No doubt. Feathered, Skybird. The name matches, too."

"Does she know anything?" Haste asked, her gentle voice full of worry.

"Absolutely not."

"How do you know? Don't doubt someone like her. Rumors spread about her like wildfire. How are we to be certain she's innocent? How can we even be sure she's a real leader?" Elise argued.

"How would she know anything if her Community stays out of other people's business? She stays in her Community, as she should. She has had no reason to be in another Community's business."

Haste watched the siblings argue, her eyes darting back and forth nervously.

"You forget why he wanted to see her. She has something nobody else has. She's dangerous. Not only to us, but to other Communities."

Orion grinned, putting a hand on his hip and bending over at his sister. "Oh, Elise. You worry too much. I won't let someone as weird, cute, and attractive as her get in the way of our history."

Elise opened her mouth to argue, then she looked away from him, her mind spiraling with thoughts. Then, she returned the grin, pushing his face away with her finger. "At least you're right about something. She is pretty attractive, if not cute."

Haste's body seemed to freeze, her eyes snapping to a raw mix of confusion and disbelief. All she could do was slowly turn her head toward Elise, expressing such a speechless, unbeknownst reaction.

13

Windy carefully stepped through the Community, watching her step. She looked out for the glowing violet torches that indicated the location of the leader's reserve. Earlier that morning, Orion had found Windy walking out of the Splinter food hut, satisfying herself with a cooked morsel. As promised, he directed her to the leader's reserve to handle her business with Shambor.

Windy looked at the glowing violet torches, thoughtful. How could fire be such a color? In fact, there were various colors of fire throughout the Community. Then, Windy recalled that the Splinters were known for their spells and supernatural castings. They must have created colors of fire to add to their Community for identification.

Windy checked her feet, focusing her eyes on the darkness. The blinding view triggered an anxiety from her chest. She didn't know where she was stepping, and the fire illuminated only so much of the surrounding area. While she was looking for the tunnel with her feet, Windy slipped on a dip, and she stumbled for her footing as her leg slid down.

Windy reached her arms out to either side of her body to catch herself along the tunnel wall. After recovering from the startle with uneasy breaths, Windy crept down the tunnel one careful foot after the other.

Nope. I am definitely not a Splinter.

The tunnel was just as dark as the Tree Kingdom, if not darker. The only way Windy knew where to go was by following the lit violet torches along the path. Even then, Windy lost her footing at unexpected dips in the tunnel, leaving her steps wary and slower.

The tunnel didn't seem to curve in any other direction than down, indicating she was venturing farther beneath the surface. The tunnel felt cool, with the exception of the quick sensations of heat along Windy's shoulders from the occasional passing of torches.

After countless cautious steps, Windy could see an illuminated cavern, which appeared to contain objects. Windy stepped in slowly, turning her head in every direction to take in the sights of such a room. This must be the leader's reserve. There were desks around the tight cavern with stray papers, likely letters from the past.

In the center of the cavern was a large engraving on the wall. The Splinter crest. The crest was a shard punctured in a tree, the leaves falling from the bare limbs. Just below the crest was a wooden, moss-padded chair occupied by a bored yet relaxed Splinter. He seemed like he had nothing to do. He wore a cape that draped over the throne-like seat and wore regal, princely clothing with its own Splinter touch. His skin was tanned, like Windy's, but with a more milky hue.

"Excuse me?" Windy spoke up from the chilling silence.

The Splinter, thrown out of his daze, looked in Windy's direction. At first sight, he gasped, jumping up as if an armed threat had walked in. Realizing who she was, he settled.

"Apologies, I thought you were somebody else." He chuckled with an underlying tinge of uncertainty. "You must be the one I am expecting, correct? Windy is the name?"

"Yes. How did you know who I am?" Windy asked hesitantly, her ears twitching with uncertainty.

"You, a Community leader, doesn't know how word spreads around Quinta so quickly? Shameful. Allow me to enlighten your mindlessness. The Vipers tell us everything! Such chatty creatures. I received an order quite recently, and oh, they talked and talked about some fascinating information about the Skybirds!"

"Assuming about me?"

"Precisely!" Shambor lifted his hand to his mouth in amusement. "They described you in the most majestic way possible. And then that letter brought by that little Skybird was like a miracle. The very Windy I have heard rumors of wants to talk! To me!"

He sounds a little too excited.

Windy nodded, her mind racing with possibilities she couldn't comprehend just yet. "Yes. Well, it's true. I have come here to talk to you about some abnormalities happening in my Community. We're not blaming your Community, we just think that you could know what could be happening." Windy stood confidently, speaking to the leader. "And you are Shambor?"

"Right! I am the leader of this Community, and I can surely assist you." He smiled, the flames illuminating an underlying threat.

"Thank you. We noticed some strange occurrences in our Community, like discoloration, beasts we have never seen before raiding the Community, and our Community life turning against each other. We wanted to discuss this because the coloring seems familiar to this Community. We're not sure if it was you or a strange coincidence. Either way, it's worth addressing."

Shambor stared at Windy, his regal, swirling facial markings hiding what lay beneath the blank, glowing eyes. He blinked once before opening his mouth to speak. "That is strange indeed. I don't know why that would happen. As far as I know, the Splinters haven't been involved in any"—he licked his lips, choosing his words—"tricks directed toward the Communities. No, we are not involved with your misfortunes."

As Windy listened, her spine chilled as she realized he must be in the presence of an experienced, well-rounded leader. He spoke with a divine confidence not even she could match.

"I am sorry this happened, and I'm sorry you all now live in fear of another odd threat."

"Another?"

Shambor smiled. "I can see you aren't that experienced with your history."

Windy glanced to the side, her fingers slowly beginning to fiddle with the softness of her skirt. What was he talking about?

"Long ago, the Communities found themselves in a nationwide dispute over dominance and rule over the Quinta continent.

Some Communities agreed, while some disagreed. But because no reasonable outcome could be made verbally, they took it physically. It was horrible, horrible. Communities were destroyed, yet they gained an unfortunate fear of the matter ever since war broke out. You live in a relatively better time. No more of that. I can say that for sure."

Windy's ears twitched, as if they were shivering from something cold. He spoke slowly, as if he were picking his words throughout his mild story. The story was indeed mild. There seemed to be holes covered by a thin sheet all over his makeshift story.

"I think there's something you're not—"

"However!" Shambor stuck his finger up, his nose in the air. "To express my concern for the history, I'm offering you refuge in our Community until such a threat settles down. After all, they say that history tends to repeat itself. I wouldn't want that to happen again, so allow me to keep you safe for the time being."

That didn't make sense. If anything, she needed to be present with the Skybirds to ensure their safety. There was something wrong with this leader. The dull, sticky feeling coursing through her body proved it.

"Thank you, but I will not accept your offer. I need to stay with my Community to keep them safe."

Shambor stood up, his cape flowing down his back. His stature wasn't the biggest, but he could be looked at from a comfortable height. He took a few steps toward Windy, radiating a certain friendliness that seemed spoiled. "I insist. Please allow our Community to keep you at bay. I would hate for you to return to your Community fatigued and troubled. Some Splinters here are kind and welcoming to outsiders."

Orion crossed her mind.

"You will be safe here in the meantime. You may stay here for the night, or however long you wish. It appears you have already had a comforting time here, so I am allowing your visit to be extended."

Windy's shoulders slumped in indecisiveness. She needed to go back to her Community and family, but on the other hand, she might never see Orion again. She looked down at him, nodding as she adjusted her posture. "Okay. But I won't stay here for long. If I do, well, you must be very good at negotiating." She smiled, giggling at her own banter.

"Make yourself comfortable. If you need anything, I have some reliable friends who could support your visit. I'm sure you've met Orion, yes?"

Something hit Windy from the inside. How did he know?

"Yes, I have. He's been very helpful so far. A welcoming Splinter, I'd say." Windy smiled.

Shambor returned the smile. "Indeed, he is. He is my assistant, alongside a few others."

That makes sense.

"Well selected. Thank you for your help and hospitality." Windy lowered her head in respect before turning around to scale up the tunnel. As she exited the leader's reserve, she could feel her trust in the Community growing.

Stepping out into the usual darkness, Windy searched the Community carefully, her eyes not completely adjusted to the darkness of the Community. She wanted to speak to Orion, who was apparently someone close to the leader. She never thought she would have been in the presence of someone of such high authority.

"Orion?"

Windy weaved between trees, calling out for the Splinter.

"Hello? Orion?"

Through the darkness, gold patterns illuminated beneath the tree. It must be a Splinter. Windy walked faster, mindful of anything in front of her in the darkness. As she got closer, she found it was a Splinter after all.

His legs were crossed as his body lay comfortably under the dead tree. His eyes were closed, and his shaggy bangs covered one side of his face like a curtain as he lay. Fireflies gleamed around him, giving an ethereal tone to his contentment.

After she took her last steps in front of him, she bent over, looking down at him. Orion looked up, shaking the hair out of his face to see Windy better. He didn't flinch at her close presence. Instead, he looked her in the eyes and smiled as he stood up. Windy straightened her posture when he stood up, keeping her brown eyes on his yellow eyes. Orion gave Windy his full attention, his face warm and inviting. Windy's ears drooped, and her face flushed, at a loss for words.

"So, Orion," she managed to spit out, "um, so, I wanted to let you know I'm going to stay in the Community for a little bit." Windy stumbled awkwardly over her words. "Not for long, though."

Orion chuckled, amused. He leaned on the tree, keeping his eye on her. "Oh, so you're joining our Community?"

Windy quickly shook her head, her hair flying from side to side.

"No, not at all. I'm still devoted to my Community, I just need some time in a different place."

The lie felt rotten as it rolled off her tongue, but she couldn't bring herself to tell him why.

I just want to see him a little more. How bad can that be?

"Hm. Perfect. That's perfect."

She huffed. "How so?"

"It's not very often we get visitors. In fact, we never get any. I thought it would stay that way, but maybe it's nice for a change every so often." He grinned, a grin that reminded Windy too closely of Shambor.

Windy looked down. "Well, Shambor told me that there were places I could stay. I assume that they're on the Community grounds, yes?"

Orion nodded. "The reservations are on the Community grounds by the fallen tree. But I need to warn you. You won't be staying anywhere unless you can climb."

Windy shook her head. "That won't be an issue."

"Ah, so you can climb too?"

"Yes. I can do a few things you wouldn't expect from a thing like me," she uttered sarcastically.

"I would expect that much from a prodigy like you. The first Skybird leader." Orion nodded. "Good to know, though. I'm sure I can find you if I need. Sooner than later, hopefully. However long that may be." He gave a sly grin, sneaking his words carefully toward Windy once again.

Windy fidgeted with the soft sleeve on her left arm, smiling.

"Thank you. You've been great to me so far."

Orion returned the gentle smile, his previously suspicious grin fading away. "Hope to see you around."

Windy walked away without another word, her head hung low.

She found that the Splinters were all like her: misunderstood. She was seen as a threat, but made up for herself. The Splinters seemed no different. They were seen as a heartless Community, Windy being told to avoid them in her earlier years. If they were so heartless, why was this Community avoided when its members were kind to others who were unlike them? If Windy had to decide for herself, she wanted a Community that acted such as this.

As Orion travelled deeper into the forest, stepping farther and farther away from Windy, his head turned restlessly in different directions, as if looking for something too important where he could find no sense of relief. The farther he travelled, the darker it became, as if he were walking through stacked curtains.

Then, he stopped walking, the darkness greeted once again by silence. "Perfect."

14

The Splinters were a Community in total isolation. Nobody left the Community, whether by choice or by force. Their method of communication was by letter, as with the other Communities, but they had no messengers.

Instead, they used their magic to quickly deliver their letters to the receiver, making their method of communication the fastest of any other Community.

Even their weapons deviated from the norm, at least what Windy knew. The blades of various weapons were all coated with a poison Windy dared not touch. But even if she wanted one, getting too close to such dark magic made her skin burn and itch. It would serve no benefit to her survival.

Windy resided in the red-ribboned tree, where the Splinters reserved tree huts for visitors who needed a place to rest. Windy jumped onto the trunk, reaching one hand after the other. The climb was never long, whether because the guest huts were shorter than the surrounding trees or because Windy could cover more ground from her height.

Most trees lacked ladders due to the nature of a Splinter's natural climbing talents. They often hid in trees, so they needed to be accustomed to climbing. She jumped onto the platform, her body making one swift movement from the ground up. The rental key was clipped to her golden-sashed belt. They were silent except for the occasional jingle from the clash of the belt clip and the metal key.

Windy unlatched the clip from her belt, unlocked the door, pushed it open, and slowly closed it, avoiding excessive noise. The interior was small, but it was suitable for visitors seeking a quick trip from home. There were wooden furnishings around the small place that added to the strong smell of nature. Overall, the room wasn't too large to take up too much space. Such a cozy setting gave a peaceful feeling to the visitor's original home.

A black woven rug was beneath Windy's boots at the walkway, which provided the only soft space in the hut from the wooden base of the hut. The bedding of the small single bed in the far back was made from packed tree leaves, all appearing to be fresh and alive. They were packed and covered with animal hides, providing a softer surface for sleepers. Windy's weapons were placed on the wall closest to the door, providing the only color in the otherwise gloomy hut.

Even though Windy isolated herself from the Community most days, she was fascinated with life in a completely different Community than the one she grew up in. Even with an unusual outsider such as Windy, the Splinters minded their own business, stealing glances at the leader. Their gazes varied from awestruck to nervous to defensive. Windy paid no mind. She was used to such reactions from people.

Windy sat by the river that ran through the Community. She could hear the water, but couldn't see it running over slick stones. The darkness was lonely. If there were nobody around in such an atmosphere, it would be a sorrowful experience. But Windy wasn't there to compress. She was there to decompress.

The river reminded her of the sound of the wind beating in her ears at home. Though closing her eyes served no purpose against the dark, she stared out in front of her, staring at whatever could be in front of her in the void. But through the darkness came a small voice. It seemed to come from beside her.

Windy looked to the side, noticing small, prominent patterns. A Splinter must have found her. She didn't know what she looked like; all she knew was that her face patterns were spotted and floral.

"You look weird."

Windy resisted a sigh; the blunt voice sounded like a child's. "I get that a lot."

"Do you have friends?" the voice said bluntly once again. There was an underlying harshness in the tone.

Windy nodded. "Yes, but they're far away from here."

"Where?"

"In a Community unlike this one."

"You're from another place?" the voice asked inquisitively. The patterns seemed to shift closer to her.

"Yes. I'm the leader of the Skybird Community. Daughter of the Wind, but I go by Windy."

"My name is Berryleaf." The child seemed to be grinning by the way her tone shifted to a more enthusiastic tone.

What a cute name.

"Why are you by yourself?"

"I just want to. Sometimes I like to spend time in places that clear my mind." Windy mindlessly picked at a piece of grass.

"Did you know you can eat here?" Berryleaf asked, her tone full of mirth.

"Huh?" Windy shifted herself towards Berryleaf, straining her eyes to focus on the Splinter.

Berryleaf seemed to look toward the river, moving herself toward the bed. "Watch."

Kind of hard.

The sound of the river was disturbed when hands penetrated the natural flow of the water, the river moving past such an obstruction. There was no sound other than the water until there was splashing.

"What's happening?" Windy exclaimed.

Berryleaf tapped her shoulder with a wet hand. "Help. I always need help. Grab it."

Windy reached out, trying to find where Berryleaf's hands were. There was something slimy and thrashing in her hands.

"See, you can eat fish here. Take it. I'm giving it to you."

Windy took the fish, straining her eyes to find the silhouette of the prey. As she strained her eyes, Berryleaf placed her hands into the river again, fishing once more. Windy didn't have her arrows on her person, so she juggled ideas in her mind. She couldn't just eat it alive.

"Excuse me, Berryleaf? How do I eat it?"

"Do you not have knives?"

"They're back where I'm staying."

Berryleaf's hands came out of the water, and she searched her body for something sharp. She must have had a bag on her because there was a clipping sound out of the darkness. From the darkness, something poked Windy's scarred arm.

"Oh!"

"Here. Give it back, please. It's mine."

What is a child doing with a blade?

Windy hesitantly placed the fish down, taking a chance at stabbing the thrashing animal. As she pushed down the blade, she exclaimed, violently shaking her hand. There was a stinging on her finger. "Ow!"

"Be careful."

Windy sighed, but she heard the fish stop struggling. She took the blade out of the fish and gave it to Berryleaf. "Here you go."

"Thank you."

Windy looked down at where the dead fish might be, unsure what to do next. "I'll have it later."

"Why?"

"So I can cook it."

"Just eat it."

"I can't eat raw food."

"You're weird." Berryleaf seemed to have successfully caught another fish. Through the flailing, there was a crunchy bite. She must be eating the fish raw. Windy found that Splinters must be able to eat both raw and cooked animals.

Windy sat with the dead fish, listening to the sound of the river once again and the occasional crunching of Berryleaf. She found the child's presence comforting, her willingness to interact with such a stranger with such kindness. Once again, a discriminated Community proving themselves wrong.

"You're nice," Berryleaf said with an empty mouth. She took another bite of the fish.

"Thank you. So are you. You're a cool Splinter."

Berryleaf giggled through the chewing. "Wha ah yu gunna du na?"

"Uh, wait until you're done eating," Windy awkwardly advised.

Berryleaf swallowed her bite, her mouth empty to talk. "What are you gonna do now?"

"I'll be leaving soon. I don't know how long, but maybe I'll get to know some more of your Community first. There are some nice people here, including you."

"That's fun."

Windy sat in silence, listening to Berryleaf eat. She allowed the child to accompany her, the presence comforting alongside the sound of the river. The child didn't say anything like Windy, only there to keep Windy company. Windy continued to find that Splinters weren't bad, so what made them such a despised Community?

15

Windy climbed down the tree hut's branches, her movements rushed with excitement. She had a fond smile on her face and bright eyes, eyes that could foresee a future that had been anticipated for weeks. She used the first step taken on land to pivot her whole body around the tree, her smile brightening. Orion stood in front of her, his physique radiating with nervousness, likely from rushing from something.

"Sorry, I'm late. Those sisters of mine were holding me back from"—he paused—"some weird girl things."

"All that matters is that you're here." Windy reached out an arm but pulled back, planning to hug but finding it awkward at the moment.

"I appreciate the understanding, Windy. Now, come on. I haven't eaten all day waiting for you."

Windy and Orion walked close beside each other, Windy feeling warm from the walk. Earlier, Orion had asked Windy for a lunch date, finding the need to accompany her while in such an unfamiliar Community. The Splinter eatery they were planning to visit was shielded by a willow, which served as its curtains. *The Splinted Tree*.

Inside, Splinters of all ages sat on individual tree trunks used as seats. There were families with children, there were Splinters on dates, even elderly Splinters with their grandchildren. The atmosphere was inviting and comfortable, given the diverse range of Splinters that attended. The lighting was relieving in the otherwise dark Community, the restaurant lit by luminescent insects in jars and by a non-flammable fire created by Splinter magic.

As they entered, Windy was the only one out of place, the Skybird colors contrasting with the dark shades of the Splinter Community. When the Splinter and Skybird walked up to the ordering desk, the attendant's eyes darted to Windy like she was an immediate threat.

"Hello," their server, Thorn, managed to say. "What can I get you two?"

Thorn focused wary eyes on Windy's presence.

"Good afternoon, sir."

How does he know it's afternoon?

Orion looked down at the menu in front of them on the counter. "Please give us a moment." He turned his head toward Windy. "What would you like?"

Windy read over the menu. It appeared that the Community was omnivorous, like the Skybirds. The diet wouldn't be too unfamiliar to Windy.

"Um, maybe the, um." Windy was unsure. Looking over the menu, there seemed to be many dishes containing internal body parts of critters and other hunted prey.

Liver, lungs, stomach, and other shredded organs.

Windy had to refrain from gagging. All she had was meat and plants.

"Excuse me, but do you have any, say, um...meat? Like, from actual body muscle and fat?"

Thorn looked lost at the question as if he had never heard anything related to such a request. He looked down at the menu, searching for something close to Windy's request.

"We have Stuffed Stomach."

"What is that?" Windy breathed, allowing herself to stay kind to the culture. But the name was enough to make her vomit.

"It's a sliced owl with berries and cooked remains."

Windy's ears twitched with uneasiness upon hearing the ingredients. She assumed that there should be some sort of tolerable meat for her to pick off.

"Okay, I'll get that, please. Do you think you could make it rare?"

"Rare?"

"I mean...lightly cooked?"

The Splinter slowly wrote down her order, confused etched on his face. "And you, mister?"

"Ah, I'll take the Diced Critter Stew. And add two cups of water for us."

That didn't sound as bad as what Windy had ordered.

The two took their drinks and then walked to their seats after Orion paid for their lunch. Windy sat down on the tree stump, looking around at the Splinters in the vicinity.

"Liking your time here?" Orion asked Windy.

Windy looked at him, her attention diverted from the atmosphere. "Oh yes. Very much! It's so different from the Skybirds, though."

"I would assume so. You're even a Skybird by the way you act."

Windy didn't know how to formally respond to that. "Uh, thanks. But anyhow, you all seem so nice. I mean, it seems like you all mind your own business. I don't know why I've heard such bad things about you."

Orion seemed to focus on the wooden table for a moment too long before looking back up at Windy. "We're highly misunderstood."

"I understand. So am I."

"That's a shame. You're so friendly, it's hard not to appreciate someone like you."

"But I'm sure you don't get that."

Orion chuckled. "What do you mean?"

"You just seem important. Whenever I see you in the Community, Splinters look at you like something to worship."

"Ah, not really." Orion shook his head. "It's really because I work for Shambor. I guess."

But why? Shambor looks up to no good.

"He has us do stuff for him that he should probably do himself. But it's not just me. So are my siblings. We're all under Shambor's eyes. He favors us more than the other Splinters."

Maybe he's one of the good ones. An outlier, like me.

"So, you all are important?"

"If you want to say it like that. Elise takes his work very seriously. I would say she's his favorite. Haste, eh? Haste is Haste. She's kind of timid. She didn't want to be pulled into this, so it's all forced upon her. And me, well, I don't care. It's fine. I find it appealing to work with a leader."

"You carry yourself like you are one."

"You tend to act like your role if you like it enough." Orion played with his fork, looking down at the table with what could be discontent.

That must not apply to Haste.

They sat in silence, drinking their water, waiting for their food. The water tasted unusual, with a spicy, tangy flavor. Windy didn't care too much about it. Different Communities had different taste palettes.

But it wasn't too long before their food was brought out. For such a busy place, Windy was surprised that their food was made so quickly.

Windy looked at her food. It was indeed a sliced owl, but it was stripped of its feathers. Windy poked the fork into the bird, and it began to bleed, just the way she likes it. But looking at its contents, Windy's ears pinned back as she gagged, covering her mouth with her hand. Orion laughed as he ate, noticing her nausea.

"Everything alright?"

Windy nodded, putting her thumb up. She breathed through her mouth to avoid the smell while she cut her food. Though the grotesque contents of such an appealing dish minimized her eating experience, she savored the taste of the bird, the meat cooked just right for her.

"It's not that bad, Windy. Just try one." Orion stabbed what seemed to be a small, sliced piece of heart with his fork. He reached for Windy, shoving the piece of meat in her face.

Windy gasped, covering her mouth and swallowing what food she had in her mouth, regardless of its chewed state. She shook her head, looking at Orion. Such a sight appalled her.

"For me? Please?"

Windy closed her eyes. She couldn't ignore such a bribe. She leaned forward, opening her mouth to eat Orion's offering. She closed her mouth as she took the food off the fork and bit down. There was a soft, chewy feeling followed by a crunch. Windy's eyes shot open wide, her brown irises outlined in white. She snatched a napkin from the table and spat out the food, gagging in the process. She kept it to her mouth a moment longer, unsure if she needed to vomit. Orion was laughing as she did, finding her reaction personally amusing.

"What a Skybird!"

Windy shook her head, quickly drinking the electric-tasting water. "Please never again!"

"At least you tried something outside of your Community."

Windy's shoulders slumped.

"It wasn't that bad. But I'm glad you did it. For me." Orion leaned in, his eyes teasing hers.

Windy's ears drooped, and her feathers fell onto her head. She looked down, bashful and nervous. She picked at her food, slowly eating and avoiding Orion's gaze. The two continued eating their lunch, with Orion enjoying it more than Windy. As Windy took the last bites of her meal, she handed the plate over to Orion.

"Do you want what's left?"

"Of course I would. If you won't eat it, give it all here." Orion took her dish, sliding Windy's leftovers into the blood-bathed soup. Windy watched the sight, mildly disgusted but with an appetite gone.

As Windy continued to watch Orion eat, she learned enough about him. Orion became dear to her, an unfamiliar feeling swelling up inside Windy. She liked the way he looked; she liked how he treated other Splinters, as far as she could tell, and he was open to activities with Windy, such as tonight.

In a Community so misunderstood, he hit a feeling close to home.

This Community doesn't feel right, but is he an outsider like me?

Windy didn't want to leave when someone like him was in the Community. But if she needed to leave, couldn't she find some way to stay with him?

16

Windy could claim she is a dual Community member if she wanted to. The duration of her stay was far longer than she anticipated. She had no other reason to reside in the Community other than her fear of departing from Orion. Such a person made her feel wanted, drawing her in without judgment.

But though Windy enjoyed such a discriminated Community, she understood she had to return to her leadership duties, and she needed to return promptly. The length she was missing was unacceptable, putting her image on the brink of losing authority.

But Orion.

Orion's behavior had remained friendly and inviting, unlike many of the Splinters like Elise or Shambor, but they weren't as discriminating as the Skybirds. But then here is Orion. Why did she care about him so much? The only person in her life she immensely cared about was her mother.

Windy weaved between trees, her eyes focusing on the darkness for a solo Splinter. Orion was known to hop between trees whenever he felt like being alone. But instead of propped under a tree to take a rest, she found him sitting outside the leader's reserve with his siblings. Her face beamed, and she ran over to the group, waving her hand. The weapons propped on her back beat against each other, creating a clanking noise.

"I don't know what your problem is, but you're taking too much time. Shambor told you to be swift," Elise barked at Orion, her arms folded across her chest in frustration.

"I know, but"—Orion heaved a sigh—"do I really have to?"

"If you don't do it, I will. And you know I won't make it pretty."

"Guys, there's no need to do this. Orion has every right to—oh. Guys, shush." Haste noticed Windy's presence, tapping them both in a rush.

Elise gave Orion a disapproving glance. Windy glanced to the side at Elise, a stinging sensation coursing through her body.

She hits deep. What's up with her around me?

Pushing Elise's to the back of her head, Windy turned her attention to her dear friend. "Orion! Thank goodness you're here. I wanted to have a talk with you." Windy paused, staying respectful. "Is now a bad time?"

Orion gave her that same grin that made Windy's body feel light, her heart fluttering with some emotion she couldn't quite picture. "No, not at all. I was finishing up a conversation with Haste and Elise. I can have a talk with you."

Windy smiled and waved her hand at the siblings. "Hello, you two."

Haste smiled and returned the friendly gesture, but Elise kept her scornful gaze off of the Skybird. An idea seemed to click within her with the way she gasped. She whipped her body around, her hands grasping Orion's shoulders.

"Go. Now! Go!"

Orion put his hands on her chest, his face nervous. He stepped back to attend to Windy.

"Let's go, Wind. I'm here to listen to you. Let's get away from these two." His tone was friendly, but his eyes were heavy with annoyance. "I'm done dealing with Splinter girls."

Windy smiled. *Wind!*

"Did something happen?" Windy asked as they began to walk.

"Oh, you'd understand. My sisters are just being boars. They've always been that way to their big brother." He swiped at the air.

"I can't imagine. Your patience is amazing around them." Windy began to speak mindlessly, her thoughts clouded by the Splinter she was walking with.

"You grow on it after a while."

Orion led Windy down the dark path, guiding her to their meeting place. Windy followed closely beside Orion, her mind buzzing in anticipation of their conversation. She could feel a burning sensation on her leg, but was unsure if it was because she had stepped on a sharp bramble. They were walking farther off from the Community, and Windy's vision, though accustomed to the darkness, became strained. These parts of the forest were especially dark, and without Orion's luminescent patterns, she wouldn't find her way.

Orion scanned his surroundings with the Splinter vision that could interpret darkness as daylight. He put his hand out to stop Windy, his hand grazing her chest. They both stood in the darkness, but by how far they walked without avoiding trees, it must be a clearing.

"Ladies first."

Windy sighed, facing Orion and taking a step back. It troubled her to break such news.

"Orion. This Community has been so lovely. I'm so glad I've had the opportunity to know you and be taken on some lovely"—Windy looked down, considering her words—"days with just us. But I can't stay here. I need to go home."

"Home? You're going home? So soon?" Orion's bright eyes furrowed with worry. He took Windy's hands as if the lack of physical touch would cause her to disappear in front of his eyes. "You seem so happy here. Can't you stay just a little longer?" Orion's composure toppled, his once-confident demeanor now overwhelmed with panic and disappointment.

Windy frowned, her naturally furrowed eyes giving her sadness an extra layer in the midst of the situation. She sighed, slouching as she looked down at the dimness beneath her feet. The weapons on her back rested on her defeated back, the silk of her flag falling over her shoulders.

"Orion, I'm a Community leader, remember? I can't just join a Community I can't be loyal to."

"Yes, yes. I understand, but I'm going to miss you. I've had such a lovely time with you in the Community. Will I see you again?"

"No, I don't believe so. Unless I have business with the Splinters, which I don't think will be ever. The Skybird Community is neutral. I respect that and want to maintain such peace."

As Windy looked into his eyes, she could tell he was deeply troubled. But lurking beneath those troubled eyes was conflict, as if he were juggling a difficult decision. "Orion. Please understand."

Orion's eyes darted to the ground beneath them, the conflict a heavy weight bearing on his emotions. "It's been two months, Windy. Couldn't you stay until the end of this week?"

Windy became firm, an urgent yet sorrowful emphasis in her voice. "Orion, I really can't. This is too long a time to be away. You would understand if you were the leader of a Community, especially as new as I am. But you're not. You don't understand what I need to do."

"Windy." He steadily lifted his hand as he tapped his fingers on the other.

"I'm sorry. If you really want a compromise, you could join the Skybirds with me. Then we'll never have to be separated from each other." Despite her stress, Windy managed an inviting smile. "You would be no different. We would both differ from what other people see as normal."

"Splinters aren't allowed to leave their Communities. Haven't you noticed this? Shambor tends to favor me. I'm one of the more important Splinters alongside my siblings."

"You don't have to let anybody know. You can leave with me, keep it silent. If there are other Splinters to take your place, let them. Orion, this is about us. Don't you want to see me if I can't make a commitment?"

"Windy. Now I can't accept that. I'm honored, but I can't."

Windy's face twisted in disappointment, defeat flooding over her. "Then there is no need to argue anymore. I'm done talking. What did you need to tell me now?"

Orion shook his hanging head, just as defeated as Windy. "There's no need anymore." He leaned in to hug Windy with one arm.

The burning sensation on her leg increased.

"It doesn't matter what I need to say anymore. But I want to compromise. Please, Windy. I think we"—he paused—"we should..."

The burning sensation went away.

A shriek enveloped the previously silent forest, the feminine shrill full of pain.

"This is ridiculous," Orion hissed, gripping Windy's collapsing body. "It's even more ridiculous that you would trust a Splinter, let alone have the entire Community know about your existence. How naïve could you be to fall for such a predator?"

Orion let go of Windy's body, letting it fall to the cold ground. He held the venom-infused dagger in his hand, the blade dripping with a mix of Skybird blood and dark magic.

"You'd think I'd love a bird like you? I never did. I never loved your Community, and nobody will. You're only one of many lazy, fake people who call themselves a Community. You don't do anything."

Windy reached behind her back as she pushed herself to sit up. The substance that coated her hand wasn't just blood. She choked on fear, the disbelief blending with the pain flaring through her body.

"If you think you can live life full of trust and sunshine, you'll find yourself right here. Consider this a lesson learned."

Windy looked up at Orion, her eyes full of rejection and betrayal as if pleading for this moment to be a dream.

Orion bent over, grinning in the same smile that would have made Windy's heart flutter with a feeling she now came to realize was love.

"It's all coming together."

Windy's mouth opened, building up the strength to speak weakly. "What is?"

Orion chuckled. "Well, if only you could see for yourself. But you've trusted the wrong person, and now you won't get to know what happens to your lazy Community."

Windy's hands planted on the ground, her muscles working at a high rate to haul herself up to her feet. Her rage fueled her strength, despite her body feeling heavy from the weight of her weapons. As she was dying, she fought back, reaching for her flag, prepared for a fight she was destined to lose.

Orion stepped back as she struggled, amused. "Your persistence was always something I've admired."

Windy's legs strode toward Orion, her adrenaline numbing the pain in her back to make movement tolerable. She could only get so far before collapsing at his feet, the flag rolling out of her limp hand. Though Orion stood over her body in triumph, he couldn't hold the pride on his face and in his veins for long. He closed his eyes, a tear rolling down his face. He continued to hold himself up even as he walked away from the body, taking no care of the situation.

17

Windy was left to rot. Love only got so far for her, but when the line was crossed, it killed her. What could make someone feel so alive, only to strip them of life soon after? The forest returned to its loud silence, the darkness enveloping any light that might sneak in. Windy's body lay until the body's rigor mortis developed, the body freezing into a shell.

But after such a phenomenon overtook the body, the deceased body showed signs of life, its limbs swelling up like lumps of clay. The body began to move and shift, discoloring to a shade barely visible in the darkness.

As the body shifted and grew, what had been a body became an entirely different entity, consumed by betrayal, rejection, and hopelessness.

The creature stood, its large hands firmly planted in the soil. Its back hooves stumbled, a sensation unknown to the once living host. Its tail thrashed, unable to control the newly acquired appendage. Its hairy body was covered in bulky flesh, with a broad upper body that tapered to its lower end. The creature resembled a bull, but with a face unseen by human eyes: a dark green skull, yellow patterns under its eyes, floppy ears that poked to the side, and sorrowful, glowing red eyes.

The beast took its first steps, each step taken lazily and unable to hold itself upright. As it stumbled around as if waking up from a sedation, it turned its head every which way, scanning its surroundings.

Though the forest was home to darkness, so was this creature. She was one with the void, such as what had become of her heart. She was now able to understand the foliage around her, the blindness unmatched by such a beast with newfound power.

Such a creature deserved no hope. Such a creature deserved isolation. This beast, once a young woman who knew nothing but compassion, was now a Creature of Darkness, the ideal punishment for love.

As the Creature of Darkness understood its new footing, it ran, striding lazily but reaching one hand after the other and one hoof after the other. Its tail trailed behind it, waving up and down with each stride. It had to leave. Such an exposed location was unsuitable for a being who craved isolation.

Through the darkness and fog, the Creature of Darkness wove between the trees, its head held low yet alert to its surroundings, searching for a domain that could welcome its heartbreak with open arms.

Its steps slowed to a trot once the trees gave way to a clearing, the earth dipping into ridged stones that shot upward from the sinkhole. It steadied its pacing, taking cautious steps as it inspected such an out-of-place hole in the otherwise clean land around it. It approached the hole, reaching its head out to get a closer look at the potential home.

Aside from the towering stones, there were fallen trees surrounding the hole, creating a sense of furnishing. The Creature of Darkness reached down to grab an exposed stone, then reached for another, descending into the sinkhole with a feline agility for its newly acquired body. It leaped down onto a tree, stepping onto the dry, cold earth of the hole.

It began to feel comfortable.

At home.

This would make a fine isolation from humanity.

Time seemed as if only the hopeful could rely on it. Now, time didn't exist. At least, not in its eyes. The only time that seemed to exist was the patience to kill. Welcome nobody and kill those who seek a welcoming presence. The pain that was endured previously was masked by a desire to eradicate everything that stood in its way. It didn't want to leave. It didn't want to find the one responsible for giving such a beast life. All was hopeless. All was lost. Any meaning was washed away by pain.

She cared not whether her previous lithe form went forgotten. This new life was the result of such mindless mistakes her previous form made. The Creature of Darkness lived her days prowling the Tree Kingdom, her territory barren besides the few unlucky wandering critters and Splinters.

She fed her emotions with the fear from others and fed her body with the result of such despair from the helpless victims. Her claws pierced the ground beneath her, leaving tracks of what was left of her torn heart, each scrape a reminder of the scars she carries.

Through the darkness, the Creature of Darkness's somber body blended into the atmosphere, the fog providing another layer of shade over the ominous territory. Though its frame was large, its steps were silent and lethal, as if a reaper were prowling in its place. The only things visible on the beast's body were its red eyes and yellow patterns beneath its eyes. It was looking for a suitable victim to satisfy its hunger, its craving for life, and the fear that came with claiming them. Though few people wandered into her territory, each day brought hope of a full stomach.

Out of the silent search, her head jerked up, her nose on high alert while her ears pinned to the side of her head. She threw her head down, trotting and tracking a scent only she could smell.

As she maneuvered through the forest, her trot was smooth for such a bulky beast. Her hands grazed the ground in a fine motion while her back hooves reached forward and back. Her tail flowed behind her, the tip swinging from either side occasionally.

She raised her head, her eyes focusing on what was ahead. Her movements slowed, her trot breaking into a slow stalk. Her beak clicked against her lower jaw, the sound echoing through the forest's silence. She hissed as she turned her body where it faced her focus point, but her head remained locked on her prey.

Her next victim was a younger Splinter with a singular glowing pattern trailing down their right eye. The Splinter, scanning her surroundings with silver hair waving messily, appeared lost, unable to track where she had been.

Through the silence, she noticed the clicking and hissing of the Creature of Darkness, her luminous yellow eyes darting toward her. Yellow eyes met red eyes, staring at each other with fear and bloodlust. The young Splinter attempted to turn around, sprinting away from the threat, but was closely followed by the hunting beast. While she strode with her life, the Creature of Darkness reached out, covering more ground than her.

The Creature of Darkness checked up on her running, veering off to the side while her back hooves dug into the ground. Before the Splinter could react to the cut, the Creature of Darkness caught her in her jaws like an eagle after its prey. Her beak sank into the innocent body as she reared up, shaking the Splinter victim.

This is what he gets!

Her hands hit the ground with a thud while her claws sank into the dirt beneath her. The body of the Splinter hung from her mouth as soulless as the dark creature was. If only this Splinter could have been the one who brought her to life.

I will destroy your Community just as you have done to me.

Satisfied with today's kill, she turned around to return to her lonely sinkhole to savor the misfortune she fished for.

These were the days of a lonely beast seeking comfort from pain. Most days left her empty, while other days left her full from others' downfall. The Creature of Darkness had no other company besides the fleeting critters or remains of those she destroyed. She favored a flat stone at the center of the hole, which stood apart from the fallen trees and rubble surrounding the sinkhole.

On a good hunting day, the Creature of Darkness would consume her victims on such a stone, coating it red, like what she envisioned the world should be.

18

Hazel fit in with the foliage around her, her dark skin complementing her bodily leaves. She hunted with a focused face, her eyes scanning the forest with a hungry desire. A hungry desire to restore peace and order. Her eyes were accustomed to the dark; her Community solely an outdoor Community, such as the Splinters. Her movements were as swift as a deer's. Her desire is as strong as a windstorm. She had a responsibility. A job that must be completed for the sake of the peace of other Communities.

Mother, find whoever committed such a heinous act and punish them well, her eyes seemed to pray. Her movements were quick yet swift, determined to complete the mission she had been called to fulfill, not for her, but for others.

Hazel of the Peacekeepers,

We hope that your Community continues to seek the peace it deserves. We are seeking a dire request, anticipating your Community's help. Our newest leader, Windy, traveled to the Splinter Community to

discuss a tragedy that haunts our peaceful Community. We were
informed that this trip would be a quick one, but our leader has
not returned to us. The only remnant we have of her is her Winged
Beast, who seemed just as worried as we were. We are hoping that
your Community could aid us in the search for our dearest leader,
Windy, the Daughter of the Wind. Her last known location was in
the Splinter Community. We are unsure if she is hurt or if her open,
carefree personality drew her into the new environment. Whatever the
case may be, we need our leader to return home to her people.

Sincerely,

Rose of the Skybirds

A beloved leader was missing from a Community that had just
found its place amongst everyone. Her anger toward such a vile act
drew her steps forward, the determination overflowing her petite
stature. She trod silently, cautious of any silent hunters of the
Community.

Familiar with the reputation of the Splinter Community, she
began her search at the outskirts of the Tree Kingdom, looking
out for any evidence that could provide answers to Windy's
disappearance.

If she had been killed, the Splinters would have taken her away
to murder her swiftly and silently, away from anybody who would
go looking for her. But if she were still alive, she would trespass on
the Splinter Community and break the peace in order to put the
Skybirds at ease.

"This is important. I must leave this instant. We cannot have a
sister Community suffer from the wrongdoings of an enemy." Hazel

spoke to another Peacekeeper. Her face was serious and tolerated no defiance. This was her responsibility. If someone were to break the peace, it was up to her to aid those broken.

The forest was thick, but the severity of the situation was thicker. She would ensure that nothing got in the way of justice, just as her Community firmly believes in. Hazel suddenly tripped over a dip in the ground, catching her unsteady footing. She looked around the ground, inspecting the flooring.

In the ground, five holes appeared to have been dug forcibly. But each of these holes was symmetrical to one another. The patterns appeared to be tracks, and Hazel traced the dirt flung from the holes to determine the direction they were coming from. She followed the tracks backward, trying to pinpoint their origin. Such hole sizes were unnatural, nothing that could have been made by a large animal such as a bear.

Hazel's eyes were glued to the path before her, following the tracks. Following the holes, she noticed there were round patterns embedded in the ground. Familiar with boars and other hoofed animals, they seemed to have large hooves.

Did this thing take her?

The printed path began to slow, its tracks becoming asymmetrical and sloppy. As the tracks neared their path, Hazel looked up, finding the beginning of the path. At the start of the path, there was a flag, a bow, and arrows all tossed sloppily on the ground. There was even a map wrapped around the upper part of the flagpole.

Hazel looked around, ensuring her surroundings were safe before she approached the weapons. She kneeled, grabbing the flag. The color, though washed from the darkness, appeared to consist of blues and whites. The pattern on the flag resembled the Skybird Community.

She found her lead.

The longer she gripped the flag, the more she felt an unusual crustiness on the otherwise slick pole. Hazel gasped, placing the flag down. She didn't realize there was dried blood on the snow-white pole of the flag. Inspecting the ground beneath her more closely, she found there were patches of blood on the grass where the weapons lay. Hazel left the property in its place, standing up to follow the tracks moving away from the weapons.

Curse whoever killed her, Mother.

Hazel could follow the tracks more quickly, knowing where the path went. She focused on the growing, steady tracks, trying to find where the trail went. Her feet were determined to find Windy's killer, and the tracks indicated the killer resided somewhere.

As the tracks spanned great lengths, the tracks began to gradually slow, spreading out in different directions. Hazel looked around. The tracks divided themselves, but they all led in the same direction.

What in nature's law is this place?

Hazel carefully stepped forward, taking each step tenderly to avoid finding herself in a place she didn't hope to be in. She focused her eyes through the darkness, fighting the fogginess of the territory against her predatory vision. Her feet slowly dipped into a crevice, indicating there must not be much more to step on further ahead.

She stopped walking, knelt, and reached her arm out in front of her. Nothing. Hazel moved her body closer to the ledge, peering down into the sinkhole. The smell of death overwhelmed her senses, and she dug her fingers deeper into the soil. Continuing the scanning of the hole, not only were there innocent victims laid out across the ground, but there was rubble scattered about, which was now destroyed.

Toward the back of the sinkhole, in Hazel's line of sight, was a ball of black fluff, unmoving but appearing relaxed. Hazel held her breath. Was that the thing that abducted Windy? Or was it another body of whatever creature took her?

Hazel dared not make a sound or investigate further. If that thing were alive, then this is where it must reside. It was surely dangerous. But if this is who took Windy, she needed to ensure this thing doesn't take any more innocent lives.

Mother, give me strength.

Hazel stepped back into the foliage, watching for bramble that could alert the beast from its slumber. As she hid herself from any threats, her body seemed as if she were a walking plant, her leaves brushing against any bushes or trees. She lowered herself into a shrub against a tree, pressing her body up against it. She unraveled the vines from her arms and legs, letting them drape out of the bush to mimic nature, giving the illusion that nobody is around.

Through the hush, Hazel whistled, hoping to attract the beast far from its hiding place so those who lost lives could be avenged for such a calamity. After indicating her presence, she reached across her body, grabbing the handle of her scimitar, prepared for a fight at any moment. Peace would be made, and Hazel swore to fulfill her promise to the Communities.

Give me strength. I must kill this beast to save us all. Keep the Skybirds at ease for just a moment longer.

19

T he Creature of Darkness' claws tore away at the ground, her hooves leaving deep imprints in the earth. She hunted with a rabid desire to rid out anybody who dared to step into her territory. As she listened for the bird, she tracked down the sound, expecting to find her prey.

Through the forest, her trot slowed as she neared her target, searching more intently. She lowered her head, tracking scents. She moved steadily, ensuring that nobody was left alive, whether it be human or animal. She slowly prowled around a tree, looking up at the leaves above her. There seemed to be no critters around.

She stared up at the trees, her ears flicking in confusion. She paced the area, growling in determination to kill. As it paced, she heard a noise come from the bushes. She turned around, staring face-to-face with what she hoped to find. Before her stood a woman with skin the color of an oak tree.

She stood about the size of the Creature of Darkness's lower arm.

Her dress was made of silk, a green and gold color adorned by the comfort and beauty of nature. She had chocolate-colored hair and forest green eyes. She had vines and leaves sprouting from her flesh, which was being wound up as they stared at each other. Whoever this brave soul was needed to go. She had no business being in her territory.

The Creature of Darkness hissed, pinning her ears. She lunged at the woman without a doubt in her mind. Her jaws were open, ready to snap her through her body. As her jaws clamped shut, there was no blood spouting onto her beak. She looked around, finding the woman standing next to her with a scimitar gripped tightly in her hand. This was no normal visitor.

How dare she look for a fight!

The Creature of Darkness stalked around the woman, her eyes focused on her small form. She charged at the woman, reaching her arm out to swipe at her attacker.

The woman would swing her scimitar, slicing her hand. The Creature of Darkness roared, rearing up and shaking her hand. She came down with a hard thud, snapping at her again.

The span of her jaw was over half the size of the woman, so a swift kill should be guaranteed. As she closed her jaws, the woman slashed the scimitar under her chin, leaving a scar down her lower jaw. The Creature of Darkness roared again and thrashed her head around, her curved horns exposed. Through the flurry, the woman was hit in the shoulder, sent tumbling down to the side. There was no pain during adrenaline rushes.

The Creature of Darkness, now having blood dripping from her mouth, circled the woman, growling and hissing. The woman kept her gaze on the beast, stepping in circles to keep her eyes on the red eyes of death.

"I don't know who you are, but I know you reap death from those undeserving of such fates. If you can answer my questions, it will be better for both of us," she said with a firm, authoritative voice. Her words were serious with no room for softness.

The Creature of Darkness stopped prowling, but she continued to face her.

"Of the possibly hundreds of people you slaughtered, have you slaughtered a tall woman with brown hair? She comes from a bright Community, so she would have been wearing bright colors. I come for the Skybirds."

The Creature of Darkness cowered, the word triggering a memory she fought to forget. She shouted as she reared up. "It's all his fault!"

"Whose fault? Who did this to you? Do you know the Skybirds?"

"Indeed, I do," she said as she planted her hands back on the ground, lowering her head to be at eye level with the brave trespasser.

The woman's eyes widened with disbelief. "Are you Windy?"

The Creature of Darkness stood defensively, her claws scraping against the ground. She snorted, snarling as she focused her eyes on the woman. "Never bring up such a name! It's his fault, it's her fault, such foolishness!"

The woman stepped forward, feeling compassion for the beast. "What happened? I need to know."

"You need to know nothing of the sort. But if you stand firm in my presence, you shall get what you beg. It's his fault. He did it. He broke something deep inside me that I never gave to anybody. He broke that Windy thing, and I'm here to make up for such crimes."

The woman's eyes shifted into confusion, but still expressed a hint of sympathy. She stepped toward the beast, reaching her hand out to touch her beak. "I think what you've felt is love. Love for someone other than your family or friends. Windy, not everybody can get along. Believe me. I know. I long for a day when we can all live together in peace, where nobody betrays one another, especially for love. You don't need to sow suffering to others who have no concern over the matter. But you can make yourself better from it. If you cause more pain and suffering, that only breaks a heart into smaller pieces. To mend yourself, you must allow others to support the process. If you win this fight, something wonderful will sprout in its place."

The Creature of Darkness stared at the woman, her eyes and body relaxing.

Is this true? Could this all be for nothing?

As she stood in a thoughtful silence, she considered her words with a grain of salt as her ears pinned back.

No. What has been done is done. I will not fall for such lies!

She made a low rumbling sound deep in her chest that grew to a roar as the despair grew in her heart once more.

"You speak pathetically, fool! My heart has no room for such sap!" She lunged at the woman again, bucking her body forward as her hands and hooves dangerously beat against the ground.

The woman stepped out of the way of the bucking bull, watching her sprint to the opposite side, facing the beast at a distance.

Quick to react, just as a fool would do.

The Creature of Darkness spread her hands apart, positioning herself in a form ready to kill, her muscles tense and her eyes full of hate. She circled her attacker, waiting for a moment to strike. Then, suddenly, she lowered her head and charged, her body stretched wide as she strode. The woman stepped to the side, reaching her scimitar out to the beast.

The Creature of Darkness sharply swerved to the side, impaling the woman and causing her to drop the scimitar. The plant woman felt a crunch in her shoulder going down her chest, but she quickly stood up after being beaten down to the ground, the blood a mere scratch compared to the brutality of the fight.

The Creature of Darkness trotted around the woman, anticipating any moment to charge once again.

Get down and stay down.

The woman darted after her dropped scimitar, spinning around to stare at her, not blinking. The Creature of Darkness broke into a quicker gait, gradually speeding up to charge at the woman again.

The woman watched the vile threat charge with her head low, her horns vulnerable. Knowing her speed, she skidded to the side and bounded forward, throwing her body at her horns, reaching her free hand as far as it could stretch.

When she grabbed hold of her horn, the Creature of Darkness jerked her head, causing the woman's body to swing onto the creature's neck, sliding down its body. She let go of the horn, allowing her body to place itself on its back, grabbing the thick fur on her neck in place of the horns.

She held the patch of fur with her free hand and held the scimitar up with the other hand. The Creature of Darkness roared, rearing up. But a gruesome pain in its shoulder caused it to frantically buck, her lower end flying above her front end.

The woman twisted the scimitar that was dug into the Creature of Darkness's muscle, causing the beast to fight harder. With each jump she took, she snarled, a warning to the attacker.

"GET OFF!"

The Creature of Darkness bucked up and then crashed herself to the ground, causing the woman to rip the blade out of her shoulder and tumble down onto the ground. Once free, the Creature of Darkness broke into a sprint, but limped with each step it took.

She turned her head toward the woman rearing up. As the small enemy charged after her, she pushed herself forward, leaping toward the woman and lowering her head to snap her jaws and thrash her head around.

Upon impact, the woman reached for her horn once again, swinging up. Understanding such a tactic, she expected the beast's response, bracing herself for such a fight.

"You leave me no choice! May you suffer the wrath of Mother Nature herself!"

As the Creature of Darkness threw its back end over herself, the woman threw the armed hand back, impaling the Creature of Darkness's back end. The Creature of Darkness stumbled, finding her footing before bucking again.

The woman swung her arm front and back, attacking her broad

front half and vulnerable backside. The Creature of Darkness stumbled with each slice, but refused to let this vermin push her around. Her back arched, bracing her muscles for a powerful jump. She leaped into the air, snarling as her body threw itself airborne. The woman felt the beast's back against her own, as if a wall had been placed from behind her.

Without a split second of hesitation, she turned around, thrusting the scimitar into her back. The scimitar dug into a patch of brighter fur. The Creature of Darkness's ears perked up, her eyes widened in terror. She reared up, practically standing on two legs. She screamed, the distorted sound piercing the darkness. The shrill, familiar to the Creature of Darkness, threw her arms up, covering her face.

She crashed down to the ground, her body pushing herself forward into a sprint, her muscles heaving her forward despite the pain. It ran around in a large circle, bucking up to get the woman off its back. As the Creature of Darkness sprinted uneasily, the woman quickly sheathed the scimitar in the case on her hip, quickly latching onto the beast's mane.

"Easy! Easy! Easy up! You're okay! I've got you!" she frantically called out to the beast.

The beast's speed and motion made it hard for the woman to keep her balance, and she constantly shifted her body to avoid falling. If she were to fall, she would surely be trampled.

"Settle down! You'll get yourself even more hurt!"

The Creature of Darkness kept striding, determined to rid itself of this scum. As she kept running, she continued to feel the weight on her back, indicating she was not free yet. But the longer the

Creature of Darkness ran, the quicker she tired out. Her movements became sloppy and weak, the ride becoming a joyride.

Noticing the change in behavior, the woman unsheathed her scimitar and slashed the beast atop her back. The Creature of Darkness stumbled, but the woman continued to fight strongly against the bumpy ride.

But she was tiring out. The woman knew this broken beast didn't have much time. She had to put her out of her misery. As the Creature of Darkness stumbled, fighting for her footing one hand after another, the woman turned her flexible body, catching a view of the bloody hole that now embellished the beast's back. She lifted her toned arm, thrusting the scimitar into her back once more.

The Creature of Darkness skidded to a halt, crying out and bucking with the last of her strength to throw the woman off. She spun around, but she lost her footing and flipped, tumbling to the ground on her side. The woman threw herself off the beast, avoiding being crushed by the bull's weight.

She picked herself up, kneeling and watching the beast's stomach rise and fall. The Creature of Darkness resisted fighting, rid of her energy and strength.

How unfortunate...

Peacekeeper Community

20

Her eyes were free of hate. Sorrow and apology were in its place. Everything she had done because of her anger fed her guilt. All the victims she claimed, all the hate toward a single being, all the isolation she gave herself. She saw the woman share the same pain in her eyes as she kneeled, placing her hand on her jaw. The Creature of Darkness twitched, her breathy pants becoming snorts as she tried to avoid the contact.

"Shh, it's okay."

The Creature of Darkness kept her eyes on the bloody plant woman.

"I'm so sorry for everything you had to go through. All the pain in your life, all the fights you had to endure. But please. Please know you impacted so many people through this pain. For the better."

The Creature of Darkness didn't resist when the woman wrapped her arms around her large head, hugging. The Creature of Darkness's head fell limp in her arms, all struggle to reach its end.

The woman let go and bowed her head, paying her respects to the Creature of Darkness and the previous life it had been blessed with. As her eyes closed, she heard a faint rustling sound in front of her.

"Where am I?" said a weak voice. She looked around, but couldn't see anything.

The woman gasped, snapping out of her prayer. "Are you Windy?"

"I"—she coughed—"believe I am. I remember being Windy."

Windy lay on the ground, leached of her strength. When the woman reached out her hand and tapped her shoulder, Windy took it, accepting the helping hand.

"My name is Hazel. I'm the leader of the Peacekeeper Community. Nice to meet you, Daughter of the Wind. The Skybirds sent for me after some concerns for your disappearance. I apologize for such a harsh awakening, but some matters need to be taken into my hands for everyone's safety."

Windy's face twisted into worry. "What happened?"

"It's not important. What's important is that you're alive and well."

Windy stared into the darkness, unsure if she was looking at Hazel. Then, she gasped. "I need to get home!" She jumped up, but winced, the pain from the battle overwhelming her.

"I wouldn't recommend it. You're not in a state to return to such pressures."

"I've been away from home long enough. I need to get back to my Community!"

"Windy. You must recover after being in such a harsh condition.

I would like you to return to the Peacekeepers with me. There, we will nurture you back to your original health so you may return to such duties."

Windy felt a sharp feeling of anxiety hit her chest, her eyes widening in the darkness. "No! I want to go home! Please, you can't make me stay anywhere else!"

Hazel sighed. "Windy. I can see this is coming from broken trust from staying in another Community. But I can promise you that the Peacekeepers are not like the Splinters at all. The Splinters are known for causing trouble amongst other Communities."

"But my Community needs me! There's a strange phenomenon happening in my Community that needs to be addressed."

"We can talk about that later. Now, let's focus on your health. Come, you can hold my hand. Once we're out of here, I have a faster ride back home."

Windy wearily took Hazel's hand, walking with her through the darkness. "How can you see a thing?"

"Peacekeepers are adapted to the darkness. It's a gift Mother Nature blessed us with for our survival."

Windy didn't comment. She trusted Hazel would lead her out of danger and into the light.

I need to get home. Why can't she accept that?

The walk through the forest seemed long to Windy, the pain and soreness in her body consuming her. But through the thick fog, it steadily brightened, indicating their departure from the Community. Windy's hands raced to her face, shielding her eyes from the brightness.

After secluding herself for such a long time, her eyes were sensitive to such profound light. Through her discomfort, she felt Hazel's hand grab her wrist.

"Hey, open your eyes. It's okay."

Windy slowly took her hands from her face, squinting. Through the reduced vision, she could see that they were out of the Splinter Forest, the green earth painting a beautiful picture.

Windy slowly opened her eyes, blinking away the soreness of her pupils adjusting. She looked around at the sight of the field, amazed by such beauty. A sight like this was never to be seen in the Splinter Community, the only thing being gloom out of the void.

This was the last thing I saw before going into the Splinter Community. It hasn't changed.

The grass beneath her felt soft, unlike the Splinter's crunchy, dying grass. The sky above her, though the sun was gradually traveling higher in the sky, glowed with a beautiful painting of blues and oranges, marking the dawn of a new day. This is where Windy wanted to be.

"It's so beautiful," she breathed, as if it were her first time seeing what was in front of her.

"Indeed. It's quite a change from all the sad darkness you're used to."

"Thank goodness I'm free. This feels like such a blessing." Her hand rested against her chest, savoring the rich feeling of the outside world once again.

Windy walked around, exploring the unfamiliar yet so familiar surroundings. Windy found the lengthy river that flowed through the Splinter Community throughout the continent of Quinta. An experience felt so close to reach, remembering that encounter with Berryleaf.

Approaching the water, she looked at her reflection. She gasped upon seeing her face. She looked older, but not like she was wrinkly or fatigued. She looked more mature, her face molded into that of a beautiful girl who walked through a forest of pain. Her body was more defined, as if being gone had shown Windy that she was still beautiful, even with her scars. She turned her head and body, checking herself out from every angle. Then, Windy heard a whistle and looked at Hazel. She stood up, limping over to Hazel.

Beside Hazel was a large deer adorned with vines and leaves. Windy froze, unsure what such an animal was. "What's that?"

Hazel smiled. "Like your Winged Beasts, this is my best friend. He's a deer. His name is Goldilock." She patted the deer's shoulder. Goldilock looked at Windy, his stature friendly but tough for an animal. The Winged Beasts carried themselves with a playful, mischievous behavior even when wild.

Windy reached her hand out, letting Goldilock smell it. Goldilock looked at her hand, then to Windy. He didn't respond, but only stood as if he knew he should give her the same respect as he did to his owner. Hazel grabbed Goldilock's thick neck, swinging herself onto the animal. She fell softly on its back, Goldilock's stature ready to listen to his owner.

"Come," Hazel invited.

"On...that thing? How do I—" Windy stammered, her eyes darting across the deer. "We only climb on our Winged Beasts because they're so large."

"Here. Just grab on." Hazel reached out her hand.

Windy took Hazel's hand, Hazel pulling her up as Windy reached her arm to pull herself up using his hind end too. Goldilock bleated in surprise, planting its hooves for support. Hazel patted him, shushing for assurance. "It's okay, boy."

Windy settled herself on Goldilock's back, unsure of seating positions. "How do I sit?"

Hazel looked back at Windy. "That's fine. I'm sure you're used to traveling atop animals."

"Yes, I am."

Hazel clicked her tongue twice, and Goldilock bounded off, running with an elegance that made the ride much smoother than anticipated.

"Woah!" Windy laughed in excitement. "I haven't felt this in forever! This is amazing!" Windy held on to Hazel for balance, uncoordinated on the new style of riding. Hazel guided Goldilock with a vine tied on his muzzle that was padded with stones on either side of his jaw.

Through the field, the contrast between the Splinter Community and the outside world was beautiful. Running through the plains gave Windy a heightened sense of ease, the misfortune of her current situation blowing away on the wind whipping past her. Hazel was focused on the ride, not turning to talk to Windy or acknowledge her.

The space was open, the hills beginning to form as they ventured farther and farther away from Splinter territory. Through the hills, animals of all kinds began to appear, some being deer like Goldilock and some that Windy didn't know the name of. As they ran past them, they only looked at their passing visitor, unafraid of their presence.

This must be the Peacekeeper Community, thought Windy as they closed in on a vast land full of huts, tree houses, and a large building that emerged from the trees in the distance. It appeared to have flags lining the border of the rounded structure. Though such buildings were still small in the distance, it gave a peaceful, natural feel to the surrounding Community of the brighter forest. A forest unlike the Splinter's forest.

As Windy looked around the land, Hazel slowed Goldilock down to stop, the deer's transitions fluid. Windy slid off first, taking slow, easy steps as she looked around the Community. Her mouth was creased open in awe at the beauty that surrounded the Skybird. She hasn't ever seen such raw nature from the two Communities she was already so familiar with.

Hazel slid off the deer's back, her feet gently hitting the ground. She turned to Windy, smiling as she reached out a hand.

"Welcome to the Peacekeeper Community."

21

The Peacekeeper Community was bustling with life. Citizens were walking back and forth, leading animals, carrying buckets of water, or simply talking among themselves. There was laughter from all directions, whether from adults conversing or from children playing. There were huts made of wood that were bound by sturdy vines. Such huts were even seen in trees, in the form of comfy tree houses, many Peacekeepers seemed to walk in and out of.

The air wasn't humid or prickling with chill. It seemed to be just right where you couldn't feel any heat or chill biting at your skin. There was a sandy path that led to each business, whether for shopping or recreational needs. The path seemed to venture farther into the trees, indicating another part of the Community.

Windy lost herself in the otherworldly sights, the Community grounds pulling her into such a daze. She found none of the unusual citizens staring at her or giving her disapproving looks. They were all just as unique as she was. The people all had qualities that reflected the very nature around them.

Some people had stylized leaves on their bodies, like Hazel, and others resembled animals, with features such as whiskers, ears, or antlers. They could be mistaken for the very atmosphere around them to the naked eye. To them, Windy was one of them. They, too, appeared to be outcasts compared to residents of the other Communities.

"Come with me." Hazel tapped Windy as she walked past her. "I have a place you may stay."

Windy followed Hazel, walking down the sandy path that wound through the trees. Goldilock was walking with Hazel as if he were an advisor of some sort and not her steed.

Along the path, Peacekeepers walked in different directions, holding bows, spears, or nothing at all. People coming from a distance seemed sweaty and tired, as if they had been training or working out, and those walking into the forest seemed to have an eager step.

Was Hazel taking her to a training facility?

Windy kept her questions to herself and followed Hazel. The Community didn't appear to have any suspicious impressions, so she felt she could rely on Hazel to take her somewhere safe. The sand was soft beneath Windy's feet with the occasional crunchiness from fallen twigs, leaves, or eggshells.

In the distance, as they emerged from the trail, stood a grand coliseum, with the same flags lining its structure as Windy had seen upon entering the Community grounds. Looking more closely, it seemed to be a performance arena, which would enlighten Windy about the Peacekeepers in different energy states coming and going from the building. The gates were open, allowing people to enter or exit freely.

"I'm staying here? In this big place?"

Hazel smiled. "Yes and no. I have a place you may stay within the coliseum."

Windy didn't press further. She continued to follow Hazel inside the coliseum. Beyond the gates, there was a stone walkway circling the building, with entrances to the staircases. There was a vast placement of seats lining the coliseum, all of which were benches carved from wood. The arena seemed to be a large sinkhole dug into the ground, padded with a mix of dirt and sand.

Inside, Peacekeepers were training in a variety of skills, whether they were warriors or everyday people. A large Community flag was draped in the middle of the coliseum, large enough to keep the activity below in view.

Hazel led Windy up a flight of stairs, ascending farther up the coliseum. There seemed to be two levels to the building, with the second level having fewer seating areas than the first.

The sound of their steps and Goldilock's hooves echoed throughout the empty floor as they continued down the building. On the left, Hazel entered an open room that led down a hallway. The stone hallway was empty, with no paintings or other adornments. The hallway seemed colder than the usual Peacekeeper's neutral temperature, a faint nip of chill along Windy's exposed arm, hands, and face.

At the end of the hallway, there was a wooden door with roots growing from it. Hazel reached for the doorknob and opened the door. The door opened to a large room adorned with vines, flowers, and other plants. The room had the Peacekeeper flag pinned to the back wall, the lining of the banner woven with ivy.

On the side was a small daybed carved from wood with a large patch of grass bedding. Across the sleeping area was a neat desk with gravel pens placed in a carved divot in the table, likely created for utensil organization. There were old but unused papers under the desk. The room appeared to be more than a normal office and more like a living space.

"This is my reserve. I will allow you to stay here until you have recovered your strength. You can sleep in my bed for the time being. I will sleep with Goldilock. I have done it before, so don't worry about my comfort," Hazel explained while she took Goldilock's tack off. She hung the plant-based tack on racks beside the grass bedding. Goldilock walked to the bed, lying down.

"Thank you so much. I truly appreciate it." Windy looked at Hazel.

But Windy soon realized something. She felt light. Lighter than usual. She patted herself on her chest and back. Her heart dropped. "Where did my flag go? And my bow?"

Hazel slowly nodded. "I found them in the Splinter Forest while looking for you. I didn't worry about collecting them because your safety was my priority at the time. We will collect them when you recover."

"But can we just get them sooner?"

"Unfortunately, I say no. I don't want you to do anything behind my back and get yourself hurt."

"You can trust me!" Windy pleaded as she closed the distance between the two.

Hazel sighed through her nose. "Windy. From a leader to a leader, I want to ensure you heal back to your normal state. You have been disfigured for far too long, suffering wounds that have destroyed your soul. You need to trust me on such a process."

Hazel was firm but still had a light layer of compassion. Windy stared into her caring dark green eyes. Hazel smiled at the silence. "Do you trust me?"

How can I be so sure this time?

"Is something the matter?" Hazel asked, noticing Windy's quiet reluctance.

"No, no. I'm okay." Windy's chest rose, and she finally breathed out, "Yes."

Hazel's face flashed with worry for a brief moment, but then relaxed into gratitude. "Great to hear. Thank you, Windy. Now, if you don't mind me asking, you mentioned some strange things happening with the Skybirds. Care to elaborate?"

Hazel listened as Windy explained the strange phenomenon that was assumed to be the Splinter's doing. She described the sudden attack by the hideous monsters, the discoloration in the Community, and how the Community appeared to be a suspect to the phenomenon.

"I wouldn't doubt that it had something to do with the Splinters. My guess is that they were so used to your Community being neutral that someone suddenly taking the role as leader appeared as a threat, when it isn't. Maybe they're attempting to put your Community back in its place."

Windy's ears twitched in confusion. To her, that didn't sound right. If that was the case, why do it in such an aggressive way?

Hazel shifted her weight, her body free from the tension. "I take it that you went to the Splinter Community to find answers, yes?"

Windy nodded.

"And did you get answers? The Skybirds made it seem like you made what was supposed to be a quick meeting into an extended stay."

Windy's ears drooped, and her face flushed in embarrassment. She had been too busy with Orion and fascinating herself with the Community that she didn't think to press Shambor further. "No. I was too busy with other things, and I only trusted Shambor when he told me that he had no involvement. I never thought it to be suspicious. Oh, I'm such a..." Windy pressed her forehead into her palm.

Hazel put her hand on her shoulder, light and comforting. "Windy. Do not stress yourself over such a mistake. You're new, and you're learning. You don't know the Communities as well as other experienced leaders. Next time, please take such issues more seriously."

"I will. I'm so sorry, I will." She let her hand fall to her leg, and she looked at Hazel.

"There is always another chance to find answers."

Windy sat down on the firm daybed. "When can we get started?"

"Patience, Windy. We can work on the dilemma while you get back into shape. I already have someone in mind who can help you in the process."

"Who?"

"You will find out tomorrow. Now, please make yourself at home. I want your recovery to be quick so we can figure out what the Splinters are really doing behind our backs."

22

Windy walked with Hazel through the coliseum. The sun was rising, so not many people were visiting the building at the moment. They descended the second flight of stairs to the first floor, walking through the opposite end of the floor.

At the opposite end from where they came was another flight of stairs, but this descended to the underground. The underground of the coliseum contained a long dirt walkway that led into a round, fenced area and out into the performance arena.

Hazel and Windy walked past the dirt trail to a closed door. Hazel opened the unlocked door, and the two leaders ascended a smaller flight of stairs. At the top was another closed door. Hazel knocked, so she must have known it was locked.

They stood patiently, waiting for a response. Through the door, a sigh could be heard, and someone violently pulled it open.

"Hazel. What are you doing here this early?" the blonde woman snapped, her hair still matted from sleep.

She was just shorter than Hazel.

Who would talk to a leader in such a way?

The blonde woman expressed no resemblance to a Peacekeeper.
She had no unusual characteristics, only appearing to be a normal

human. She had hazel eyes that had a fiery tone in the lighting from her room. Though her hair was messy, it was thick, with shaggy bangs and shoulder-length.

"Brook, please understand. I'm so sorry, but as you can see, we have someone who is in need of care." Hazel clasped her hands together.

Brook narrowed her eyes. "I've never seen her around. Who is she?"

"Windy. The Skybird's newest leader. She found herself in an accident in the Splinter Community, and she needs to heal herself before she can leave to her Community."

Brook adjusted her position, crossing her arms across her chest and barely raising her eyebrows. "Oh, the Skybird's first leader. This is the one who's got everybody talking. So, what do you want me to do about it?"

"Help, maybe? You overlook the status of our Community defenders, so no doubt you could bring Windy back to health."

Brook looked at Windy, her eyes narrowing again but with a scowl. "What does she need fixing?"

Hazel tapped her fingers against her leg. "Well, imagine someone was raised from the dead. They'd be weak, right? Well, she needs to get herself back in shape."

Brook stared at Windy a moment longer before looking at Hazel again. "Yeah, she does look pretty bad. But you know, giving her to me will mess her mind up."

Windy jumped into the conversation. "I've been through a lot. Trust me."

Brook glanced at her as if she didn't want Windy to join in. "Okay. Give her to me. You go worry about all your high and mighty responsibilities while I take care of my own."

Windy glanced at Hazel, in awe of how a leader allowed their own citizens to speak.

"I trust you, Brook. You've done many things for us in the past. Have fun, you two." Hazel waved as she walked off, leaving Windy with the sour Peacekeeper.

Brook's eyes shot back at Windy. "Give me one moment." Then Brook closed the door in Windy's face.

Windy flinched, startled at the gesture. She stepped back, waiting for Brook to return. She grew awkward in the situation, unsure how to comply with such a rude Peacekeeper. But a few minutes later, Brook came out looking more kempt than before, her hair smoothly brushed and wearing a brown dress with a green sash.

"Let's go. We have many things to discuss."

Windy followed Brook, keeping a reasonable distance behind her. She didn't fear her; she just kept herself on edge from her unpredictable actions. Brook led her into the performance arena, walking to the stone railing and hopping on the ledge as a seat.

"So tell me, Skybird leader. What in Mother Nature's name got you in such a bind?"

Windy looked down awkwardly. "Well, it's kind of hard to explain. All I can really describe is that it feels like I woke up from a nightmare that affected my whole body in some way. I think? And my back feels terrible."

Brook began to disassociate at the thought. "So other leaders can be useless. Great. Tell me, do you have any combat experience?"

"Archery and blunt weapons."

"Lucky for you, you aren't totally lost. Yes, Hazel is holding you back for your safety, but, unlucky for her, she set up an archery race competition in a few months. If you could show her how far you've come, you'll be out of here."

"What is an archery race?"

"As the name says. Contestants race against each other to hit all of the targets the quickest and make it back to the line. It's harder than you think."

"I'm sure I could do it."

"Okay, but not today. You seem like you'd be good at stepping on ants the fastest."

Windy stared at Brook.

"Why the sour face? It's true!" Brook clapped, smiling.

"I lost my weapons, and Hazel won't give them back to me unless I recover," Windy dryly added.

"Oh, Hazel." Brook pinched the bridge of her nose.

Is this common for Hazel to do?

"Listen. If you know where they are, I'll get them for you if she won't. She can't stop me from doing what I want to my students. Where did you lose them?"

Windy's ears perked up at the sudden question. "Um, somewhere in the Splinter Forest, outside of the main grounds."

Right where that murderer was. If only he could be gone.

Brook sighed. "Of course, somewhere I can't see. Okay. I'll get someone to collect them for me. They'll listen to me."

Windy's gaze jumped up and down Brook's body. The Peacekeepers could see in the dark. Why couldn't Brook?

"Now, you mentioned your back is all jacked up?"

Windy nodded, squeaking. "It feels terrible."

Brook hopped off the ledge and stepped over to stand behind Windy. Her eyes could bulge out of her face if she were to widen her eyes any further. The torn fabric of her dress revealed a large, nearly black scar. Brook didn't make a sound. She walked around Windy once again before sitting on the ledge. Her face looked troubled.

"What happened?" asked Windy.

Brook closed her eyes. "I should ask you that. Are you not aware you have a scar as ugly as a rotting bear on your back?"

Windy gasped in fear, trying to twist her body to look at it. Every movement she made gave her pain, her eyes squeezing shut as she avoided making any noise.

Brook waved her hands, scrambling to keep Windy in place. "No, no. Don't look at it. Take my word for it. What happened, anyway?"

A lover happened. Or, should I say murderer. If only he could feel what I had felt. That... Orion!

Windy pressed her hand against her aching head.

"I don't remember." Her stomach felt uneasy at the act of lying.

She wouldn't have believed it.

Brook nodded, sarcastic. "Yeah. How do you not remember an injury such as that?"

"I tend to forget embarrassing incidents." Windy messed at her skirt, refusing to look at Brook's harsh eyes.

"So, you were being careless?" She folded her arms.

Windy shrugged. "More or less so."

Brook sighed, rubbing her face with both of her hands.

Maybe it was good that I said that. I would have been in for a beating if I said what had happened.

"Okay. I know how to get yourself feeling better and coordinated after your injury. It might be a painful process, but you need to trust me on this. In case you are still wondering, yes. Our Community is one with the forest," Brook said with a dreamy delivery, but her words were emphasized with sarcasm.

What is she trying to get out of this?

Brook waved her arm as if she were holding a sprite's wand. "We are friends with the animals, and they trust us with whatever we want them to do. That said, I'm sure you're familiar with the Community using animals for transportation or for leisure activities, correct?"

"I mean, I rode on the back of a deer with Hazel on the way here."

"Oh, you did?" Brook asked with false amusement. "Well, how was it?"

"A little uncomfortable. I'm used to riding larger creatures."

"Well, would a bear be right for you?" Brook grinned teasingly.

"What's that?"

Brook gripped the stone beneath her tightly. "Right. You're a Skybird. You don't know these things. Well, bears are just a really big animal. But getting back on track. Riding an animal is very good to help with your soreness, as well as other things you might not get out of whatever you do with those cats with wings."

"So, is that what we'll be doing?"

"Just to get you feeling back to yourself so we can work on getting your defense skills back. It's still early in the morning, and you aren't prepared at all. But now that you know what to expect, we will start tomorrow. For now, I'll give you some mint paste for your back. It should help with the pain until we get started tomorrow."

"Mint?" Windy wrinkled her nose.

"It's a natural numbing remedy. We use it all the time when we're ever sore."

Windy nodded, processing the overload of information.

Brook led Windy out of the performance arena, back up the flight of stairs to leave. Peacekeepers who passed them all waved at Brook, only receiving a nod in acknowledgement. However, nobody talked to her.

Brook must still be likeable even though she acts like a thorn in my eye.

Beyond the forest the sand trail passed through, they reached the Community grounds, which seemed emptier but were beginning to flourish as the morning sun rose higher in the sky. Brook beelined to a tree with a rope ladder, knowing where she needed to go. Windy followed Brook, trusting her instincts as a Peacekeeper.

"Up here." Brook climbed the ladder without waiting for Windy or helping her.

Windy grabbed the rope, carefully stepping on the small logs that were the steps. She struggled, given how weak she currently was. She gripped the rope with straining arms as she pushed herself up each step. Never did she struggle as hard to climb a ladder, no matter if it was sturdy or flimsy like this one. At the top, Brook looked down at her slow climbing, irritated. Windy took her time, keeping herself safe from her weakness. At the top, Windy grunted, pushing her body weight onto the platform where the hut rested. Brook only stared at her, unhelping.

"Could you help me?" asked a weak Windy.

"No. If you want to get better, you need to do these things by yourself."

Windy sighed, pushing herself even harder on the platform. Once she swung her leg over, she adjusted herself on the platform to stand.

"That was terrible to watch. Okay, the medicine is in here." Brook led her inside the tree hut, walking through draped ivy.

The medicine shop was small, but it had everything a Peacekeeper could need from remedies to bandages neatly lined along shelves. Though created from the trees, it gave a sterile feeling in the atmosphere.

Along a small shelf were healing herbs in bags and herbs mixed into a paste that was placed in a wooden container. Brook inspected the paste containers carefully, her hands shuffling for the mint. Windy wandered off to look around, checking out what the Peacekeepers used for medicine.

Chamomile.

Ginger.

Aloe vera.

Lavender.

The area smelled pleasant, as if the very plants being sold could be used as a fragrance to draw customers into the shop.

There's so many natural remedies here. The Skybirds would be so lost at these substances.

The Skybirds relied on ice and wraps for pain or wounds, which were nothing like the Peacekeepers' culture.

Windy distracted herself to the point where she didn't hear Brook calling her name. She was tugged on the shoulder while reading about an herb, being pulled back.

"When I call for you, answer me. Do you want this? Take it." Brook shoved the mint at Windy's chest, walking out the opposite end of the shop that was marked as an exit. There was a rope to slide down to get back on the ground, and Brook slid swiftly. Windy looked at the rope, unsure of how to do such an act.

"Hey, Brook?" she called out to Brook, who was already walking away. "How do I get down?"

"Do what I did. Just let yourself fall while holding the rope."

"How do I do that?"

Brook's mouth moved, but Windy didn't hear what she said. Then, Brook raised her voice: "Grab the rope and hug it. Let yourself fall."

Windy tried to process the shallow instructions. She grabbed the rope at the base, holding the container of mint between her teeth. She stepped off the platform, fell, and slid down the rope. Painfully. She squealed in surprise down the rope, hitting the ground with a thud as she crashed down. Brook, as usual, didn't help her.

"You're okay. Get up."

Windy took the container out of her mouth. "I burned myself!"

"You'll live. Now, put some of that on your back, and I'll see you tomorrow in the performance arena." Brook continued to walk off, leaving Windy behind. Windy assumed she would return to Hazel's leader's reserve, apply the medicine, and then take the day to rest by herself.

At least she had a steady day before the work kicked in.

23

W indy stood inside the performance arena, waiting and smelling of mint. The coliseum had a relaxed glow from the afternoon sun. She woke up early and spent the morning waiting for Brook. For how punctual Brook is, she thought she would be here by now.

What could make Brook so late?

She watched the Peacekeepers train, working alone or with friends, occasionally checking the gate entrance. The only people she saw coming from the gate were arriving Peacekeepers.

When Windy checked again after waiting a moment, Brook approached her, leading a deer and carrying a large woven bag on her shoulder, a flag popping out of it.

"Sorry, I'm late. My delivery boy took longer than I wanted him to. But anyway, here's your stuff. My friend I sent out also found something a little weird, but I'll leave this with you so you can keep it wherever you're staying."

"Thank you, Brook. Are we going to be doing anything with these, or should I keep it to the side?" Windy held her belongings tenderly, but it was almost as if the pain of the Splinters radiated across her hand.

I can't believe these have been at that forest all this time.

"Keep it to the side. We need to get your body back in shape." Brook turned to the spaced out deer beside her. "This, I'm sure you already know from Hazel, is a deer. A doe, to be specific. They're one of the quickest animals we have. They require a lot of balance to stay on, so I figured we'd use this one for your recovery."

I should have expected her to pick a difficult starting point.

The deer had the same kind of bridle Hazel had on Goldilock, except it seemed to be more casual.

"Get on," Brook commanded.

Windy looked at the deer. The last time she had to mount a deer, she had help from Hazel. But if she used the same concept without the addition of being helped by someone else, she could at least mount the deer. Windy walked up to the side of the doe, grabbing its rump with her right arm and using her left arm to grab its scruff. The doe bleated like Goldilock and it shuffled around, not liking what Windy was doing to it.

Brook walked up to Windy, shaking her head and swatting her hand. "No, no, no! What are you doing? Stop!"

Windy let go of the doe, looking at Brook.

"You do it like this." Brook pushed Windy out of the way, taking her place. "Stand by the face, but face the opposite direction of where it's facing. Put your arm on the back of the neck and swing yourself on." Brook did as she was told.

Windy watched, confused. How could she do that in her current state? When Brook slid off the doe's back, she slowly repeated the steps Brook demonstrated to Windy. She stood beside the deer, facing the opposite direction the deer was facing. She put her left hand on the deer's neck, and she got a running start to swing on. But Windy didn't get far. She only got her leg halfway over the deer's body, her body stuck in her current twisted position. She quickly got off, crouching down.

"That hurts!" Windy cried out from the pain in her back.

"The only thing that hurt was watching that sorry excuse for a swing. Keep doing it until you do it right."

Windy huffed, standing up again. She attempted to do the same thing Brook had demonstrated, as she had done last time. But each attempt was as unsuccessful as the last, leaving Windy breathless and in pain. Her leg never made it over the deer's back, and she found herself stuck in the same position as the other attempts.

"I know what's wrong. You're not getting yourself off the ground high enough. Treat it as a jump," Brook advised.

Windy attempted the swing again, getting into the usual starting position. She gave herself a few hops to prepare for the jump. Once she was ready, she got her running start and leaped off the ground, swinging her leg over and rolling the rest of her body onto the deer's back. She had done it right this time, feeling as if a weight had been lifted off her shoulders.

"There. Now you see how to do it. I want you to gently kick the deer twice. Like, tap your heels against its belly."

Windy's longer legs reached just below the deer, but she carefully moved her legs so her feet could tap the deer's stomach even if they went below.

When she tapped her heels twice against the deer, it moved into a fast but swift trot, its long legs reaching out. Windy exclaimed, struggling to find balance on the deer. Her body moved from side to side, and she fought to shift her weight to keep her balance.

"Are you cat ladies this uncoordinated, or is it just you? Center yourself on its back! You're making yourself look like a fool in front of everyone!" Brook called out to her.

Windy tried to find her balance on the deer, but the trotting was too much for her in her current state. Windy slid off the deer's back, letting go of the vine reins. Though she fell to the ground with a hard thud on the dirt, the deer didn't run off. It stopped trotting, unsure why its rider was on the ground. Brook walked over to her, ignoring all the concerned Peacekeepers in the arena. Windy kept herself on the ground. The pain in her back from the fall was now unbearable. She waited until Brook was staring down at her, unapprovingly.

"Can you help me get up?" Windy asked, her ears going limp as they faded to a red hue.

"Get up."

Windy sighed, whimpering as she pushed herself up.

"You have a lot of work to do. But the more you do this, the more you'll get used to it and improve. We are not done yet. Now get on."

Windy returned to the leader's reserve, exhausted after her first day of training with Brook. She set down the bag she had been given earlier that day and searched its contents. As Brook promised, her stuff was inside, the flag sticking out of the bag as if to announce its returning presence with Windy. The bow was also sticking out of the bag, but not as much as the flag.

While Windy was alone for the time being, she rolled the flag and slid the bow underneath the bed to hide it from Hazel. She couldn't wear them on her harness just yet. But even with the weapons taken out, the bag wasn't empty. There was something else at the bottom.

When Windy reached inside, it felt cold and slick, the object even having some weight put on it. She reached into the bag with both hands to take it out. Windy's heart dropped at the sight.

The object before her seemed to be a dark green skull of some kind, with yellow markings beneath the eyeholes, and its horns curved back, with a muzzle resembling a beak. It seemed to be missing the lower jaw. Its ears seemed to be connected, but not floppy. They were hardened, like the skull.

Windy felt along the skull. Given its weight and thinness, it seemed durable and unbreakable. The sight seemed like a bad memory to Windy, but she couldn't recall what bad memory it reminded her of. She couldn't tell if it reminded her of something she didn't want to remember or if it was a nightmare. Just looking at it gave her a feeling of hopelessness, as if the skull was made from some kind of voodoo magic.

Though such an object was embedded in her mind, she was unable to tell where she had seen such a figure before. It seemed personal and made of hardened bone, the skull mask thudding against the floor. But if it was actually hers and she couldn't seem to remember, she needed answers.

Windy sat on the bed, the minutes ticking away as if they were hours. Her eyes remained fixed on the skull placed in her hands, her mind generating questions to ask when Hazel would surely return to the leader's reserve.

What is this?

Where did it come from?

Why was it given to me?

I need to be secretive about this. I can't let her know I got my stuff back.

Just as Windy's mind began to exhaust itself with thoughts, the door opened, revealing a steady Hazel making her return. "Good evening, Windy."

"Good evening to you, too." Windy's legs fidgeted restlessly on the bed. "I need to ask you something."

Hazel turned her head, her gaze focused on Windy.

Windy bit her lip, considering her question. "So, Hazel. What is this?" Windy held out the ominous skull in front of Hazel, the eyeholes staring maliciously at her.

Hazel's curious face fell, her eyebrows lowering against her eyes as a wave of memories flooded into her mind. Her head bobbed up and down as she understood her question. "Yes. I know."

Windy shifted her body toward Hazel, her body jittering for answers.

"Windy. Do you know what happened in the Splinter

Community? When you met me?"

Windy shook her head, her body hunched over. "I don't remember. It's all so hazy in my mind. All I remember is being stabbed and then waking up. What happened?"

Hazel hesitated. "Well, I was involved with your awakening. I received an urgent letter from the Skybirds concerning your disappearance."

"You were?" Windy's eyes widened as if she were a child once again.

Hazel nodded. She began to tell the story of her fight with the Creature of Darkness, gently reaching for the skull from Windy's hands. Her eyes were stuck on the mask as she retold the sorrowful story.

Windy listened with erect ears, unable to fathom the situation Hazel was sharing with her. "That was me? This thing came from me?" Windy looked down at the skull, a piercing feeling growing in her chest.

This is terrifying. Was I terrifying like that?

"Precisely. You must have been resurrected from some sort of Splinter magic. If you had been murdered, this is exactly the Splinter's business, whether Shambor admits it or not. The Splinters have a reputation for such lies, never to be trusted. Especially, if I recall correctly, their target to eradicate any weak or threatening Communities." Hazel focused on the skull, her explanation recovered deep within her mind.

So it was their fault! How are the Skybirds? Does this involve them?

"I am not a Splinter. I do not know what this object's capabilities are, if any. But just looking at this horrifies me just as much as it does you. Whatever the case may be, you must keep it. It's yours, and it might be useful down the line. Who knows?"

I really need to get back home now.

As Hazel handed her the skull back, Windy clasped the cool object in her hands. She looked back up at Hazel, her eyes almost pleading for comfort.

"I wish you a good evening, Windy. Please recover well." Hazel said with a gentle motherly tone as she returned to Goldilock, who was already taking place in the corner.

That night, while Hazel was occupied with sleep, Windy reached for the flag beneath the bed, placing the items on the floor as she began to search the room. She looked on the shelves, looked on the floor, and searched through the drawers.

Does she have any string?

Then, when she opened a drawer on Hazel's desk, there were small pre-cut vines tied together neatly. Windy took the vines and untied the bundle, placing each of the sturdy natural ropes on the ground. She took a few in her hands, tying them together to create a longer rope to loop the string around the horns and through the eyeholes, providing a sturdy hold.

She took her flag, tying the end of the string under the rubber cap of the pole. She rolled her flag up, protecting the ominous skull from the elements.

The Splinters will make up for what they have done. I need to be sure of that.

24

The deer trotted through the arena with ease, being guided by other Peacekeepers. The afternoon sun showered the Peacekeepers in heatless light, creating a comfortable atmosphere for all the athletes. Such an atmosphere was perfect for Windy, who was riding the trotting deer hunched over. She felt uncomfortable with the balance of the trot, but the extra stability from leaning forward assisted her. Her back felt sore, but nothing like the day she began training.

"Sit up!"

Windy heard Brook's guidance, and she hesitantly sat up. She continued to guide the deer around the arena, though she felt bumpy. She focused on what was in front of her, keeping her mind off the fear of falling off once more, like on previous days.

Windy had been working with Brook daily, with all of their training taking place atop a deer to help Windy rebuild her strength and balance, which had eased her bodily pains from the resurrection.

Windy rode around the arena for a few more laps, finding her comfort zone in the trot. Brook watched her, a smirk playing on her face.

"Alright. Take it in." Brook waved her over when she rounded the corner.

Windy trotted toward Brook, shushing the deer to stop, as she had been taught in her previous teachings.

"I want to have you start something new today. Get your weapons, but don't let Hazel see you. If you see her around, tell her that I need her in my office. I'll be waiting for you."

She submissively walked off, travelling down the coliseum alley, stepping up the flight of stairs. She walked down the first floor of the coliseum, traveling up to the second floor to the leader's reserve.

When Windy opened the door, Hazel was sitting at her desk with her legs crossed, writing on a piece of paper. She had been in the reserve when Windy woke up.

She must be doing something important.

Windy hesitated, looking down.

Just tell her that Brook needs her.

"Excuse me, Hazel? I don't mean to interrupt what you're doing, but Brook sent me for you. She's not happy."

Hazel placed her utensil against the desk with a thud. "What's happening with her today?"

"I don't know. All she told me was that she needed you."

Hazel sighed, pushing her papers to the side. "Where is she?"

"In her office."

"I will go see what she needs from me. Thank you for letting me know." Hazel stood up, walking out of the leader's reserve.

Windy waited in place until Hazel left, ensuring she had a safe return to Brook. She walked over to the bed, reaching under to collect her weapons. As she grabbed each of them, she clasped her flag on her back and put her bow across her shoulders, the quiver resting on her back.

Now that Hazel was gone, Windy left the leader's reserve, walking back to the performance arena. The weight on her back was familiar but new at the same time. At this point in her training, she was well enough to carry her weaponry. She walked down the stairs with ease, able to carry herself with the additional weight.

She walked past the open gate, turning the corner to walk toward Brook, who was leaning on the rail.

"I see you made it back in one piece. Good to see you can carry weight safely."

"I sure did!" Windy proudly announced. "I'm ready to start!"

"Whoa, there. Not so fast. I want to see how you've been handling yourself while using these. I don't know how you've learned, but it's not as easy as you think. There's not one right way to do it, but there's a better way than others. Let me see your archer form."

Windy took the bow from her shoulders, reaching for an arrow behind her back. She nocked the arrow on the bowstring, pulling the string back and getting into form. Brook shook her head, walking toward Windy.

"You call that archery? I thought you were this professional trained fighter. Everything about that is wrong."

Windy lowered her bow.

"No, no. Keep yourself up and don't whine about your fatigue. First off, look at your arm. You look like you dislocated your shoulder. Keep your arm straight." Brook adjusted Windy's right arm, leveling the raised limb. "And this." She pointed at her face. "How can you see where you're aiming with open eyes? Close your left eye and tilt your head toward the arrow. You're aiming, not guessing."

Windy did as Brook instructed, focusing on a certain spot on the railing. "It feels weird."

"It feels weird because you aren't adjusted to it. It feels weird because you're doing it the better way. If you keep this up, you'll be even better than you were before."

Windy lowered her bow, her burning arms relaxing. "You're right. I guess I've been a little off with my aim whenever I do archery."

"And I am here to make you know your stuff. From now on, we will work on your archery. We have a little time before the tournament, but if you want to go back to your Community, you need to win and show Hazel who can fend for herself."

"So, what do you think I should do?" Windy asked quietly.

"You've made great progress working with me every day. But you can't keep relying on me to do things right. I want you to work on what I teach you by yourself so you can truly learn."

"But what about Hazel?"

"Hazel." Brook rubbed her face. "If she gives you any problems, tell her that she trusted Brook to put you back into shape, so that same Brook is telling you that you can start giving yourself some physical therapy."

What did she have against Hazel? "If you say so."

"I very much say so. Now, let's stop worrying about her and let me show you why you should adjust. Come with me. We're done here." Brook turned around, exiting the performance arena with the deer Windy had been using for the majority of her training.

Brook led Windy outside the coliseum, walking down the sand path in the forest. She stopped walking and took the bridle off the deer so it could run free. Brook walked into the forest, her steps loud and crunchy. Windy stayed put, unsure where Brook was going.

"Well? What are you doing just standing there?" Brook looked over her shoulder. "Come."

Windy silently followed Brook, quickening her pace to catch up with her. The girls walked through the forest, Brook looking around the trees. The forest made Windy feel uneasy. Her stomach churned with nervousness, the cramp uncomfortable. It brought back memories of the Splinter Community she desperately tried to forget. She had to know that the Peacekeepers kept peace, not disrupted it. *These are good people. They know what's right and wrong.*

"Here." Brook stood in the middle of a clearing, surrounded by trees. The area wasn't packed like the Splinter Forest, so light filtered through the trees, giving the land an ethereal breath. "We are going to do some target work using the techniques I showed you. Now get into form."

Windy, still holding her bow, raised it, taking an arrow from her quiver and nocking it. She pulled the string back instinctively, resorting to her bad habits.

"Lower your arm."

Windy lowered her arm. She tilted her head to the side, closing one eye.

"Now focus on the tree right in front of you. I want you to hit the lowest tree branch. That one." She pointed.

Windy focused on the tree branch, noticing that her aim appeared better with Brook's advice. Once Windy found her comfort, she released the string, the arrow flying from the bow it was once housed. The arrow pierced the tree branch that Brook told Windy to fire at. Windy's eyes widened in awe, slowly lowering her bow.

Brook had a crazy grin on her face. "Do you see what happens when you find a better way to do things?"

"Oh, yes. It's been very helpful."

"Okay. Don't get all teary-eyed on me, please. It was no problem at all, truly. I want you to keep working on this. Now that I've shown you what to do, keep working on this technique. If I need to suggest something else to you, I will." Brook held herself with overflowing pride.

"When will you check back with me?"

"I think every other day will be fine by me. Tomorrow you can have a day to apply what you learned, and then the next day I'll check in with you."

Windy nodded. "Okay."

"You can go now. We've had a good day." Brook waved her hand, brushing Windy away.

"Thank you again." Windy turned around, walking down the sandy path to return to the coliseum.

Please let this mean I can go home soon. The Splinters could have finally destroyed the Community and I never knew.

Walking into the coliseum, Windy knew her way around, walking through the large structure with ease. She traveled down the hallway that led into the leader's reserve, opening the door. Hazel was inside, lying beside Goldilock.

Hazel gave Windy a brief smile, but upon seeing the vivid blue and white weaponry on her back, she took back her smile. "Windy, how did you get those?"

Windy's body tensed. *Just be honest.*

"Hazel, listen. I'm so sorry, I'm going against what you advised me to do, but Brook thought I was ready to start transitioning into combat. We've been working on recovery, and she has seen so much progress."

Hazel didn't argue. She had to be glad Windy was recovering. "Okay. But how did she get them?"

"I think she sent for someone to retrieve them from the Splinter Forest." She began placing her weapons against the wall.

Hazel rubbed her face with one hand. "Yep. That's Brook. Well, I'm very glad you're making progress on your therapy. Give yourself a little more time, and I will consider you leaving. But now that you're here, we need to talk." Hazel stood up, motioning to her desk. "Take a seat."

Windy sat down at Hazel's desk, looking up at her, who was leaning on the table.

"About your dilemma with the Skybirds."

Oh no.

"We need to address this promptly. I've been sending letters to the Skybirds regarding the issue. Yes, this appears to be more than a mere coincidence. They described everything that's been happening and, well, as you have seen from the Splinter Community, it matches.

"The coloration, dying of plants, and the strange psychological illness that's been corrupting the citizens. I sent out a follow-up letter not too long ago because, well, it's been quite a while since I've received a message from them. I'm trying my best to maintain order and safety for your Community. They miss you very much, Windy."

Windy looked down as she spoke, processing such information. "Then can I please leave now? If they need me, what will become of them if they don't have me?"

"No, Windy. You aren't well enough to defend your Community yet. If you were to return now and find yourself in reckless danger, then your Community will fall into a bigger pit. It's for the sake of your Community and your safety."

How could she be so defiant if my Community is in desperate need?

Windy nodded coldly. "But Hazel. I would hate to return and see that my Community has been taken over in my absence. If this is the Splinters, then—" Windy gasped. "Wait! That's probably why they lured me in! That's probably why they tricked my feelings into getting me killed! Oh, no. Oh no." Windy's hands shook as her body began to sweat. "What if they are in danger? What if they've been attacked and I don't know about it? I could have been thinking right all along!"

Hazel bent over, putting her hands on her shoulders. "Windy. Calm down. That hasn't happened. Remember, I've been talking to them."

"But you said that you haven't heard from them!"

"Windy. Calm. Need I inform you that you have an ally right here speaking to you? Everywhere you look, you have allies. We are on your side. If you return to your Community and it is demolished in the worst-case scenario, you have a second home right here."

"But what about the last Community? The Viper Community? I've heard about them, but I don't know what their status is with my Community."

"The Vipers are the delivery service of the Quinta continent. They know everything that could possibly be happening. If it will put you at ease, I will speak with the next Viper that enters the Community regarding the Splinter's curse on the Skybirds."

Windy nodded, her hair flying up and down. "Yes. That would be so nice."

"Okay. I will do that. But Windy, please know that I am by your side in all of this. I know how new you are, and I know how scary this can be for you. But you need to trust me on this. My Community is not like the Splinters. In fact, we are against them. You have someone to fall back on. Please know."

Windy's composure settled, her body relaxing into the chair. She stared at the wall behind Hazel, thinking. She found that she could trust the stubborn Hazel, but anything could happen. She had a Community to lead, and that same Community was in danger. Windy stood up from her chair, rubbing her head from the growing headache she was getting.

"Excuse me," she said. "I need to lie down. I had a busy day."

"Of course. Please take care of yourself," Hazel said.

Windy lay down on the soft mattress she had gotten used to sleeping on. As the muscles in her body slowly began to relax, she could feel her earlier stress seep into the pillow, her mind left only with exhaustion. Before long, her eyelids sank against her brown eyes, all thoughts replaced by the comfort of sleep.

This Community had to do something. For the sake of humanity, they surely needed to help. But if they weren't...

25

The main Community grounds bustled with sunlight and cheerful life, especially in the afternoon. Peacekeepers walked to and from shops with children, friends, or older family members. There were weapon repair shops, outdoor cooking, food supplies, and even a daycare pen for those with forestry pets. Peacekeepers interacted with one another everywhere, smiling as if they were a large family.

Windy sat with a group of Peacekeeper children, watching them play. The children played in a pit of sand, building structures, playing with toys, and interacting with one another. Windy has never seen a playpen such as this from the Skybirds or the Splinters. She thought all the kids stayed inside with their parents, as she was raised. The sight was interesting—to see the new generation beginning to know each other and get along.

"Hi there!" said a young Peacekeeper that seemed to be younger than Windy.

"Hello." Windy smiled, looking at her.

"Is one of these yours?" she asked. She had a wooden horn on her forehead that branched into two other horns, each adorned with jewelry. She had small, pointed ears and fangs. She had patches of green fur on her shoulders and wrists. Even with how animalistic she looked, she didn't have a tail.

"Oh, no." Windy shook her head. "I'm just watching them. I've never seen such a place before."

"You've never seen a sandpit?" the Peacekeeper asked, confused.

"No. Where I come from, we don't have such things."

"You're..." She tilted her head, inspecting Windy. "You look familiar, but I'm not sure where I've seen you before."

"I'm a Skybird. I'm staying here to recover from an injury I got from another Community."

"Oh. A Skybird. I didn't think that. You looked like something else, but I must be having déjà vu. How long have you been here?"

"Well, a few weeks, at least a month. I'm not allowed to leave until Hazel thinks I'm good to go."

She nodded. "Oh, that's Hazel alright. But she's doing the best for you. Know that. We will take great care of you. You look good, though. What happened?"

Windy looked down, glancing at a child who was destroying their sand mound. "I had a freak accident. But I do feel better. I'm planning on attending the archery race tournament to prove that I'm well enough to leave."

"Oh, that sounds fun! I love the athletic tournaments Hazel and Brook plan. They're so breathtaking, watching each Peacekeeper fight for the first place, knowing we all still love each other in the end." The Peacekeeper clasped her hands, lifting her head joyously. Now that she saw her hands, Windy noticed she had green claws.

"I've done something like that, but not quite like it. I'm hoping I do well. I really need to leave."

"Totally understood! I know you miss home. I would want to go back home, too."

"It's more important for me to go home, though. I'm the Community leader."

The Peacekeeper gasped, her hands covering her agape mouth. She reached out her hands, waving them at Windy. "You're the Community leader! Oh my gosh, I'm so sorry I treated you so casually! My name is Kirsty." She reached out to shake Windy's hand. Kirsty's hand felt cold, but unusually soft. "Yes, yes. You need to return to your Community ASAP! That means 'as soon as pronto!'"

Windy chuckled, though the energy caused her head to grow into a dull feeling. "I agree. I have some business to take care of there." She sighed.

"Understood, understood. Please take care of yourself, of course."

Then, out of the peace, there was a shriek. Everyone looked in the direction it came from, their eyes wide with fear. Windy stood up, running in the direction of the sound. She wove through a flurry of scattered Peacekeepers, pushing her way into the chaos.

"What's going on?" she shouted.

"A beast killed our animals!" a Peacekeeper replied in horror.

What? What beast?

Windy kept running against the flow of traffic, approaching the start of the chaos. By the time she made it, the crowd was already gone. The sight in front of her caused her to slide on the gravel to a stop, in pure disbelief at the sight before her.

It can't be! How?!

There was a red and black creature with horns, hooves, and a stomach the color of cerulean. It looked around, just as scared as the Peacekeepers were. In its jaws was a large boar; below it, a bloody, bitten deer.

It was a Winged Beast.

Windy's Winged Beast.

"Nodin!" Windy ran toward her Winged Beast, her arms outstretched. Nodin looked at her, his ears perking up. He trotted toward her with the boar in his beak, blood dripping in his path.

"Get it away!" a Peacekeeper shouted.

"No. He's safe! He's not dangerous! He's a Winged Beast, an animal native to the Skybird territory." She turned to Nodin, rubbing his face. "Yes, you missed Mommy, didn't you? I know. She was gone for too long. I can't believe how worried you must have been!" she cooed, scratching his face.

Nodin chirped, dropping the boar and pressing his face against her. Windy scratched his face along his forehead and jaw.

"Such a good boy! Such a good boy! You were just hungry, and everyone got scared. I'm sorry."

The frightened Peacekeepers gathered, watching Windy interact with such a beast. In her peripheral vision, she noticed the crowding

Peacekeepers and turned around.

"Everyone, this is Nodin. He's a Winged Beast. They are native to the Skybird Community and are not aggressive. I apologize with all of my heart for the animals he killed, but he was just hungry. Please understand, everyone." She stepped aside to show everyone the invading animal.

The Peacekeeper's eyes widened, marveling at the animal. Then, from the crowd, someone shouted, "Can I pet him?"

"Yes! You may! Whoever wants to see him, come up. He is friendly. I promise."

Peacekeepers approached Nodin, talking among themselves and laughing with excitement. Nodin lowered his head, looking at each of the Peacekeepers. His ears twitched, and his chest rumbled, but he remained friendly. Little kids, teenagers, adults, and even the elderly were all fascinated by Nodin, relishing the once-in-a-lifetime moment. What was once a chaotic moment became a heartwarming moment for the Community.

A voice rose from the crowd. "What is happening? What is that?"

The crowd stepped aside, making way for the announcing Peacekeeper. It was Hazel. She gripped the scimitar at her hip as she approached Windy and Nodin. "Windy? What is that thing? Why is it here? Why has it killed our animals?"

"Hazel, this is Nodin. He's a Winged Beast. They're from the mountains."

Nodin reached his head toward Hazel, curiously sniffing her. Hazel stepped back, disturbed by such a beast. "This thing isn't a cat, a bird, or a goat. How strange."

"He's friendly. Winged Beasts are friendly animals," Windy gently reassured Hazel.

Hazel looked into Nodin's eyes as if to read the creature. She reached out a hand, cautious but open. Nodin tapped his beak on her hand, chirping as if to assure her he wouldn't hurt her. Hazel's eyes focused on Nodin, a new sense of familiarity between them, with the way she was calm toward him. Windy smiled, watching the two.

"How did he get here?"

"I don't know. I assume he went looking for me after I disappeared. I told him to wait outside the Splinter Community, but I bet he became nervous when I never returned."

Hazel nodded, continuing to gaze at the Winged Beast. "Interesting. He is indeed far from home, but a loyal companion to have if he made the long search for his owner and remembered her."

"He is a very good boy. That's right, you're a good boy!" Windy scratched his chin.

Hazel stepped back, giving them some space. "If he is here for you, then he needs to stay with you."

Windy looked at Hazel, thoughtful. "Stay with me? But where? Is that fine with you?"

Hazel nodded. "He is welcome here, just as you are. As long as he doesn't bring forth destruction to the Community, he may stay."

Windy shook her head. "Oh, no. Winged Beasts aren't destructive at all. They usually prefer to mind their own business or stick with their owners."

Hazel grinned. "I see that he follows the latter in this situation.

Okay. I trust your word. I know you're around these creatures every day, so you know what's best."

"Thank you, Hazel. I appreciate it. I truly do. May I bring him into the coliseum? I want to spend some time with him."

"Yes. I only ask that you stay safe."

Windy looked back at Nodin, motioning with her head for him to follow. "Come, boy."

Nodin followed Windy as she walked off, staying close behind her. The Peacekeepers stepped aside for the two, giving them room to walk, especially for Nodin. As they walked through the forest, Nodin looked around, chirping uneasily. Windy reached her arm out, comforting him.

"Shh, it's okay, boy. I know this is new. Nothing will hurt you. Do you want me with you?"

Nodin looked at her, intrigued. He kept his eyes focused on her even as she stepped to his side. She grabbed his feathery pelt, climbing on his back. She struggled, but managed to adjust herself on his back.

This was way easier than the deer.

"Walk," Windy said as she grabbed his mane to guide him.

Nodin began walking but kept looking around. He peered into every dark space, every bush, every tiny hole in the ground.

"Shh, it's okay, boy. It's safe here." She reached her hand out, patient with his feelings. They continued walking toward the coliseum, the towering building closing in on them. When Nodin saw the large building, he stepped back, chirping and flapping his wings in fear.

"Nodin! Shh, it's okay. We walk inside it. Go. Walk."

Nodin shook his head, lashing his tail. Windy moved her hand along his shoulder, feeling the soft feathers of the Winged Beast. Her touch was light and comforting, full of patience for the frightened animal. "Walk."

Nodin looked at the building, watching the people walk in and out of the gates. Peacekeepers who passed by startled themselves at the bright red figure, the monstrosity new to them. They must not have been at the site where the fiasco occurred. He stepped to the side, unsure why they were scared of him. But their fear fueled his own, and he didn't want to move forward.

"Nodin. Please. Walk."

Nodin refused.

Windy sighed, running her hand through her hair. She fought herself to maintain her patience. She slid off of Nodin, stepping forward. She faced him, reaching her arms out. "Come."

Nodin looked around, but when he saw that his owner wasn't afraid or in danger, he walked toward her, his steps cautious. Windy stepped back, guiding the beast slowly toward the gates. She kept guiding him to follow her, her voice slow and soft. Nodin looked around the building as he walked, chirping and growling. Windy snapped her fingers, maintaining his focus. Nodin continued to walk toward Windy, taking his time. Windy then stepped onto gravel, then rock, indicating she had made it past the gates. Nodin froze, looking inside at the dark interior.

"Come. Come." Windy waved her hands.

Nodin looked at her, then continued to walk. Windy stepped

toward him when he made it just before stepping onto the rocky floor of the coliseum. She scratched his face, petting him in the process.

"Good boy! See, you're safe. Now let's go in." Windy got herself in place to climb onto Nodin, her muscles burning. One time was enough for her recovering state. "Walk."

Nodin walked into the coliseum, nervously looking around. Peacekeepers screamed at the sight, startling the Winged Beast.

"He's not dangerous! He's mine!" she alerted the Peacekeepers. "You're scaring him!"

She patted Nodin again, and he continued to walk.

"Stop," she commanded when he approached the seats surrounding the performance arena. She adjusted herself on his back, repositioning her hands on his back into a suitable flying position. "Fly."

Nodin flapped his luscious wings, the beating of the wings echoing through the first floor. He flew forward, out of the first floor. Windy felt the wind against her face, a feeling she never realized she had missed. The feel of Nodin's feathers beneath her hands and the cold air brought her comfort.

I'm so glad you're safe.

She guided him above the performance arena and around the area. He confidently responded, his fear from before gone with the wind. As he glided, Windy sat up, looking at the coliseum from below. The training Peacekeepers seemed like ants from how high she was, and the arena was also significantly smaller.

In the distance, she could see the fields that the Peacekeepers claimed, the empty land a vast sight. Far in the distance were trees, and in another direction was arid territory.

The Quinta continent was beautiful, even if Windy could only see a small portion of it. As she gazed out at the view, she quickly snapped her head to the side, thinking she saw something in the corner of her eye. She gazed out at the walls of the coliseum, straining her vision to find what she could have seen.

She turned Nodin around, gliding toward the other end of the coliseum. As she approached, she couldn't see anything other than a fuzzy black spot in the distance.

Was it a shadow?

As Windy approached the wall, she noticed a fuzzy discoloration that looked like an imprint, but it seemed suspiciously out of place. There were claw marks surrounding the shade, as if something had been there.

"Down," Windy commanded.

Nodin landed on the ledge, his claws gripping the brick. Windy slid off his back, stepping over to the shade. In the patch of shade, there seemed to be footprints a shade lighter than the blackness beneath, which could barely be seen.

Windy wondered what could have caused this, if it was natural or unnatural. But she didn't know this Community completely. It could have formed from a fire a long time ago. Windy kept it in the back of her mind, but didn't think too much about it. She had other things to worry about, like getting home.

Windy mounted Nodin, guiding him back into the sky. She dove into the performance arena, landing near the entry gate. They were greeted by terrified Peacekeepers, who ran away from the large beast. Windy dismounted Nodin, stepping in front of him. "Stay."

She walked off, looking for a somewhat steady Peacekeeper she could talk to. She walked to a Peacekeeper sitting down on the dirt, who was holding a flask of water. The Peacekeeper had patches of white and brown fur on his body and had long whiskers on his upper lip.

"Excuse me, mister?"

The Peacekeeper looked up at Windy. "Hello there. So, you're the one causing trouble with that thing, huh?"

"No. He's with me. He's not dangerous. Look, I'm interested in the archery tournament that's coming up. I need to compete to show Hazel that I can go back home. I haven't been in the best condition, and she's been reluctant to send me back. Where do I sign up?"

The Peacekeeper pointed to the entry gate of the arena. "In there, there will be a clipboard hung in the warm-up pen. From what I've heard, not many spots are left. I don't know how many are left, but with it being so close to the day, you need to go there now if you want to participate."

"Okay, thank you." Windy gave a respectful nod and walked off toward the gates. As she passed Nodin, she pointed at him firmly. "Stay. Still stay."

He looked at her, but didn't follow her. Windy walked along the dirt path in the underground, which would lead her to the warm-up pen.

As she stepped on the mound of dirt, she noticed that there was a clipboard hanging on the rim of the pen, where Windy walked past. She grabbed the gravel utensil from the clipboard and searched down the list. Names were written on all the lines except for one.

Windy quickly wrote her name down, securing her place in the event. She smiled, placing the writing utensil back on the clipboard. She walked back out of the warm-up pen to retrieve Nodin.

Nodin obediently listened to Windy, flying to the second floor with ease, though timidly. She led him through the hallway of the leader's reserve, showing him where he'd stay. He fit through the hallway despite being such a large beast. But if Hazel's deer had to fit, so could Nodin.

As she opened the door, Nodin stepped back, nervously looking inside the room. Hazel wasn't inside, but Goldilock was. The deer saw Nodin and immediately stood up, bleating. Nodin chirped in fear, rearing up.

"Hey! Guys! Guys! No, shh. Don't be scared. It's okay. Nodin. Come." Windy walked into the leader's reserve, guiding Nodin carefully. Nodin looked at the deer, trying to stay away from him as much as possible. Windy led him to the daybed, pointing at the floor beneath the bed. "Lay."

Nodin lay down, looking up at her.

"Stay." Windy sat down on the bed, and Nodin didn't get up. Windy had to teach him that this was now his space for the time being. Windy sat down, looking at him. Just the sight of the Winged Beast reminded her of home. But she would be going home soon; she just needed to prove herself in the upcoming tournament she caught by just barely according to Hazel.

Please let me go soon.

It was soon time for her to prove herself once again for the sake of her home.

26

The nightly air of the Peacekeeper Community wafted unnoticed, not a degree warmer or colder than equilibrium. Insects danced happily through the forest; peace was promised to all living creatures, including the critters. Peacekeepers slept in the comfort of huts and tree houses, respecting the ethereal atmosphere with silence.

Sheltered away from the citizens of the Community, Windy and Hazel found solace in the leader's reserve, the room just as peaceful as the outer atmosphere of the Community. But earlier in the night, such peace was yet to be found.

"Windy! What is that in your arms?" Hazel's hands clutched the doorframe, her body stabilizing against her startled body.

"Hazel, don't worry. This is Nodin. He's a Winged Beast. They're domestic animals at the Skybird territory." Windy's hands gently caressed the neon red feathers sprawled along her open lap, the feline chirping in response.

"So they are. I apologize for my concern. I understand how special they are to your culture."

Hazel scribbled on a worn sheet of paper, eyes focused on the majestic letters against the dirty background. Windy sat with jittering limbs as her plumes fluttered against her skin.

"Hazel?" Windy spoke up against the silence. "May I ask you a few things?"

Hazel lowered her pen, gently sliding the dirty paper across the table. "Of course. What do you need to ask?"

"It's about the Community. The more I live here, the more I find myself drawn in. The people, beliefs, your life."

Hazel's body twisted toward Windy, her eyes deep with care.

"You all look so different. Honestly, I'm jealous of that. I'm jealous of how you treat one another. I never got that in my Community growing up. But I feel accepted unlike any other. It feels weird. But if your Community truly trusts me that much, I want to ask you where I come from, if you have any idea at all." Windy leaned toward Hazel, her clasped fingers picking at one another. "I look like the Community, but I've always been told I'm a Viper."

Hazel's head bounced up and down as she carefully stepped toward Windy, placing herself closely beside her. "I can see your confusion. We, Peacekeepers, value peace. To achieve peace, we must learn to accept one another and our looks, beliefs, and actions. Some people, especially Communities, cannot understand that. But you indeed look like one of us, with your quilled body.

"However, I do recall a Community far, far back that apparently had bodies such as yours. But this Community fell years and years ago. It would be impossible for them to flourish after such a time. I apologize, but with honesty, I do not know who you are. Peacekeepers appear unusual, and Vipers have the same bodily tint as you.

"I have doubts you originate from an extinct Community after years, but if you truly seek answers, may Mother Nature guide you on this path of succession, peace, and identity."

Windy lifted her hand as she shook her head, dazed and unsure. "I hear you say this all the time. Who is 'Mother Nature' and why do you put, well, her into everything you say?"

"A respectful question from someone of a different culture. My Community worships the very being who gave us life. Mother Nature gives us life, freedom, and peace. Such is the way we live. We ask her for help on these qualities, should any of them be broken."

"You worship this thing? Where is she?"

"All around us. The very trees created, the grass that breathes beneath our feet, the very animals who graciously give their lives for all that walks. She is within you, as you have been created from the very environment. Without each other, we wouldn't exist."

"I don't get it." Windy's eyes glanced at her feet as pressure rushed through her body.

"Do not feel bad. She understands your confusion. The spirits all around us understand. Those whose lives that have been stripped from mortality."

Windy's mouth seemed to lock, unable to speak any further about the subject.

"Though, within her, she gives us the opportunity to see our loved ones again as she sees fit. But do not be afraid if she blesses you with such a gift. It's how she allows us to live on with life forever with our loved ones."

Windy lifted her head to meet Hazel's enthusiastic forest-green eyes, the barrier between understanding and naivete solid across their Communities. "I don't think I'll ever understand, but thank you for sharing your life so openly with me. I truly appreciate it."

"Happy to enlighten such a new leader on our world."

"I should, um, get ready to sleep. Brook won't be happy if I show up to her version of physical therapy." Windy adjusted her seating on the bed, her body flattening out beside Hazel.

"How has that been for you? Has Brook been treating you well?" Hazel asked as she stood up, freeing up space for her guest.

"Well, Brook is Brook. I'm sure you know how she would be working."

"Of course. I hope I can get a report from her soon so I may evaluate you for your journey home. But for now, rest well and continue to keep yourself safe."

As the silence around Windy began to sink into her mind, darkness soon followed, leaving her with the unanswered mystery of her existence, whether this Mother Nature could confirm it or not.

27

Brook's steps were heavy and deliberate. Unlike the other Peacekeepers, her eyes were focused and condescending as she approached the burly creature in front of her. "Windy! What in Mother's name is that thing? Is that your little kitty?"

There's that reference again. Even Brook believes such a person.

"Stop," Windy commanded Nodin. She had been trotting, allowing a free Nodin run around the arena to get familiar with his new surroundings. He was easing in, but remained timid about minor things around the Community. "Hi, Brook! Yes, this is Nodin. My Winged Beast."

Nodin stepped back when he saw Brook. He didn't like her. Brook stared at the Winged Beast, her eyes staring into his dark beads. "Why do you ride him like that? That's a weird way to do it."

"This is how all of the Skybirds do it. It's because we primarily use these animals for flight."

"Eh. I kind of see. But I don't see. Anyway, more important

matters to be worried about besides being a crazy cat lady. Are you ready for the tournament? It's next week. Do you even know what to do?"

"Well, now that I have Nodin, I figure I can just use him. It's a race, after all. And he's a strong man."

Brook barked a laugh, which startled Nodin. "Use him! Wow, you really don't know anything, do you?"

Windy looked at Brook, uncertainty all over her face.

"I figure I should tell you this now and not the day of. So, yes, the name suggests it's a race, so do what you can to win. But no. We don't rely on animals for what could be done by ourselves. You, by yourself, are racing against other people to hit the targets, which means running on foot. Which I assume you have never done that?"

"Not necessarily." Windy shook her head.

"Great. So, we need to work on that this week." Brook sighed, putting her hands on the sides of her head. "This is great."

"Um, what do we need to do?"

"Get to it—that's what we need to do! Let me see if there's anything in the back over here we can use. Stay here." Brook walked off toward the gates, her steps loud against the dirt, practically taking out her frustration on the ground.

Windy glanced at Nodin as if she could speak to him with her eyes. She leaned against the large animal, waiting for Brook. She didn't feel the need to complain. If she wanted to get out, she needed someone to teach her how to win. Windy gazed at the training Peacekeepers, wondering what they were doing. Was it for themselves? Was it for what was coming up?

While Windy was busying herself watching the Peacekeepers, Brook came up to her while holding a circular slice of wood.

"Here. Warm up, and we will get started."

Windy adjusted her bow in her hands, stretching the string until her muscles loosened. As the tension felt lighter with each movement she made, she took an arrow from her back, setting up in front of the target that Brook adjusted against the railing.

"Remember what I taught you."

Windy's eyes were not blinking as she focused on the target, holding in her breath. Her body felt light and relaxed, finding comfort in her new stance. In her eyes, the arrowhead fell in the middle of the wood, indicating a perfect aim. Windy's fingers slid off the string, the arrow flying toward the wood. Though Windy anticipated a perfect first shot, the arrow hit just above the center of the target.

"Keep your arms relaxed as you shoot. Moving your arm will change how the arrow penetrates."

Windy continued to warm up, keeping what Brook said in mind. She continued to warm up, her body steadily relaxing during the activity, further supporting her warm-up accuracy.

She continued to fire arrows at large, only deciding when she would be finished. Brook focused on Windy, inspecting every move she made. Even Nodin was mindlessly watching Windy. Windy's tan body shone, the warmth up exerting her body.

"Okay. Let me talk to you." Brook waved her over. Windy kept her arrows stuck in the wood, focusing on listening to Brook.

"Now, as I have mentioned before, this is an archery race on foot.

You need to shoot all of the targets on foot and return to the timeline once finished. It's easier said than done, but there is a strategy to it so you don't lose control over your body. That will be your biggest breaker in this competition. First, I want to test your reflexes." Brook stepped back, giving herself distance between her and the wooden target. "Stand here."

Windy placed herself where Brook guided her.

"Sprint down, but stop when you get in front of the target. After you make a complete stop, start running again. As fast as you can."

Windy's mind raced with confusion, but she had to race her body out of her state of mind. She ran, her head facing the target that she approached. Windy's feet slowed, taking quick steps to bring herself to a complete stop. Then, she sprinted again.

"Bring it in!" Brook called after her.

Windy turned around, jogging after Brook. Her chest heaved as she ran, her legs weak.

"I think you completely missed the idea. Let me show you." Brook got into position, as she had directed Windy. Her body seemed to tense with pent-up energy, begging to be set free. Once she sprang forward, her feet beat against the dirt, sending the pounded substance flying behind her.

Like Windy, her eyes were focused on the target she was lining herself up with. Her dress flowed behind her like a horse's tail, the elegance remaining apparent despite the athletic trainer's performance. When she was about a stride before the target, she slid on the dirt, her body pushing her forward rather than her legs.

Once she passed the target, she leaped forward, her legs catching the ground and her body propelling forward. She slowed to a stop once she finished the demonstration, jogging her unfatigued body back toward Windy.

"What did you notice?"

Windy's eyes widened in awe, unable to fathom such an action from Brook. "Well, uh, you made everything smooth and fluid."

"Exactly. Anything else?"

"Uh." Windy shook her hands, her mind unable to find the right answer.

"I positioned myself as if I were going to hit the target while continuing to move. Yes, I slowed down, but I continued to move. This is a race. The more you can control yourself, the better results you will have. Now do what I did."

Windy blinked, unable to process the sudden demand. "Now? Aren't you going to tell me what to do?"

"No. Do what I just did, and I will adjust you when I see something off."

Windy's steps were hesitant as she adjusted herself back at the starting distance from the target. Then, she launched herself forward, her legs darting her body forward with their long strides.

When Windy lined herself up with the target, she tried to suddenly stop against the dirt like what Brook had done, but her body toppled over as if the very air shoved her into the ground.

"Woah!"

"Get up and get over here," Brook snapped.

Windy brushed the dirt off her now off-white and blue clothes, stood up, and sheepishly walked to Brook, her steps slow with embarrassment.

"I said get over here, not stroll over here!"

Windy picked up her pace, striding to Brook. Brook's condescending eyes looked into Windy's guilty eyes, her gaze preparing her criticism.

"What was that?"

"I don't know." Windy's ears drooped, her feathers limp on her head.

"Well, if you don't know, you sure won't get anywhere. If you did that out there, you're done. You slide, not fall."

"But how do I slide?"

Brook grinned. "I'm glad you asked. First, you don't plant your feet. You stop moving, but position your legs so they can catch momentum on the dirt."

"This is easier on a hard surface," Windy commented.

"Then this is why you adapt. We won't get anywhere if you can't do this because when we add a bow into the mix, you're going to hurt somebody."

Windy ran forward, not worrying about positioning herself in line with the target. She ran forward, practicing what Brook explained to her. She suddenly stopped, placing her legs one leg in front of the other, her feet catching the ground but not as fast as Brook. Windy turned around to face Brook, her damp face asking for approval from her mentor.

"Not quite. Do it again."

Windy sighed, walking back to Brook. Though her chest felt heavy and her limbs light, Windy continued to drill until she approached success. With each attempt, Windy's body weakened; the weight of her own body was too much for her legs. After she drilled round after round, her chest heaved, gasping for air.

"No more. Please."

Brook looked down at Windy, who sat beneath Nodin's paws. "How can you get better if you don't push yourself? You perform in a week."

"Okay, well, can we do this later tonight? Or tomorrow? Please, I can't go anymore." Windy's voice trembled as much as her body did.

"If you want to, go ahead. I'll see you later." Brook turned her back, walking off without another word, leaving Windy's weak form to herself.

Windy watched her shrink into the distance, disappearing through the gates. She looked up at Nodin and pushed herself to her feet. "Lay," she commanded Nodin. When he lay down, she threw her heap of bones onto Nodin and adjusted herself lazily on his back. "Fly."

Windy reeked of the unusual scent of sweat and mint. Her movements were fluid, and she worked tirelessly. Such twisted body parts moved in harmony, working together to create a common outcome. Her feet kicked up dirt, kicking it in different directions. Her once uncoordinated legs now moved in mutual synchronization with the speed her body generated.

She moved like a swift hunter, aware of every movement its prey might make and anticipating any sudden move from its focus. Arrows dug themselves into the wooden target, making contact with a satisfying thud from different distances.

"Back in!" Brook waved her hand at Windy.

Windy ran back to Brook, her legs striding with comfort despite the slickness of her skin.

"Do you feel like a different person?" asked Brook. She smiled like a mother watching her child walk for the first time.

"I do!" Windy bounced on her feet, her excitement radiating off the sweat that gleamed on her body.

"And do you care that I was so hard on you?"

"Not anymore."

"Good. This is what happens when you allow yourself to be tough and work a little harder than you're used to. Relax yourself. I have faith in you for this weekend."

"Thank you, Brook! Thank you so much!" Windy crossed her bow across her shoulders, clasping her hands together as she shoved herself into Brook's face.

Brook leaned back, her face unchanging from the excited gesture. "No need to thank me. Thank yourself for allowing me to help you."

Windy giggled as she spun around to mount Nodin, reaching her hand for his pelt and throwing herself onto his back.

That evening, Peacekeepers worked in the performance arena, stepping on ladders or hanging from balconies to decorate the coliseum. They adorned the vintage building with fabrics in green, brown, and yellow while Peacekeepers below rode forest animals to ensure the dirt was raked and flat for what was to come.

Windy assisted the Community in preparation for the event. Earlier, she helped pin flags and banners in places Peacekeepers couldn't safely reach with ladders. She helped assemble rakes for the working animals in the performance arena. Now, she was helping decorate tables with Peacekeeper adornments, the banners and table pieces placed just right.

The evening fell lower in the sky, greeted by silver sequin stars above the Community. Though Windy's muscles burned with progress, she found no problem in helping the Community that graciously provided her with a home when she couldn't return to one. Peacekeepers around her expressed their appreciation, thanking her and waving.

Even when they didn't need help, Windy found something to do for the Community. After all, the Community didn't need to help Windy, but they found something to do for her, and now she would emerge as a leader stronger and wiser than before.

28

The Community was at its peak. The sound emitted from the coliseum could be heard even outside the Community grounds. Members of the Community cheered until their voices were soundless and hoarse. They all clapped until their hands were glowing with a red hue. Peacekeepers filled the seats, squished together to enjoy a shared experience. Tree nuts flew from the hands of Peacekeepers, their excitement flinging such snacks like confetti.

Overlooking the performance stood a balcony draped with a large, burned Peacekeeper flag. It was placed strategically so you could see the activities below without being too far or too close. Stepping onto the balcony was Hazel, who formally held her hands behind her back and tilted her chin up.

Upon the leader's entrance, the crowd gradually lowered its volume in respect. Once the crowd hushed, Hazel raised a megaphone, lifting her free hand.

"Greetings, Peacekeepers! Welcome to today's quarterly

Community championships! Before we introduce our contestants, let's open with a moment of silence."

The color of the crowd rolled into a mix of black, brown, and blond heads as the Community began their personal prayers. The religious silence continued until Hazel raised the megaphone to her mouth, projecting her voice.

"Thank you, Mother. Now, to introduce our contestants!"

Peacekeepers flooded out of the left side of the gate, which was now divided for the event. Peacekeepers of all forms and sizes ran against the dirt, waving at everyone while they held bows in their hands.

The very last contestant who followed them wasn't a Peacekeeper, but Windy. Windy ran with the Peacekeepers in a single file line, nervousness flooding her mind. She knew this very moment would signify her departure to her home Community, so every moment mattered the most.

If I win, I will be one step closer to protecting my people from this threat that infected our Community for years.

Windy's nervous eyes gazed at the cheering crowds, the noise filling a hole in Windy's chest. The weight felt heavy on her, her head thumping with adrenaline.

Please, let this be it.

Once everyone had spilled back through the right gate, the crowd's volume began to drop, indicating that Hazel was starting the tournament. The first five participants lined up on the left side of the gate while the remaining participants returned to the warm-up pen. A Peacekeeper with a clipboard and a piece of paper monitored activity inside and outside the performance arena. Windy walked around the warm-up pen, stretching her tense arms. With each step, Windy felt her body tense as if the coliseum only gave her such karma. As she flexed the bowstring, her muscles burned as if the anxiety were an inferno on her body.

Windy could see participants dash in and out of the gates, but couldn't keep up with each time they received one by one. There were so many of them. Some ran out tense but returned in a much more relaxed state. Some ran out with large egos and returned with faces wet with tears. Some ran out with smiles, only to return with rough scowls. Whatever the results, they were sure to vary based on the reactions of the finished contestants. Fifty in, fifty out.

The warm-up pen gradually diminished its contestants, leaving the final ten participants, including Windy. But when a distraught Peacekeeper stomped through the warm-up pen, the last ten contestants were called, everyone's steps just the same as everyone else's as their moments closed in.

A Peacekeeper with deer antlers, Bucky, was pushing a female with a similar build, as if they had come from a herd of deer. His sister, Ollie. Her eyes were glued to him while her brows curved down. She was shouting just as loudly as the male.

"You're the oldest, which means you have the oldest time!"

"Mistaken, mistaken! You've always been the slowest, so let's see just how slow you are today!"

Windy watched the two interact.

Once Bucky was at the gate, Ollie shouted, "Bad luck, Pudu!"

Why would they talk to each other like that? How harsh!

Ollie poked her eyes through an opening in the gate, mumbling to herself and hissing under her breath. The crowd cheered loudly after what seemed to be every second. But before Windy could blink for the fifth time, Bucky raced in, slowing down.

"Beat that, sis."

Ollie raised her arm with an arrow pointed at him, but paused once the gates opened for her. She threw her body around, sprinting out of the gate with loud feet. Bucky began shouting at her from the gate, ensuring he could be heard by the competitor.

Windy lowered her head, closing her eyes. The longer she breathed, the longer she could settle. She needed to relax. Relaxing meant success. Her mind went blank as she drifted into her own white world, drowning out all sound, even her own heartbeat. But she opened her eyes when the shouting beside her began.

"I'm sure that was slower than me. And I'm always right."

"Go get your antlers stuck in a tree! I cleared the first target faster than you!"

"If you blinked, maybe. But I kept my eyes wide open, unlike you, blind girl."

"Just because I looked down once does not make me blind!"

Windy ignored the two as they left, resuming her peace. There were only two performers before her now, yet her mind was thunderous. She clamped her trembling fingers over the handle of the bow, her knuckles bleeding into a white hue.

Though her body was beginning to feel light, she was startled out of her world, hearing her name being called. She sprang forward instinctively, her legs working without the responsibility of her mind. She darted her head around the arena, locating the eight targets lined up.

As she ran, scanning her surroundings, the otherwise neutral atmosphere around her began to chill, clouds forming in the sky.

Everyone was focused on Windy.

She positioned herself in formation as she passed the faded white line marked in the dirt. Applying the skills taught by Brook, her body naturally set itself up for the seamless firing strategy.

"That's one," announced Hazel, but her announcement hinted at an underlying fear.

The sound of Hazel's voice assisted in the launch of Windy's body, her long legs striding as much ground as she could take in. Windy slid against the dirt mindlessly, her body and arrow in line with the target as she fired the next arrow.

"Two."

Windy's legs pumped, her body fueled by a concoction of fear, anticipation, and adrenaline. Each target was shot seamlessly, her body continuously running like a machine.

"Three."

"Four."

Windy's chest heaved with a dull pressure.

The sky continued to darken.

"Five."

"Six."

Two more.

"Seven."

Windy used the last bit of energy to race to the last target, her body naturally preparing for the slide as she controlled the preparation of her bow. Windy's hair flowed to the side as she hovered above the dirt, effortlessly demanding the arrow fire into the target.

The crowd gasped

Windy's heart sank.

Windy turned her head to face the target that should have been penetrated, but was left clean. Windy skidded to a halt, her body jerking back into formation. But as she prepared herself for the redemption of her mistake, a large shadow blanketed the coliseum.

What had been a beautiful moment marked by cheering was now replaced by screams of terror, the crowd bustling uneasily.

Windy lowered her bow, not realizing her body was stinging with adrenaline. She looked around, finding any Peacekeepers who could be motioning toward the sight. She looked up, noticing that the smiling sun was now interrupted by an ugly sight.

This wasn't the Peacekeeper Community.

The arrow Windy had fired was on the padded dirt, and a sprout emerged from the shaft. The darkened Community began to chill with rain, the sudden storm disturbing the clean Community.

Her chest expanded with oxygen and was exhausted with a screeching whistle that tore through the screams. This was no normal behavior, and Windy needed to find out what was happening at once.

Nodin dove as if his gravity was greatly increased, speeding toward his distressed owner. Nodin didn't plant all four of his feet on the ground when Windy ran toward him, grabbing his fur and placing herself on his back. "Fly! Now! Go!"

Nodin's wings beat furiously, screeching in surprise. He took to the skies like the very arrows that were fired from the Peacekeepers, battling the puncturing rain. The coliseum was now a place of chaos as people ran out for their safety.

As Windy flew through the storming Community, Peacekeepers were beginning to find shelter within the Coliseum, removing themselves from the discord. But as they ran, they saw puddles of water rapidly forming from the destruction.

But the water wasn't any normal water. It was murky with a rough, blueish color.

What in the world is happening?

Windy's mind spiraled with thoughts, her attention barely focused on the phenomena.

Where did this come from?

The storm tore through the peace until there was none left. Thunder roared across the sky as lightning struck down on the territory, destroying anything in its path. In the dark sky, Windy's body steadily grew damp from the forbidden liquid. She couldn't find the source of the chaos.

But her ears appeared to stand up straight, her eyes frantically scanning her surroundings as her mind screamed a chilling revelation at her.

She knew this from before.

It hit way too close to home.

The home she didn't know existed or not.

Windy led Nodin closer to the surface, her gaze darting to the muddy ground beneath her. While inspecting the Community for any other threats, such as those the Skybirds had fought years ago, she found only mud in the performance arena.

Defeated by confusion, Windy returned to the trembling Peacekeepers, her bright colors standing out from the gloom. She gracefully slid off Nodin, her skirt trailing down his back as she sprang forward through the crowd.

"Hazel! Hazel, are you safe?" Windy called out, her voice tearing through the uneasiness of the crowd.

Windy swiftly weaved through the crowd, her body twisting through each person like poles. She felt her oxygen levels diminish through the fear, her breath shallow, no matter how hard she breathed.

"Over there!" A Peacekeeper's finger darted from the crowd, guiding Windy in her desired direction.

Following the Peacekeeper's assistance, Windy's brown eyes closed in on Hazel's green form, anxiety meeting anxiety on equal levels.

"Hazel!" Windy's hand shot in the air.

As if she were listening intently for her, Hazel's eyes locked with Windy's at the first call of her name, her face brightening up amidst the darkness of the Community.

"Windy. Do you know what's happening?" Hazel asked over the deafening shrieks of thunder.

"I may, but I'm not entirely sure. All I know is that I've seen this before. In my Community."

Hazel's bright face darkened once again with horror. "Don't tell me this is what you meant."

Windy nodded, just as wounded as Hazel.

Hazel put her hands on Windy's shoulders, her determined eyes looking into Windy's pained eyes. "You cannot wait. We cannot wait. This threat is becoming too dire. We must let the Vipers know. They must know what's coming for them!"

"But what about you?" Windy asked as she put her shivering hands on Hazel's.

"I will be fine. What matters now is that we spread as much information as we can. And that means informing the Vipers of this threat."

But I don't know them. Why do I have to do it again?

"But—" Windy's voice caught in her throat, her anxiety gatekeeping any sound coming from deep inside her.

"Do not worry, Windy. You may go now." Hazel gently punctuated her words with a smile.

The only thing she could do was wrap her grateful arms around Hazel before weaving through the crowd once again, returning to her loyal best friend.

She had freedom now.

Freedom to do what she wanted to do.

And the first thing she wanted to do was go home.

SKYBIRD COMMUNITY

29

Windy's face grew numb from the wind against her face. She and Nodin had been flying for several hours, racing to get home. Today would be the day she returned home, and she couldn't reach any farther. Nodin's feathers were damp from the activity, and Windy's body cleaned itself from the glistening sweat she showered herself in at the Peacekeeper Community.

Home.

Hurry! Hurry! Lives are on the line!

That was where she needed to be. In the distance, the stretching mountain range grew larger, the once-fuzzy peaks becoming sharper.

Though Nodin's flying became bumpy and uneven while he panted, Windy patted his shoulder, pushing him farther.

"Just a little more. We're almost there."

Windy knew where to go. After spending most of her life in the mountains, she felt a sense of familiarity with her surroundings. Her eyes rested on the sight of the incoming mountains, memories of her childhood flooding in.

She spent years trying to prove her worth in the Community. She spent years trying to earn the trust of her own people. But she never knew she had spent her entire life preparing for the new role the Skybirds graciously offered her.

Nearing the mountains, Windy's ears twitched nervously, her hand reaching into the leather pouch on her harness. Grabbing her map with trembling hands, Windy inspected the Skybird Region. She noted the colors marked on the map that reflected the Skybird's elegance and beauty, which the Community basked in.

Windy looked up in front of her.

This wasn't the Community she remembered.

She pushed Nodin faster just enough to quicken their arrival, a sense of urgency to ground herself.

"Down."

Nodin landed in a hurry, his feathers flying and his sides heaving like a balloon being blown in and out. Windy quickly dismounted Nodin, striding forward a few steps. Her furrowed brows seemed to lower, a hole forming in Windy's chest. She folded the map and returned it to the pouch on her chest, looking around the Community.

Her worst fears came true.

The Skybird Community appeared to be a variation of the Splinter Community, its beauty once treasured, now infected with colors of despair, the thick fog shielding the sunlight from blessing the Community. Windy's steps naturally carried her through the grounds, her home still traversable from experience. Windy's eyes registered each site of devastation: wilted trees and flowers, crunchy grass, destroyed homes, and the stench of death lingering in the fog.

Windy paused, staring out into the fog. Her mind was blank. She couldn't think about anything else when the home she desperately longed to return to was now alive with the worst thought from her mind. She looked at her hands, gray and hazy from the fog.

Was she truly the leader the Skybirds needed?

Were they better off without a government after all?

She had let them down.

Everyone she loved could be dead.

Mother...

As her mind flooded with failure, her eyes fell to the golden cuff on her right arm. The gold shade was now a stoney yellow color in the fog. Windy pictured Feral. As she looked down at herself, she could see that her clothes were discolored. Her blue, red, and yellow hues faintly tore through the fog, but out of the Splinter's curse upon the Community, she was standing amongst one of them.

Then, as a revelation flooded her mind, she fell to her knees, crying. Feral wasn't just any clone. She was the very Splinter embodiment of Windy, if she were to be raised as one of them. Orion. She realized he wanted to turn Windy into such a creature. Her answers were beneath her feet and in her very surroundings.

If I hadn't gotten in the way of that night that started it all, would this be different?

Tears fell down her face, her sobs the only sound in the bone-chilling silence. Sounds of hooves clomping behind her grew in intensity. Then, through her pain, there was a light but cold beak tapping her shoulder.

She knew it was Nodin.

She reached her hand up, acknowledging his presence. The Winged Beast bumped his forehead into her hand, silently comforting her. Continuing to cry, Nodin pushed her. He needed her to stand up. He chirped, continuing to push her.

"Fine, fine." Windy stood up, her eyes heavy.

Nodin pushed Windy again, and she looked back at him, her disheveled face ordering him to stop. But when she looked back at the view, she noticed that the same beasts that had invaded the Community years ago were lurking on the grounds, their goat-like figures eerily ethereal, as if they were lost spirits Windy could empathize with.

"Come," she whispered as she jogged off. Nodin trotted after her, following close behind like a guard. Windy and Nodin's movements echoed through the Community, gathering the surrounding beasts' attention. She ignored them, relying on her Winged Beast to support her.

They carried themselves to the Skybird village, their feet moving at a restless pace. Windy's legs strode in front of the houses, her eyes struggling to catch a sense of familiarity.

But one house undeniably attracted Windy's attention, her body snapping to the door.

Nodin stood behind her, a faint purr rumbling from the animal. Windy took no second thought before opening the door and stepping inside. The first steps taken seemed to drain her strength little by little. She looked around the home, the devastation no match for the nostalgia coursing through her veins. She stepped through the home as if the ground would cave in at any moment.

This is where she grew up, where she was sheltered during her childhood.

Windy stepped into her old room, the contents untouched but slightly shuffled. It seemed as if nobody had entered the room, but disaster left a mark of devastation. Windy fell back in time as she gazed at the room. Her childhood might not have been alive with other children, but it was precious to cling to. Her rapid maturity throughout the years left no scar on her life. It only provided the tools for the future. Windy stepped back, refusing to enter the room as if her presence would further harm the preservation of such serenity.

Windy moved toward the kitchen, looking around at its state. Her inspection came to a heartbreaking stop when her head turned in the opposite direction. Her hands shot to her mouth, her eyes shiny with threatening tears. She sprinted to the far end of the kitchen, throwing her body on the floor, sliding.

"Mom!"

Rose sat motionless against the wall, tangled in vines. Her hair had streaks of silver in it as it fell over her hanging head.

Don't be dead. I can't lose you first!

"Mom?" Windy repeated silently.

The hanging head lifted itself slowly, revealing soulless eyes. They made contact with Windy's weak gaze, familiarity welcoming the emptiness. "Windy? Is that you?"

"Yes, Mom. It's me." Windy's voice broke through an empty child.

A child that grew up too fast.

"You look different. So different. But the same as I've known you." She carefully gazed at her daughter.

Windy's ears pricked toward her voice, straining to listen to the volume.

"I know. It's been too long. But I'm home now."

Rose shook her head as if it were controlled by a string. "No. This is not home anymore."

Windy moved the twisted vines off of Rose. "What do you mean? What happened while I was gone?"

"Listen. My child. Those Splinters," she began, her voice violent with hate, "are no good. That Community is gardeners, and their seeds of destruction have grown into something terrible. Stay away from them. Stay away from them! They took our people. They took our land. They took everything from us! I still remember those words. 'We will now move on with our plan now that she's all gone. The Entropy will soon dominate this continent.'" Rose hung her head, her words drowning in agony. "I didn't want to believe they meant you. I never wanted to. But when you never returned, I had no choice but to accept the situation."

"Mom, I'm here. I'm alive." She leaned forward, comforting her mother. "What happened to the Skybirds? Are they"—she choked on her words—"dead?"

"I hope not. Oh, I hope not. I saw some of them escape. Hopefully safely. But most of them were captured by the invading

Splinters. Such terrorists. Who would cause harm to people who were never involved with their business? Once."

"But what happened to you?"

"My injuries? I tried to protect the Skybirds while you were missing. But I'm not suited to be a leader. I can't do what you do. I can't. Oh, Windy. I'm so sorry."

"Mom. No. Please don't apologize. It's my fault for running off with a Community I have no idea about." Windy clasped her hand with Rose's, helping her to her feet.

The moment Rose stood on two feet, hunched, she hugged Windy, her child returned after years of disappearance.

"Windy. You need to stop this. You can't let the Splinters get away with such a curse. This Entropy. But know. Please know. If you don't make it, always know that you are the best daughter I've ever had. I don't know who your parents are, but they would love you just as much. They would want you to live on. Enjoy every second of your life. You don't know when it's going to fall apart."

Windy's grip on Rose tightened, using all her strength to cry out her tears on her shoulder. She didn't care that she had been adopted. Someone had always wanted her from the beginning, even if they couldn't properly care for her. She never had to prove herself around people like these, whether she knew them or not. She was always good enough to have been brought into this world. She rubbed her face on Rose's shoulder, giving her troubles and any traces of sadness to Rose.

Windy squeezed Rose before releasing her, stepping back to leave her childhood home. She took all the time in the world as if looking away would cause Rose to disappear into thin air. If this were the last time she'd see her, she wanted to make it last.

But she had to live on for those impacted by such a powerful threat. Not only were the Skybirds in danger, but the entire continent of Quinta.

VIPER COMMUNITY

30

Since the establishment of the Quinta continent, the southeastern territory of the vast land promised turmoil. The heat, unlike any other Community, slowly bit at its unsolicited travelers, eating their lives away. Though such a deadly threat prevailed across the plush sand, the Vipers lived their lives as any other Community members would, with the steaming temperature their best friend.

Within the Community grounds, there was an unusual visitor within the Community walls. Not only did the visitor appear unusual amongst the Viper population, but her survival from the journey to the Community was unusual. It was a feat to navigate the Desert of Turmoil alive, and this woman took a remarkable risk.

"Excuse me, mister?" Windy bent over a Viper sitting in the sand, holding a cup of coins.

"Anything on you, beautiful girl?" The Viper reached his cup out, his voice hissing with shade.

"I am armed. That's what I have on me. I'm not here to donate. I'm here for business. My name is Windy, the Daughter of the Wind. I am the leader of the Skybird Community, and I need to make an urgent warning to your leader. What is his name and where can I find him?"

"A coin for every question, m'dear."

Windy looked around. The eyes of the Vipers seemed to be attracted to Windy, an unreadable grin on each of their faces. Windy stood up, walking away from the beggar. As she walked through the Community of brown and white, she avoided eye contact as if it would kill her.

"Would you like to buy this, dear?"

"Not interested."

"Real diamond necklace for three coins."

"No, thank you."

"You look hungry. Allow me to help."

"I ate not too long ago."

Windy shuffled through a village of tents speckled with sand blown onto the fabrics over the years. Some tents were zipped, and some were open. Only a few Vipers resided openly in the shady tents, their heads moving in Windy's direction. Windy left the residence, walking through an alley to return to the main grounds. As she walked, the blistering threat within the territory was catching up to her.

Earlier in the day, when Windy arrived at the Desert of Turmoil, she stepped onto the golden fibers of the desert with hesitant steps, her eyes fixed on the direction of the Viper Community from her map.

I must find these people. If this kills me, that would do nobody good.

The sun was at midday when she ventured across the vast desert, the temperature beating down on her like a weighted blanket. Despite the actual heat, Windy's body felt as though the weather were a little less than warm. For the safety of her Winged Beast, she left him behind, knowing from her knowledge of Winged Beasts that they can't withstand such temperatures.

What a shady place.

Windy searched the area, her eyes scanning for any sign of the Viper leader. Vipers passed by, their laughs just as dark as the shade their white robes gave upon their brown faces. She quickened her pace, her feet clamping loudly against the sandy tile on the ground.

Exiting the alley, she came across the desert town, standing beneath clustered palm trees and large shops that had brimmed roofs. The shade protected her from the heat, but that protection wouldn't last when the heat was the biggest threat to outsiders.

As she continued her search, Windy began to feel the effects of the rising sun; her body was fatigued. She searched for a place to rest, her head swinging side to side in panic. The gorge, high above the Community, stood in the distance, a worn trail in the sand indicating its location.

From how deep the trail was, Windy assumed many Vipers regularly traveled to such a canyon. But what was it for? As she followed the trail, she found it led outside the walls of the Community grounds into an empty land of sand.

Leaving the main grounds was a wooden sign painted in faded red

print. TRADE FACILITY AND LEADER'S RESERVE. Windy
stepped out of the open walls, confident she was going in the right
direction. Windy's body shook as she heaved each step in front of
her, fighting against the sun. The trail was empty, with no Vipers
traveling in and out of the large stone wall. She knew about the trade
facility from mentions by other people. If this were where Vipers
worked, then there would be little to no activity along this trail at
this time of the day.

Arriving at the rocky wall, she closed her eyes, letting her body
collapse against the hot wall. She sat near a cave opening but found
no strength to push herself to move inside. Her face was flushed red
from the bites of the sun's rays, her sweat working tirelessly to cool
her body off. But the warm sand beneath her served no help in her
condition.

Windy's body felt heavy as the sun crept higher and higher in the
sky, threatening to collapse. Windy suffered alone, no Vipers in sight
to help. Windy huffed a sigh before her body toppled over to the
side, softly landing on the soft sand. Her limp body lay on the sand,
the heat continuing to eat at her body ravenously.

But the sight of such a vulnerable leader interested the Vipers as they
emerged from the cave, having finished their shifts for the day. The
sun slid down the sky at this moment, and they found their perfect
chance to slither in to bite. Vipers gathered, crouching by the body.
They searched her for valuables, specifically coins. They cared about

nothing else.

Their voices cackled among themselves, their evil deeds only a mild amusement to the thieves. The cackling attracted other, exiting Vipers like buzzards, and soon enough, the working Vipers were poking at Windy for money, fighting each other for coins obtained by the gatherers.

In the midst of the collection, a tenor voice boomed from the cave, causing the robbers to screech. They scurried away like mice, holding the stolen money like a baby.

Vipers screamed as the invading Viper neared the body, the trail deepening from fearful fleeing. Their eyes were wide with panic as chaos erupted through the desert. When the area tree was clear of sinners, the respected Viper stood above Windy, his feet giving hair lengths of room from the body. He kneeled, picked the body up, and took the body away into the cave.

Windy's eyes opened to shade. Shade, unlike she remembered. Her vision blurred with awakening, her eyes blinking into focus. She sat up, rubbing her eyes. Her body felt weak. Weaker than it has been before.

She checked her surroundings. A nicely shaded area with a wool rug leading up to the stone platform where she lay. There were papers dusted in sand scattered throughout the tent, carelessly thrown out. Lining the tent were golden beads that eventually draped over the curtained entry.

As Windy's memory returned to her, this wasn't where she had been before. She was certain she had been outside a moment ago.

Where am I? Who took me here? Was I abducted?

"Rise and shine, sleepyhead!" a tenor voice behind her sang.

Windy looked behind her, noticing a Viper sitting cross-legged on a woven chair decorated in jewels and gold to give the impression it was some expensive throne. "Who are you? Where am I?"

"Well, you're in the Viper Community. Surely you know that if you came all the way here, Skybird," the Viper teased. "But surely you also know who I am, yes?"

Windy shook her head, focusing on the Viper's features. He had one earring in his right ear and a snake tattoo that slithered from his pectoral muscle to his cheekbone. He wore white fabrics accented with black and gold, reflecting his regal presence in a Community of sin.

"Shame. Well, allow me to introduce myself. I'm the head of the Vipers. Heatwave. Best known for my good looks, obviously." He ran his fingers through his shoulder-length hair, a cocky grin slapped on his face.

"From a leader to a leader, hello."

Heatwave's mouth curved into a sparkling smile of amusement. "The Skybird leader! So, that's you! Why, the Skybirds are quite fortunate to have such a pleasant-looking leader like you."

Windy's body frame stumbled, her ears pinning against her head as her face faded into red. She squeaked a whimper, her hands shivering against the warm stone beneath her. She looked to the side, lifting her hands to her churning stomach. "Yes," she whispered.

"I'm sure they are all very grateful."

Heatwave chuckled deep in his chest, the low vibration reverberating through the tent. "Now, now, now. Let's switch to another topic. I think the most important thing to address is you. Here. What brings you here?"

Windy adjusted her posture, turning around to face Heatwave. Sweat ran down her face as she struggled to maintain eye contact with him. She lifted her hands and explained what was happening with the Skybirds. "And we need to get all the Communities involved. Even if mine is scattered, and so far, only one has accepted their place in the cause. They cannot harm another Community for their selfish practices."

Heatwave lifted his fingers to his chin, his lips puckered. His eyes narrowed, looking down at the stone beneath Windy. "That does sound terrible. A big no-no. But my Community is in no state for such an interference. The Splinters must not be underestimated, clearly. But as I mentioned, my Community is in no state to go against a Community like them."

"But couldn't you arrange something with your Community in preparation for our invasion? This doesn't just impact my Community. It impacts the entire continent."

"It's a rough decision. I'm still not sure about my Community. If we were to go in just as we are, our Community would die, and that would get nobody anywhere. I don't think it's worth it."

"But think about it this way. You won't be fighting by yourself. You'll have two Communities to back you up. I've proven myself to be a leader like no other. I'm capable of many things the Splinters cannot wrap their heads around. They already sealed their fates when they launched the curse on our Community many, many years ago. Everybody needs to be ready to fight regardless of whether a Community backs out or joins."

"Hmm. Well, that is a good point, but I need some time to make a final decision. It's dangerous, and I need to put my Community first before anybody else."

"I thank you for your consideration, Heatwave. I appreciate it. I truly do. May I stay here for the time being until you make a decision? I have nowhere else to go that's safe. My Community is in shambles, and the Peacekeepers have already been terrorized by their curse."

"Yes. Absolutely. I have a spare tent in the chest over there." He pointed to a worn chest at the edge of the tent. "Take one and set up wherever you wish. I suggest you stay here within the trade facility, considering the state I found you in outside the cavern."

"What happened?"

"Well, you got heatstroke. Not a heatwave, but you do have me here now." He chuckled deeply, placing his hand on his gold neck adornments.

"Yes." Windy's eyelids drooped, her shoulders slumped. She turned over her shoulder, stepping down the stones to the chest directed by Heatwave. The chest was unlocked and opened with ease as Windy pushed the lid back. Large, neatly folded fabrics were stacked within the chest, each tied with a leather bag. Windy grabbed one of the tent sets, softly closing the chest and exiting the leader's reserve tent.

Inside the canyon was the Viper trade facility. Large stations were placed throughout the area, each marked with a different Community flag. The canyon was shaded by large white drapes hung along the walls, creating shelter from the overbearing sun. At dawn, the drapes cast an illusion of night, blocking the sun and keeping her world from a glorious new day.

Windy walked along the sandy rock, far along the canyon, where she could be secluded from the Vipers. She couldn't fully trust the Vipers, as her first impressions weren't the best, but they weren't welcoming her with arms full of lies, as the Splinters had done to her. The farther down she walked, the smaller the large trade facility came into view.

Once her feet reached padded sand, she placed her folded tent down. She untied the fabric, opening the bag that was tied to the tent. Inside were tent necessities like stakes that were bound by ropes needed for assembly.

Windy took out the stakes and began assembling the tent. Her hands and mind worked roughly as she figured out how to assemble the tent. Her ears twitched up and down as she worked through the assembly.

Once finished, Windy examined her work. The tent was slightly uneven and wrinkled, but it would work. Windy didn't want much for her time at the Viper Community, after all. She crawled into her tiny living space, disappearing without a trace from the Community that proved itself shadier than any space beneath a tarp.

31

As the afternoon sun was shielded from the Community below, the liveliness of the Vipers beneath the tarps was very different from that on the main grounds of the Community. Vipers shouted demands at each other, some jogging out of the facility, some scrambling to toss items into Community stashes, and some moping about with heavy eyes. Though in poverty, the Vipers who worked treated everyone as family.

As Windy walked through the trade center, she noticed that this Community had actual jobs, unlike the other three Communities. The previous Communities, as noted, lived together to survive.

But the Vipers spent their days working without care, their Community untouched from harm but overrun with a lack of decent wealth for its members and even workers. Heatwave's leader's reserve was at the far end of the trade facility, overlooking the progress made by the laborers.

Windy took a seat against the rock wall of the canyon,

comfortably watching the Vipers. As she sat with her leg propped up, she noticed a gruff Viper approach her, Cactus. While firmly holding a piece of paper, he had a visible tattoo of a lotus on the back of his hand. "Here for pickup, Skybird?"

"Oh, no, sir. I'm just watching. I'm staying here until I hear a response from Heatwave about an urgent matter."

He lowered the piece of paper. "Good. We have a bad reputation with Skybirds picking up orders instead of being patient. But if you're here with nothing to do, make yourself useful. You know what your Community needs. Find an order form and start placing your resources in the carts. We're light on Skybird orders, so it ought to be quick work."

Windy frowned, her ears limp. "Well, you see, that's because the Community is in ruin from the Splinters invading."

Cactus's eyes widened, staring at her as if she had admitted she was one of the Splinters in charge of such an act. "Oh. I'm sorry."

"I spoke to Heatwave about it the other day, but he wasn't very sure about letting the Community help us."

"Of course. If you're waiting, expect to be here for quite a while. He takes his time on decisions."

Windy nodded, grimacing.

"Well, we have all of this stuff for the Skybirds. I guess we don't need it anymore. Take what you want. Stock will clear out slower, so might as well keep the pace up even for a day."

Windy stood up, her face etched with uncertainty. "Are you sure?"

"Yes. Take whatever you want. We need to declare a shortage soon enough if the Skybirds can't provide their share of materials."

Windy shrugged. "Well, thank you so much." She walked off toward the large section marked with the Skybird flag.

The Skybird supplies included items that reminded her of home. There were supplies of bird feathers, dyes, yarn, large pieces of flint, and other items found in the mountains.

Windy searched the pile for anything that could be useful to her, but the Skybirds provided nothing she needed. Many items were cosmetics or accessories used for crafting, which Windy didn't need at the moment. She stepped away, the sight of what came from her home unbearable.

She walked up to Cactus, who was now shouting commands at the workers. "Excuse me?"

"Find anything?" he retorted.

"No. I don't really need anything from my Community. Can I help clear out the stock, though?"

He checked his worn paper, eyes squinting at the text. "We would have an easier shift if you were to work. Find a cart and fill it with orders from the list provided. And make sure everything gets done. I don't need any more unhappy people stomping into our job and telling us what to do when we know what to do."

"I'm on it!" Windy smiled, raising her hand. She walked over to the station full of empty carts, claimed a dolly with four empty crates, and read the list inside the first crate.

SKYBIRDS -

SPLINTERS - HONEY [LARGE x3] (PE), SILK [x2] (SK), ARROWS [x50] (VI)

PEACEKEEPERS - FABRIC [x3], ARROWS [x100], ROPE [x23] (SK), SCRAP METAL [x14] (VI)

VIPERS -

Windy held the list, pushing the cart to the Splinter station. Reading down the list with descriptions and quantities, Windy searched each Community stash, ensuring there was stock for each request. She paced the facility back and forth, collecting supplies as she passed.

Each time she returned to the crate, Windy placed each item into the second crate marked with a purple sash, neatly organizing them so they would all fit and would be placed together safely.

Once the crate was completed with its orders, she placed it down on a stand beside other finished crates. As she moved the cart over to the next station, the Peacekeepers, she glanced around at the Vipers. They were all busy with something, whether it was pre-assigned or if they were being shouted at. None of them seemed to be off task or getting themselves into shady work.

Windy focused on the Peacekeeper's orders. She once again paced the facility, gently placing each item into the crate, taking care to preserve its integrity for the long trip to each Community. The Vipers didn't seem to mind the foreigner helping with their work. In fact, the Vipers thanked her as she passed by, nodding in respect.

Once the Peacekeeper crate was complete, she placed the green-ribboned crate on the Peacekeeper stand, completing the first set of orders. Windy worked the next few hours at the same pace, ensuring everything got done quickly for the overworked Vipers.

Windy sat down at the edge of the canyon, overlooking the trade facility, as she caught her breath, watching each worker continue to bustle with hard work. In the distance, her ears motioned toward the sound of footsteps, her head following her ears to see who was approaching. It was a tall, burly woman named Shah. Her hair was cut short, and she walked with a frame full of pride. Even the gold adorning her body indicated she was of a higher status.

"Miss. Are you Windy?" she snapped.

"Yes. Do I need to leave? I'm sorry, I was curious about your trade facility." Windy stepped back, her body hunching over.

"No, no. Not at all. I am Heatwave's assistant. I must speak to you. More specifically, I need to give something to you."

Windy's mouth opened to a gap, her mind thinking about what she needed to give her. Did she drop something when she came to the Community?

"Heatwave and I were speaking. Check yourself. Are you missing something?"

Windy twisted her body, looking behind her. Flag and bow present. She placed her hand on her upper harness, running her hand down. Her hand slipped down to the pocket at her waist. Her eyes flickered in confusion. Then, she gasped, patting the harness over her chest. She was missing the long, wallet-like pocket in her harness. Her own wealth was gone.

"Ah, precisely. You see, when you fainted that one day, some Vipers—well, you could say vultures—took all of your money."

"They did what?"

"Yes. It's a wonder why we haven't changed our name to the Vulture Community rather than the Viper Community. Apologies, the Community targets anybody who isn't one of them, and when they're most vulnerable, they take what they have. But Heatwave allowed them to keep what they stole. We spoke endlessly about the situation at hand. Correct, you are a Community leader. Even though I am a Viper, I have morals. I know it is wrong to commit such acts such as this, especially from someone who is supposed to be helping our Community. More so from a Community with a bad reputation. So here. I'm giving you a rough estimate of what you lost, including a little extra." Shah held the same attachable wallet that Windy once kept on her harness, but it appeared fuller. "My gift to you."

You're more worried about giving me money than helping your leader speed up an important decision? "Thanks." Windy grabbed it from her with a light smile and adjusted the binding on the worn harness.

"You don't seem too happy. What's the matter?"

"I'm still waiting for Heatwave's decision on my request." Windy's eyebrows creased in the middle.

"Yes. Heatwave spoke about that once. Then never again."

"You're kidding? Please tell me you are. My Community is already either dead or its members alive in danger." Windy's ears flattened against her head.

"I understand, unlike him. If I could make a decision, I could whip these Vipers back into shape myself. But I cannot do anything without Heatwave's approval. I apologize."

"At least you can do something. Anything. Just anything to help us. I'll wait a few moments longer. If I don't hear anything from

Heatwave, I'm going back to the Peacekeepers so we can make adequate decisions ourselves. In a reasonable time." Windy wrinkled her nose.

"Understood. I trust you can ensure safety to the communities better than our own leader. I am limited on what I can do to help. Apologies, once again."

Windy's chest heaved a hot sigh, her hands lifting to cover her mouth. "Thank you, miss, for at least trying to help when you can't." Windy turned around to leave, Shah watching her go. Behind her, she could hear footsteps moving farther back across the golden terrain, their space steadily increasing.

32

The afternoon sun beat down on the Viper Community, yet the Vipers remained unaffected in the canyon. The sandy ground was marked with thin lines, indicating scaly visitors had passed through the territory in the middle of the night. All had been calm. All had been peaceful. The Vipers maintained their peace within the scorching sun and chilling moon, their lives free from outside stress.

Windy walked past the working Vipers, her body motioning toward the cavern that marked the exit of the trading facility. She avoided the leader's reserve, let alone glancing at it. Heatwave was to be avoided like the plague if he were unwilling to help.

The Vipers were in dire need of joining the rebellion against the Splinters, but the Community seemed to take the matter with a grain of sand, brushing it off their shoulders like dust.

The workers went about their jobs as if today were another day. The Community continued to rob others of their wealth as if this were the common life for the Community.

Windy entered the cave that led to the outside. At first, the path was dark. But as she ventured deeper into the cave, torches lit the path that spread out along the perimeter of the space. Windy stepped into the illuminated cavern, noticing faint markings on the stone. As the patterns came into view, she noticed they were paintings faded into time. She paced the walls, reading the paintings with careful eyes.

Drawings of people overwhelmed the walls. People with spears ran through the space, as if reliving a heroic tale told by a bard. Carvings of snakes were embedded in the dunes, painted on the stone. On the far side, where the engraved warriors were running, stood two people facing each other. Both held their hands out to each other. The two people, though different, appeared to be sharing some kind of possession. If not sharing, then giving.

Windy stepped back from the stone tapestry. She couldn't assume these were Vipers. They appeared to have none of what the valiant people possessed. They seemed prosperous, while the Vipers lived in harsh conditions.

Windy stepped out of the cave into the scorching desert. Sweat ran down her face as she ventured onto the Community grounds. Vipers were in every corner of the town, whether sitting down or walking through the establishment. She searched the area, looking for Vipers that didn't seem untrustworthy. But each Viper she made eye contact with was hunched, wearing white hooded garments with eyes barely peeking from the shadows. She sighed, continuing to walk.

"Hello, Skybird."

She ignored.

"Wanna buy some earrings? These would look great on you."

She ignored.

But as she walked, a female Viper sat beneath a palm tree holding a toddler. The little Viper was asleep in her frail mother's arms, unaware of the hopelessness in her eyes.

"Miss?" Windy asked as she walked up to the Viper.

"You. Please. Help me," she begged, sitting up to ensure Windy could hear her weak voice. "I was betrayed by my own people. My people, they took everything I have. There's nothing. Nothing for me and my son. Please help me. Anything. Just anything."

Windy's ears perked up, though her brows supported an extra depth of sadness. Betrayed by her own Community? Did the Vipers scam each other for their money? Windy reached into her wallet pocket on her harness, taking out a handful of coins. "I was given too much without asking, so here. I'll give some of it to you."

Though the Viper was desperate, her hands gently took the coins from her hand, holding them close to her son. "Thank you, miss. Thank you, thank you."

Windy kneeled in front of her. "What happened? Why would someone in your own Community do this to you?"

"Foreign Skybird. You don't know what happened to our Community. A brute force we trusted turned on us when our backs were turned, when we were least expecting. No. When we never expecting."

"Who? Do you know who did it?"

"Those Splinters. That Community that uses people like toys."

Her eyes widened, her eyebrows continuing to demonstrate her compassion. "The Splinters harmed my Community too. At least you all still have a Community to live in. They destroyed mine."

"Oh, child. Oh, child, no!"

Windy sighed. "I actually talked to Heatwave about it. Your leader. But he doesn't seem to acknowledge the severity of the situation. He's implying he's too worried about you all rather than what could happen in the future."

"But why? He knows what happened to us. Why wouldn't he want to crush our enemies? If anybody wanted them gone, it would be him!"

"I know. I'm only staying here to wait for an answer other than an 'I don't know.' But I'm going to leave soon if this doesn't get addressed. There are more important matters to take care of."

"I would do the same. But Skybird, I support you. I thank you for helping me. The Vipers need to know what is happening outside the sand. They don't know what is happening. I didn't know. But we need to know. Skybird, help us. Help us help you. Heatwave will surely see how desperate we are to return to our glory. Please, Skybird. Help us."

Windy looked around at the Vipers within the walls. "Could you help me spread the word? If Heatwave somehow comes to an agreement, the Community needs to be ready for the Splinters."

"Yes, Skybird. Yes. I will help you."

Windy smiled at the Viper and stood up, turning around. In the distance was a water well planted in the sand. Windy untied the rope, hung on one of the reams, and gently let the pail fall into the water with a calm splash.

As the pail filled with water, Windy pulled the rope to retrieve the water bucket. She held the wooden pail to her lips, drinking the water. For such a poor Community, the water tasted fine, its quality better than the Splinters' electric-tasting water.

"Need something for that?" a Viper holding a crate hissed behind her.

Windy swallowed the last bit of water she collected, hanging the rope back on the hook and turning around to acknowledge the Viper. Her eyes were hooded like the clothes he wore, and her smile was anything but inviting. "Are you trying to sell me something?"

"Indeed, so. You seem to be in need of something to carry water. Here. Let me provide you with a handy water flask. Ten coins and it's yours." The Viper reached into his crate and held a circular water flask to Windy's face.

Windy inspected the item carefully, considering it came from a Viper. "No, thank you." The water flask had tiny, subtle holes Windy would have missed if she hadn't focused as hard. "But do you really need to keep doing this?"

"Miss?"

"Do you need to keep scamming people out of their money for trash? There are Communities outside here suffering because of one dominant Community. I know you know what I'm talking about."

The Viper slowly set the water flask in the crate.

"The Splinters took my home. They destroyed it! I have nowhere else to go, but I'm not making other people's lives miserable, like what was done to me. You think that because someone who hurt you makes you do the same? Those in our lives aren't just things in a dream. They're real. They have feelings. They need help. They need help from others who have suffered. To save us all."

"You know too much." The Viper slowly took his hood off. He had a tattoo of scales on his forehead.

"Please help us. The Peacekeepers and Skybirds are fighting for their lives against the Splinters. They are plotting to take over the continent of Quinta. Your devastation will become unimaginable if you don't try to help us." Windy reached into her bag, taking out twenty coins and putting them into the Viper's hand. "I don't mean to bribe, but let me help you help us. Your Community needs the money more than I do."

The Viper looked in his hand. He stored the coins in a pocket on his waist and grabbed the crate, holding it below his hip. "To help us, I will help you."

Windy returned to her tent, lying in the cool of the desert night. She closed her eyes and let her mind drift into hope. Hope for the Community. Hope that they would open their eyes. Hope for the future. She closed her eyes, allowing her body to relax into sleep, in hope for the coming day.

33

The desert was a glittery snowfield as the moon sat high in the sky, watching down on its inhabitants. The sand of the desert was a cool navy color, unlike the fiery apricot of the sand fueled by the sunlight. The air was quiet in sleep, desert inhabitants taking shelter from the fierce chill.

The stars danced by themselves in the sky, joyous for the precious time they had in their hands. Hidden in the sand were traces of life daring to present themselves to the chilling moon. Slithering tracks, paw prints, and even footsteps trailed along the dunes.

Elise, shady as a Viper, trekked the sandy region, her legs trudging through the grit like mud while her feet kicked up sand in front of her. She kept her head low, eyes focused on the sand below her. She walked with confidence. She knew where she was headed. Her hair flowed easily down her neck, undisturbed by the stillness of the night.

A dagger sat in a sheath on her hip, swaying with the movement of her hips. Her eyes were sharp with vengeance, the slits all the more menacing as she marched her trail of death. The chill against her arm was but a minor inconvenience, nothing she wasn't used to.

The Viper Community was as silent as the desert and as dark as a pit of vipers, the sleeping predators as silent as they kill. Not a flicker of light could be seen in the vast darkness, promising the Community's only moments of peace. But in such a territory of danger, there would be a new predator, almost as if a hunter prowled into another hunter's line of sight. Elise's footsteps quickened, but she remained silent as she padded through the sandy Community.

Within the walls, the trespasser passed through the gates, completely avoiding inspection of the inhabited inner walls. Her head didn't turn to glance at anything that could be of use to her. She left the back walls of the grounds, her bright eyes focused on the towering gorge ahead.

Her hand came down to sit on the hilt of the blade that rested on her hip, her body in preparation for what was to come. She navigated the darkness of the desert like broad daylight, the moon's faint glow upon the sand useless for her navigation.

Stepping into the agape cave opening, her fingers twitched, her body itching with adrenaline with each further step she took toward the Viper trade facility.

In the trade facility, the woman stared out at the large stock of Community goods, noticing traded materials from her own Community. She passed the grand storage stands of supplies, turning right from overlooking the facility.

"She told me she's here. I shouldn't be too close," Elise whispered to herself. Her voice was tinged with scorn, the faint hiss fueling the menace in her actions. She prowled in the distance, exiting the barriers of the trade facility.

Up ahead, she could see a tent closing in, the small figure zooming in as her feet strode faster. Her fingers clutched the hilt of her blade, slowly unsheathing it. She fell to her knees and crawled to the back of the tent. Sand sprayed around her and into her heeled boots, but the discomfort went unnoticed as she closed in on her prey.

Crouching at the back of the tent, Elise sliced open the fabric as if dissecting a wolf's prey, but was silent so that any little sound would not draw attention to her actions.

Inside the tent lay Windy, fast asleep and unarmed, with her weapons placed beside her. Her natural features made her appear as if she were having a bad dream of some sort, but she slept immobile, not a twitch in a limb. Elise stared down at her, her own glowing eyes fixed on such a peaceful leader.

"Oh, what a shame he fell for you," she mouthed, avoiding making any noise.

She lifted her arm, the dagger's sharpened point threatening certain death. Her body shifted forward, preparing for the impact of the killing blow.

"Excuse me, miss?" a low voice asked behind her.

Someone's here!?

Elise's concentrated body jerked, hustling out of the tent. She quickly sheathed her dagger and stood up. Though she was breathing rapidly, she made no sound. She turned around, stood up, and stepped toward the intruder. "Who are you?" she asked, just as silent.

The hooded Viper clasped his hands, a crate slung over his shoulder with a strap. "Ah, yes. Good. May you please come with me, miss?"

"Why should I?"

"I have the opportunity of a lifetime you wouldn't want to pass up. I know who you are, and I can help you on your little mission." He chuckled.

Elise stepped closer to him. "Go on. I'm listening."

"Follow me. We must talk away from the victim." The Viper turned around, his hooded person a mere black figure in the environment. Elise followed him, staying a far enough distance away from him. Every so often, the Viper looked over his shoulder, checking if she was following him.

This guy is weird. This better be good. Oh, it better be.

Leaving the trade facility, the Viper led Elise as far away from civilization as possible, their feet venturing through plain sand once more. Once the Viper Community was as far away in the distance as possible, the vendor turned around, facing her.

"Splinter, yes? I know who you come for. We Vipers are intuitive. Our unfortunate skill your Community fated us with became a strength. You may have won, but so did we." His voice hissed with the venom of a snake.

"Tell me why you brought me out here. I have something to do, Viper. I don't have time to hear your sad stories." Now that they were away from Windy, she could raise her voice to her usual volume. Her voice was dominated by an authoritative demand, her hand waving violently.

"Ah, yes. I mustn't hold you away much longer. We have many swift-murder supplies to aid you in your assassination. Poisons, cacti, spears." He shook his back, a mounted spear swaying back and forth. "I will make a deal with you. Hundred coins and they're all yours." He grinned.

Elise cackled as she tossed her head up. "A hundred coins is insane, Viper. I know your dirty work. Don't think that scamming me for something cheap will work. I'm smarter than you think."

"Oh, no. I can assure you these are crucial. We're Vipers. We're known for our swift methods of killing, not just robbery."

"Lies."

"How unfortunate. Well, if you're simply window shopping, I must ask you to leave my Community. We have no need of such casualties."

"Don't tell me what to do, peasant. I do as I please, and I won't let people of low lives as you boss me around. I'm a Splinter! Shambor's assistant! I have more prestige than you!" She sized the Viper up, snatching the dagger from her hip.

The Viper threw the crate in the sand, cackling as he smashed the empty wooden crate with his foot like an eggshell. His former suspicion was replaced by a storm of high leadership, as he took off his hood to reveal his tattooed face and boisterous persona.

"More prestige, eh? Be careful who you talk to, Splinter. I must inform you that you have been speaking to the Viper leader all along!" Heatwave cackled once again, giving her a show of hands as he threw his head back.

Elise lunged at him, swinging her arm to slice him. Heatwave dove forward, disappearing into the sand. Elise stared mindlessly at the sand beneath her, searching for Heatwave. Through the sand, she couldn't pinpoint where he could have gone. She spoke not a word as she hunted for her prey.

Behind her, the sand divided, a jumping Heatwave pouncing at the Splinter with his spear in hand. He threw the spear at the Splinter like a harpoon. As they pierced through the darkness like an arrow, Heatwave watched with awe as the arrowhead dug into the invader's shoulder. Elise's shriek echoed in the night, an animalistic cry spilling from her chest.

She twisted her body, yanking the spear out of her shoulder, and held both weapons in her hands, stalking up to Heatwave.

"Big mistake," she warned in a low, predatory voice.

Heatwave disappeared into the sand without another word, the Splinter's feet shuffling as she pivoted in circles, tracking Heatwave.

Through the stillness, Heatwave sprouted through the sand like a tree, his legs thrusting him up to snatch the spear from the Splinter's hands when her back was turned.

"Think again!" he announced, raising the spear high above his head.

Elise turned around. Her body fell back from the shock of his presence, barely avoiding his attack. Her eyes gleamed brighter as she pointed at him, a lightning strike crashing against the sand behind him, causing him to lose coordination on his attack.

He stumbled forward, his hand occupied with the spear, crashing down. Elise slashed his chest as he fell, the cutting edge ripping through the layers of fabric Heatwave wore to impersonate the Viper vendor. She checked the blade of the weapon, noticing there was only a fine line of blood, none of what she expected. She watched Heatwave return to his feet, anticipating his next move.

"Oh no you don't!" Elise stomped her foot against the sand, the soft terrain melting into dried earth. She reached for him, throwing her body forward and stretching her arm as far as it could go.

Heatwave parried her attack with the wooden shaft of the spear. The knife stuck itself inside the spear, but Elise recovered it as the two simultaneously jerked their hands back to steal their weapons from each other.

Though Heatwave couldn't swim in the sand, he fought just as well on his feet as if he were using his swimming tactics. Elise's arm flailed around in a flurry of swipes, whipping through the air as she ruthlessly fought to see this leader dead.

She sent another lightning strike, slicing through his clothes as Heatwave shook on his feet. The fabrics were thick enough that any impact upon his flesh was padded by the clothes. Heatwave used his elbow to knock Elise off her balance, rapidly thrusting the spear at her.

She felt the arrowhead pierce her body in various places, causing her to drop her intended murder weapon. She allowed her body to crash down on the cracked ground, missing an attempt from Heatwave. She used her position to knock Heatwave off his feet, putting him at ground level with her.

Heatwave crashed down on top of Elise, giving her an opening to attack. Her hand thrust into the rough plane of his upper body, jabbing the meat of his ribcage. Heatwave groaned and thrashed his body. His cries broke free when she twisted the dagger.

While tearing the blade from his body, blood splattered on her face. Heatwave caught her eyes, enraged and venomous. He dealt the same blow against the Splinter, digging his spear deeper and deeper into her petite body, the same way she had done to him.

Elise shrieked, the sound equivalent to a roar. Her body stopped resisting, dropping her blade and throwing her hands to the spear Heatwave was controlling. She pushed against the force, fighting for her life.

"Okay!"

Heatwave paused his attack, looking into her weak, desperate eyes. The slits in her eyes dilated, staring at him. "Okay!"

"Are you done causing more problems for my Community? Will you stop? How much more could you do?" he shouted, his voice booming in the night as he hunched over to talk in her face.

"No. But give me mercy. Let me return to my Community."

"How can I let you leave if you won't keep your promise?"

"I'm not here for you or your Community. I'm here for someone else."

"I know exactly who you're here for, and I won't let you hurt her. If you want to put on a fair fight, I'll let you go. But don't come back here unless you want to be thrown to the snakes. The next time you see us, your Community will suffer the consequences of your actions. You will watch your Community fall into the sand farther down than our Community has been destroyed!"

"If you think a weak Community such as yours could go against a Community full of supernaturals, be my guest. This was boring anyway. I would want to watch your Community die under our hands myself."

Heatwave shoved the spear farther into the Splinter, unfazed by the scream from her throat. "Watch us die, or we'll watch you die. We may be broken, but we still hold the legacy we cherished years ago." He ripped the spear out of her body. "Now go. Be prepared for your downfall."

Elise collected her blade, sheathing the failed weapon. She clutched her body as she ran through the night, her figure disappearing into the dunes.

The mix of adrenaline and rage spurred the speed in her footsteps, determined to return to her Community to keep her promise. The Vipers were weak, anyway. This was just the Community leader.

Once the whole Community was gone, she could have revenge ordered to her on a golden platter, savoring the delicacy of such a feeling.

34

The sun charred the Viper Community, taking the honor of baking the region now that the moon slept peacefully. The Community lived their days innocently, knowing things only their overseer knew. But ignorance was bliss. The Community continued with their lives, but under the influence of Windy's ideas.

They no longer scammed each other out of their wealth.

They no longer treated each other like foreigners in their own Community.

They no longer lived lives that destroyed the trust of others.

Though they were still the lowest Community, they supported each other, aiding each other in food collection, water distribution, and wealth gain. Instead of a Community fighting against each other, they were now a Community growing together as a family once more.

Windy had her ripped tent patched up. When she noticed the rip and the footprints, her mind was haunted with speculations about the evidence of the intruder around her tent.

Who was looking for her?

How did they know where she was?

Feral?

Windy could feel her pulse as she took in her surroundings, but she had no reason to leave. She didn't know who had tried to disrupt her peace, and nobody, not even Heatwave, knew.

This day in the Viper Community was unusual. Windy watched the workers of the trade facility clump together, their eyes wide, brows furrowed, and arms swinging. Nobody was working. They were too preoccupied to work.

But as Windy sat watching them, her body felt cooler. Not because she was sweating, but because, though the sun was at its peak, the temperature was dropping. Her skin felt as if she were back at the Peacekeeper Community, rather than her tan skin being cooked by the overhanging sun.

Though Windy preferred such a temperature, she knew in her mind that this wasn't normal for the Community, which surely would send the Community's frame of mind amiss. She assumed correctly as she watched the Vipers converse, unable to understand what they were discussing. Concerned for the Viper's traditions and well-being, Windy steadily walked over to the Vipers, cautious yet inviting.

"Excuse me, everyone? Isn't the trade facility supposed to be open?"

"No orders." Cactus turned his head over his shoulder.

"Have you had a quiet day like this? I'm assuming not, by the way you're acting."

"Never!" a Viper in the crowd exclaimed. "Our record keeper returned empty-handed. What is happening?"

"I'm scared. When I made my rounds this week, I checked the Skybird Community again, but they were still ghosted," said a young Viper who was equipped with various accessories and weapons. If he's the one who collects orders, it's understood he needs to know survival management. "I went to the Splinter Community next, but they were gone. Missing. I didn't care to go to the Peacekeepers. Something was wrong, and I didn't want to be outside my home if I was in danger."

Windy's ears drooped, and her brow furrowed. That wasn't good.

"Something's up," said Cactus. "I don't know what it is, but it's not good. Does anybody know if Heatwave is aware of what's happening outside our territory?"

"No. I didn't tell Heatwave. "I told you first," said the record keeper.

"Where's the other one that left? Scale?"

"Scale is still out. I didn't intercept him when he was supposed to leave the other morning."

"Strange but concerning. Let Heatwave know. He needs to know about this now. Our Community might be in trouble next."

"I can go for you. I need to ask him about something anyway, so I'll address this while I'm at it." Windy raised her hand halfway up her body.

"Thank you so much, miss. You have been a great help. As for everybody else..."

Windy turned to head over to the leader's reserve, more worry etched on her face than frustration. Upon entering the leader's reserve, Windy noticed Heatwave lying on a blanket, his cheap, makeshift throne placed to the side. He sat with a thoughtful expression, his face worn as if he had been thinking for much too long of a time. His advisor was standing beside him.

"Windy. Welcome." She pointed at her.

"I need to tell Heatwave something. It's urgent."

Heatwave sat up, looking at Windy with a twinkling grin. "Ah, Windy. So wonderful to see you're alive and looking fine."

Windy pinned her ears back for a split second, appearing as if her ears twitched. "Yes. I am. So, Heatwave. I need to let you know about something important."

He sat up all the way, sitting cross-legged. "What a coincidence. I wanted to inform you of something, too. I was just waiting until later in the day. But ladies first. Please."

Heatwave was bandaged from the waist up to his chest, with some bindings on his arm. He had a healed scar peeking from the chest bindings, the snake tattoo on his body appearing to be sliced from the neck.

"I'm not sure if you're aware, but I was speaking with the working Vipers outside."

"Are they doing sketchy crap again? They better not be. Who do they look like? I'll take care of them." Heatwave raised his hand to the side of his head, his eyebrows heavy.

"No, no. Listen. Please. They noticed something unusual happening with the Communities. The Viper, who takes all the orders, told us. And apparently one is still missing."

"Oh, so our record keeper not only did his job but also served as a spy?" Heatwave grinned, amusement shining through his wounded body.

"Well, I guess you can put it that way. But Heatwave. Listen. Please. They said that not only were the Skybirds still corrupted, which would be no surprise, as I've come to terms with. But the Splinters are missing from their Community as well."

Heatwave's grin swapped to concern, his relaxed eyes tensing. "That is some news."

"Yes. He didn't check the Peacekeepers because he felt unsafe outside his Community, so now we are aware of something suspicious happening outside your grounds."

"Hm." Heatwave's tense face slowly dissolved into guilt, as if he wasn't telling Windy something crucial. "It's good he's safe in the Community. But if the Splinter Community is empty and the Skybirds are already infected, that's no good for us and the Peacekeepers. Hopefully, the second—well, I guess we can call him a spy—comes back with new information. I'm not aware of any threats posed to my Community, but the Splinters are clearly up to something. Hmm."

"Well, on that topic, I actually have something to admit to you. Now, I have been thinking about your request. And, as you can see, I've found myself in an unfortunate situation." He moved his arms away from his body to show Windy his wounded state.

Heatwave returned to the leader's reserve as silently as he left, his weakened body limping with every step he took. Though the sand was dapped with a bloody trail, it would be gone by the time the sun and wind made its way to life.

"Heatwave! Did you get attacked by a real viper?" His assistant took a hurried step toward him, her arms reaching out, ready to help.

"It's Windy. She's in real danger."

"What's the matter with her? Did anything happen?"

"It could have if it weren't for me. But none of that matters. The Splinters. They're after her."

His assistant stood, her eyes focused with undivided attention.

"She needs help. We need help. I cannot let my Community sit by any longer when the Splinters are beginning such evil once again."

Heatwave waved his hand. "But it is none of your concern how I became this way. Just know that how I became in such a way has helped me push to make up my mind."

Windy's face brightened in anticipation. She listened to Heatwave, eyes pleading with hope.

"Yes, Windy. I will allow my Community to help in some way. I'm not sure how we could do it, but I'll find a way for us." Heatwave gave her a wink, as if sealing the promise.

Windy's breath came sighing out deep within her chest. She was so tight with anticipation that she didn't realize she was holding her breath. She reached forward, shaking his hand and bowing her head. "Thank you, Heatwave. Thank you, thank you, thank you."

Heatwave chuckled, finding her gratefulness amusing. "No need to thank me. As I mentioned before, I've come across something that helped me make my decision."

"Well, whatever it was, I'm glad you're alive and well from the result. Thank you. I will be sure to keep your Community in touch."

"So, does this mean your time here at our Community is up?" Heatwave raised his hand to his chin.

"Unfortunately, yes. I need to talk with the Peacekeepers about the news. I might have abandoned them after they got invaded, but it's my responsibility to return and discuss future plans with Hazel. However, I thank you for everything, Heatwave. I greatly appreciate it."

"I'm thanking you for showing up. I had not met a Skybird leader, and I'm glad to know you're an attractive one."

Windy pinned her ears back. She didn't comment. She couldn't comment. But as the leaders made their final acknowledgements, a Viper barged into the tent, flapping a note in his hand. It appeared to be the other record keeper, Scale. His chest heaved as he caught his breath. His body was shining with sweat, which is something Windy hadn't seen a Viper do while she was around the people. "Heatwave! I've seen things!" Scale cried.

"Woah, Scale. Calm your snakes. That's a very broad statement. What exactly did you see?" Heatwave was intending to be funny, but in the midst of the tension fuming in the atmosphere, his joke didn't land with anybody in the tent.

"So many things!"

"Scale, just settle down for one moment."

"The Peacekeepers!"

Peacekeeper Community

35

Not again.

Windy and Nodin shot above the bloody yet dry Peacekeeper Community like a jet. It wasn't raining this time, but below, a flurry of green and purple clashed together like hot and cold air, forming a tornado of death. Peacekeepers on foot quickly tumbled to the bloody earth, their peace pouring out on what was thought to be a calm land.

Animals were dying in their own homes, a place where they sought to live a free life. Screams of innocent victims slaughtered to death created the soundtrack of the tearing scene. The minds of children, adults, and warriors were all maimed, the bloody scene embedded in their minds if they survived.

What was once supposed to be a Community that kept peace now had its traditions fall through its fingers like muddy water.

On the battlefield, through the epileptic flashes of Splinter magic and ear-bleeding scrapes of metal against metal, the enemy team began dropping dead as they were moments away from slaying an innocent Community.

Rescued Peacekeepers turned their heads, desperately trying to pinpoint their hero. In the sky, they pointed to the darting red color, arrows flying from its source. Amid the shouting, survivors cheered, thanking their savior. The color of a miracle grew larger, revealing itself as they dove into the coliseum's performance arena, which was more like a battle arena.

Windy's flag waved behind her as if announcing who she was. Nodin ran furiously on paws and hooves as if knowing where to go. Windy shot down Splinters from all directions, relying on Nodin to keep themselves safe. The blue color deviated from the Community, which is packed with purple, green, and red, raising the alarm that a new threat has arrived to support the Peacekeepers.

As Windy weaved through the mix of Splinters and Peacekeepers, her body alternated between sniping down Splinters and looking for their commander. If the entire Community was here, Shambor had to be here, too.

But that meant Orion would also be here.

Windy's stomach churned in a painful mix of fear and anxiety at the thought of facing Orion and announcing her resurrection to the one who was meant to kill her. As she passed by, Splinters distracted themselves with the sight of Windy, their mouths agape.

To many Splinters, Windy would be the last thing they see in the chaos. Splinters who got away with the shock of standing in Windy's presence, fled the scene, many shouting, "She's still alive!" and "We need to tell her!" as they dashed away from the Peacekeepers.

Who is "her"? Is that the commander?

"Easy, boy," Windy softly told Nodin as a select few Splinters removed themselves from the fighting and retreated into the distance.

Confused but safe, the Peacekeepers looked around, glancing at Windy as if they were asking her what their sudden behavior was about. The Peacekeepers, continuing to fight, caught the upper hand, Windy serving as an unintentional distraction.

"Where's Hazel? Is she okay?" Windy asked one of the Peacekeepers, though her tone came off as shouting rather than a normal question.

"I think she's alright. Nobody told us she's dead yet." The Peacekeeper lowered his bow, looking up at Windy.

Yet. I don't like the sound of that.

Windy sprinted out of the coliseum with Nodin, dashing through the coliseum and trotting upstairs to the first floor. They dashed through the broken gates, jumping over metal debris. Outside the coliseum, the fighting only continued, unlike at the settling coliseum. Splinters continued to kill Peacekeepers as they defended their land.

Windy ran through the crowds, her body molding itself into position to swiftly kill more Splinters with every stride she took. She followed the sandy trail into the forest, where the fighting was eerily silent. She slowed Nodin into a walk, inspecting the area closely now that they were safe.

Windy could only see bushes, bramble, trees, and everything that seemed to be in place, but Nodin walked off the path, his ears leading his footsteps. He lowered his head, sniffing at a fuzzy tail and a tan cat ear poking from the bush. Whiskers peeked from the leaves, unmoving.

"Leave that alone!" Windy tugged Nodin's mane, knowing that it was a hiding Peacekeeper. She guided Nodin back on the dirt trail, walking to the Peacekeeper's main grounds, but taking their time to catch their breath. They'd surely need it.

Most of the survivors must be here. No wonder the Splinters aren't doing anything here. The Peacekeepers are making them think it's just a forest.

The moment they exited the forest, the Skybird and her steed bounded off as if they were racing. Windy's eyes widened in horror, the sight in front of her eyes triggering a memory she couldn't forget just yet.

The Peacekeeper Community bled of Splinter essence, their grass discolored and dead, the trees wilted of their bark, and in place of the life that should have been the Peacekeepers, there were Entropy Beasts prowling with the support of Splinters, fighting off the remaining survivors of the area. In the same state, Windy found the Skybirds.

She kicked Nodin's sides with her heels, her rage fuelling the strength of the kick. Nodin chirped in surprise, his feet kicking up dirt as he scrambled to dash off, his legs running at a high speed, and his back arching up.

Windy sniped each Splinter and every Entropy Beast her eyes fell upon, leaving no room for mercy. Every Splinter could only glance at Windy until they were met with flying arrows backed by hate and rage for their crimes against such an innocent Community, one that gave her a home when she had nowhere else to go.

"YOU TOOK MY HOME FROM ME!" Windy's voice distorted as she roared, each arrow impaling beasts and Splinters as if they were one. Her eyes flashed red as her body fought a supernatural force.

Enemies fell to the wilted grass, falling on top of the victim's lives, which they selfishly took for themselves. Wounded Peacekeepers stared at Windy as she took the work from their hands, in frightened awe at her newfound power.

"Leave if you wish to see another day!" Windy demanded the remaining Peacekeepers in the camp. They stumbled into the forest behind Windy, fear pushing them toward safety.

As her allies were out of the area, Windy began chasing the threats in her line of sight, her eyes returning to the chocolate-hued hazel in the dim sunlight. Splinters had little time to react, though Windy's reaction time was quicker. Between their dark magic and Nodin's experience in battle, Windy kept herself safe, only worrying about the enemies in sight.

But behind her, a violent shake in the trees in the forest caught Windy's attention. The forest was quiet just a moment ago. Why was there commotion now?

What is happening now?

Windy forced Nodin's head around, violently turning him around to check out the unrest within the trees. In the forest, Windy's eyes darted through the trees, locating the source of the noise. Nodin slowed to a stop, chirping in front of him. He stepped back, hissing.

In front of them stood a Splinter and a blonde Peacekeeper archer fighting each other with dark magic and arrows. Windy recognized both fighters. Haste, the Splinter and Brook, the Peacekeeper. But veering in from the side were a swift deer and a woman adorned in leaves and vines supporting Brook.

At last, Windy found Hazel, who was injured but alive. Judging by their conditions, they must have been fighting for a good portion of the day, just now falling back into the forest to continue their sparring.

Though the colors red, white, and blue were in their lines of sight, their minds could only process each other as enemies, which was their main focus. Windy once again jabbed Nodin with her heels, sending him forward down the path. Windy focused the arrowhead at Haste's hands, which were forming a heap of dark magic toward the dashing Peacekeepers.

As if they popped out of a hole under their noses, Nodin dashed by the attackers, Windy's arrow gleaming as it hit Haste's palm, causing her spell to fail. She shouted, her eyes darting to the arrow that seemed to appear in her hand. She jabbed the tiny spear out of her flesh, turning to face Windy, who was barreling toward them once again. Haste dashed to a tree, climbing it as swift as a Peacekeeper.

"You! I thought you were dead! Orion told us all you were dead!"

Windy forced Nodin to stop, his paws and hooves spreading out as he slid on the sand. "Never trust what other people claim."

Haste leaped out of the tree, her hands glowing with another deadly enchantment in the making. She hit the ground, her hands slamming into the dirt beneath her. Flashes of yellow and steel blue flashed across everyone's faces, the electric poison beating against everyone's bodies. The girls gritted their teeth, groaning as their bodies felt like tiny prickles of glass were slicing their bodies.

Nodin reared up, thrashing his body around from the unusual pain. Haste spun around, dashing away down the path. Hazel, Brook, and Windy chased after her, the speed of Windy's and Hazel's animals allowing them to take the lead.

But through the chase, Windy threw her body back, a cry tearing from her throat. The jolt caused the hand grabbing Nodin's mane to tug him, telling him to stop. Brook turned around, her eyes darting to Windy and then gasping at what was behind her.

"Windy!"

"Go! I can handle this! You need to stop Haste, and this will all be over!"

Brook stared at what was behind Windy a moment longer before striding after Hazel, her small legs pumping with speed.

On Windy's shoulder blade perched an arrow. She reached behind to remove it, ignoring the blood pouring out from her body. As she reached behind, she saw her attacker.

Atop a black Winged Beast was Feral, chasing after her with another arrow loaded.

"Go! Go! Run!" Windy reached out her hand, and Nodin obeyed the gentler command. Windy copied Feral, aiming an arrow at her like she was doing. Now that they were anticipating the same thing, Feral paused any attacks, waiting for Windy's call.

As they stood chasing through the forest, Feral reached her hand up, her body planting down on the Winged Beast.

"Fly!"

Windy soon heard wingbeats behind her, her ears facing the sound. She snapped her head over her shoulder, her neck making a popping sound from the movement.

Her mouth fell agape, and her eyes widened so that the white outlining her dark brown eyes brought forth just as much panic as the Peacekeepers were in.

Behind her, chasing after her in what appeared to be a black Winged Beast with a pointed beak was the feral clone of Windy she faced years ago at the Skybird tragedy.

How feral.

Feral!

Arrows began flying from below, focused toward Feral. Feral looked down at the fleas below her. "Futile."

Windy gasped. That voice was exactly hers.

What is this thing?

As they flew, they played a game of deadly tag as they tore through the air, flying over the coliseum.

Feral's Winged Beast blasted itself after their prey, its black feathers falling to the ground with grace. If Feral was going to attack from the sky, Windy needed to know what she was doing.

"Go!" Windy copied, Nodin listening to her order.

Windy followed Feral, the sound of beating wings nothing but common ground for her. Windy reached her hand past Nodin's neck, urging him to fly faster to catch up with Feral.

Windy's free hand gripped her bow, her knuckles turning white. She wouldn't use it. She had to rely on Nodin, since Feral would only copy her every anticipated move.

As she put her trust in her loyal companion, Windy's mouth opened wide, and a deep shout was emitted from her chest while she pushed Nodin toward their threat. "Fight!" Nodin began stretching his arms, reaching for the Winged Beast. Feral turned sharply in the sky, going nowhere with her directions, but Nodin followed, his damp body working tirelessly to catch up with the alien Winged Beast. After ripping through the air, Nodin caught up to the Winged Beast, pouncing on it from the sky as if he were on land and sinking his claws into the black feathers.

The Entropy Winged Beast screeched, kicking its back hooves in Nodin's face. "Attack! Don't stop until she's dead on the ground!" shouted Feral. The two animals began their aerial combat, hisses and shrieks, claws tearing through the darkening sky.

Feral turned her body, nocking an arrow as she twisted and fired at Windy while she was at the lower end. Windy's eyes darted toward the arrow in her bow, reacting just in time to miss the attack. Windy attempted the same move, but her attack was rendered useless as Feral hit her arrow with her own.

She knows what I'm going to do. What can I do now? I have nothing else up here. What else can I do?

"Down!"

As if Feral read her mind, her Winged Beast kicked Nodin in the face, swooping down. Nodin followed her, his command still fresh in his mind. Feral turned her body around, her back resting against the diving Winged Beast. Windy also focused an arrow at Feral. If she stayed like this, she wouldn't do anything. If they could get on solid ground, she would be safe and could call for backup.

Windy fired the arrow, alerting Feral to also fire her arrow. A triumphant smile emerged on Windy's face as the arrow found its home in Feral's dark heart. But though Feral's disappearing death was a silent one, a screeching cry filled the gap. Windy felt herself tumble in the sky, losing her balance on her Winged Beast.

Windy's back faced the impending ground beneath her. She closed her eyes. Maybe if she were to start sleeping up here in the air, she wouldn't feel a thing. She won't feel or see a thing.

If she could plummet just a bit slower, she could have more time to welcome death with the same friendliness she gave everyone. Maybe she could see what the afterlife held, if there was one. Her eyes started leaking through shut eyelids, the residue chasing after her through the air. But she was too fast.

She grew up too fast.

She fell too fast.

She couldn't fall asleep fast enough, but so many lives beat her to it.

Please let it be over with.

Windy's body heaved with a thud. But the thud wasn't painful. It was uncomfortable, but it promised her life. The thud nearby didn't.

Windy took a moment to reassure her body that she was still alive, allowing her nervous system to feel the hands clasped under her back. She opened her eyes, her wet face greeted by a panting Hazel.

Brook stood beside her, pacing with a disheveled face. Windy looked around. The Community blossomed with death, the discoloration spreading throughout the entire Community rather than the main grounds.

Her eyes scanned her surroundings a hair too far, revealing to herself a sight that would scar her entire body and mind. Her body flailed out of Hazel's arms, running to the dead Winged Beast beside her. His wings were sprawled out, lifeless but still so beautiful.

Windy fell to her knees as she reached her hands out to her best friend. Before she could touch his soft pelt, her figure broke into sobs, her hands covering her face with a slap. Her back heaved with tense muscles as if she could explode all of her sadness out of her body.

Windy heard footsteps behind her.

"Windy. I'm so sorry," Brook said in a much softer tone than her usual commanding seriousness.

"Please take a moment here. Brook and I will gather the Community survivors and start cleaning up the Community. In fact, take as much time as you need." Hazel put her gentle hand on her shoulder. "I'm sorry. I can understand the pain you're feeling."

Windy didn't acknowledge the departing Peacekeepers. She kneeled above Nodin, crying as if her tears could save his life.

I can't handle this.

36

T he Peacekeeper Community was silent. On any other day, such silence would ensure peace, bringing tranquility to its members. But today, such silence indicated mourning for lost peace, hundreds, if not thousands, of bodies of people and animals now finding peace with Mother Nature. Peacekeepers stood in the stands, bowing their heads in respect for the lives taken from their Community.

The crowd shrank to a group; what had once been a full Community filling the coliseum left room for many others to watch. But there was nobody else but the Peacekeepers and Windy.

In the midst of the standing Peacekeepers, Windy sat down, clutching her stomach and letting her hair fall beside her to curtain her from her cries. Nodin lay amongst the other animals who unwillingly gave their lives to the Splinters, joining the Community's union of defeat. The Community was stripped of its beauty, replaced by the ugliness of the Splinters and their seeds of hopelessness.

"Thank you all for your respect." Hazel's voice interrupted the silence. "We are all here to express our sorrow for the innocent lives taken from us, but also to express our gratitude to our battalion, who fought with their lives to protect us. Let us see this not as a loss but as an opportunity to show our killers that we can emerge from defeat stronger than before. A tree cares not if a boulder sits on its roots. It will eventually tear through the weight, proving its strength."

Windy stood up and left the funeral. She kept her head low, avoiding eye contact with those who might watch her leave. Windy's steps through the coliseum were drowned out as Hazel continued speaking, allowing Windy to have a quiet departure.

She knew her way around the Community that had taken her in as its own child. She stepped up the flight of stairs leading up to the second floor, her legs queasy with grief. In fact, her whole body was queasy with grief.

In the leader's reserve, Windy lay on Hazel's bed, taking no care that Hazel claimed it once again after Windy left. Windy needed a place to rest her heavy body. She needed somewhere to go to avoid the heaviness of the situation she threw herself in once more.

She closed her eyes, unable to look at the dead plants in the leader's reserve, now tinted with remnants of the Splinter's attacks. In here, Windy was alone. She had no one to keep her company. She could only hear her own breath and not the calm signs of life from Nodin. She needed to know someone was alive. There were too many people dead in front of Windy's own eyes.

But now, time in Windy's life seemed to pass as if one second in someone else's eyes was a thousand years for Windy. Each day felt as if a million years or more had passed by. She lost her own Community, her allies, and now her best friend. If anything else were to happen, just let it happen now. Windy didn't care. She didn't care about her surroundings. Everyone was hurting, so why care?

The door behind Windy silently opened, footsteps entering the leader's reserve. She sat up, turning her head to see who had come in. Her weary eyes landed on Hazel and Brook, and she slumped her body back down on the bed.

"Windy, how are you holding up?" Hazel kneeled in front of her.

"You haven't said anything to us for a while. Are you okay?" Brook added.

Windy shrugged. "As good as someone who lost their best friend can be."

Hazel nodded. "I understand. Recovering from pain takes a long time, but emotional pain takes the longest."

Windy scoffed, her body twitching. "That's funny. Why do I worry about the pain? I've experienced it enough. I should be fine by now."

"You cannot rush the healing process. You will only hurt yourself more. But while you are here and listening to us, we have some things to share with you." Hazel stood up, glancing at Brook.

Brook cleared her throat, her voice returning to its serious commander tone. "So, when I was facing Haste, the commander of the Splinters during the invasion, she was rambling on about some stupid nonsense. But she kept repeating the word 'Entropy', so I'm assuming this is what we're up against. Entropy."

So, it is called that.

"She went on about the Splinter's greatness and their natural dominance for Quinta. If you ask me, it sounds like they're trying to force us into a dictatorship."

Hazel nodded. "I agree. This Community needs to be put down. We cannot have a threat such as them wandering in our land."

Windy sat up, punching the bed beneath her with all of her strength. "Why did I ever trust them? My Community would have been safe if it weren't for me! This is all my fault!"

Hazel put her hand on Windy's feathered shoulder. "Do not blame yourself. The Splinters have a history of dominance. They're only trying to fulfill what they started so many years ago."

"They took my home, my best friend, your home, and stripped families of their lives! You're saying after all this time, they got away with their selfishness?"

"The continent assumed they stopped, given how long we have been living in peace."

"So, the killing isn't over yet?" Windy asked, her eyes pleading.

"Unfortunately, not. We need to push through one more time before the Splinters increase that number."

Windy groaned, falling onto Hazel's lap.

"How can we possibly return to battle like this? We are all broken. If we were to go off anytime soon, we would become extinct," Brook asserted, her hands moving up and down.

"About that." Windy sat up. "I have some news to give you, Hazel. After Feral invaded the Peacekeeper Community after the tournament, I left for the Skybird Community."

"Pardon my interruption, but who is Feral?" Hazel lifted her hand.

"That Splinter copy of myself. Apparently, the Entropy curse also pertains to a clone of myself, but only if I were to be a Splinter instead of a Skybird.

"I left for the Skybird Community. Now, I'm here because, as I've mentioned before, they took my home. It's demolished. Barren. In fact, it looks pretty close to the state the Peacekeeper Community is in."

"That's why you're nomadic. I'm so sorry, Windy. This must be even harder for you to bear." Hazel looked down.

"Now you see. But after I left my ghost town of a Community, I traveled to the Vipers and met Heatwave to discuss our situation and, well, it was quite lengthy. If you know Heatwave, he isn't the fastest at making decisions or very responsible with his time."

Hazel nodded, closing her eyes. By the look on her face, she knew exactly the struggle Windy faced.

"But he eventually came out and told me he would place his Community into our cause. Now, the Vipers are really messed up. And so is Heatwave. I'm not sure how honest that promise is, but if Heatwave has been working since I left we might have a chance."

"How did you even know what was happening?" Brook asked.

"One of the Vipers, a part of the delivery service, saw what happened and rushed back to the Community to let us know. Then, I rushed here to give you support."

Brook nodded in understanding. "So, what's the plan? I feel like the Splinters are just making their bed more and more comfortable to lie in with everything they're inflicting upon us. Hazel? What do you think we should do?"

Hazel took a moment to think, her careful face demonstrating her thoughtfulness. "I think we inform the Vipers. If Heatwave doesn't have them prepared after such desperate callings, that's on him. But we cannot wait a moment longer. Brook, I need you to start arranging everybody in the Community. We need every hand we can get."

"Yes, ma'am."

Was Brook respectful just now?

"As for you, Windy. I already know how capable you are in battle. You need to focus on recovering your heart and mind. Without those two things working hand in hand, you'll go nowhere far."

Windy nodded. "Thank you, Hazel. But are you sure I can't help in any other way?"

"No. We need you to feel your best so you can fight your best. We cannot lose a valuable asset like you."

"I understand. Thank you again." Windy clasped her hands together.

"That's it. Move out! We need to start right away!" Hazel announced, but it was only directed to Brook as they strode out of the leader's reserve.

Now all that was left was Windy, who let herself fall onto the bed. She opened the floodgates of her mind, allowing her mind to overfill with words.

I'll have to avenge what has been lost, she thought. *If I don't, everything that I've gone through will have been for nothing. I need to trust that our new allies will prove themselves useful. The Splinters can't reign forever.*

Windy was allowed to make herself comfortable in her returning domain. She was their secret weapon, apparently. Everyone relied on Windy. That was apparent ever since she was assigned the role of a Community leader. If everyone relied on her, she needed to uphold such standards so everyone could live in the home they loved. And loved.

Everyone needed to place their share of work in the cause if they all wanted to emerge victorious. Without the Skybirds, only two Communities would charge into battle, either victorious or prove themselves to be the peasants the Splinters saw them all as. If Windy wanted to see her home flourish in freedom, she needed to move on. After everyone who's been killed, she needed to fight in their place if they couldn't any longer.

But it still hurt.

37

Windy ran through the fields of Quinta, her hair flowing elegantly behind her. The air tickled her in goodness, the freedom like a blanket upon her soul. The grass of the continent showed no signs of illness, its health untouched, as all things should be.

As Windy frolicked through Quinta, her bounding strides taking up space as she strode, she could see a familiar face up ahead.

Rose stood in the field, a smile on her face. Her arms spread out, inviting her adopted daughter for a hug. Windy's bouncing happiness quickly burst into a sprint. "Mom!" Rose didn't appear to be wounded by the Entropy curse. She appeared in the same condition Windy left her before she traveled to the Splinters.

When Windy ran into her mother's arms, she could feel the same hug Rose gave Windy when she returned to her after too much time had passed. "Windy. We're all here." Windy broke the hug, looking out to see what her mother was talking about.

Behind Rose were Skybirds and Winged Beasts walking toward the two, their steps confident and full of the same Skybird pride Windy knew her Community to have. Windy watched her people close in, stepping back in otherworldly astonishment. They were here. They were alive. She found them. She looked into the faces of every person and Winged Beast, basking in the feeling of returning to her Community. They all stared back at Windy, misfortune plastered on each of their faces.

"Mom, are they okay?"

"We have been looking for you. You found us. Now save us all."

Windy watched as they all dashed off in terror, their screams carrying the essence of pain and suffering. Windy looked around at the Skybird stampede, her heart racing. Through the storming Skybirds, Rose's face melted into the same terror the Skybirds were experiencing.

"Mom? What's happening?"

"Windy! Save us all!" Rose screamed as someone jumped from behind her, a glowing dagger shoved into Rose's chest like a sword into a pedestal. Orion murdered Rose. Windy screamed as she tried to save her mother, but she couldn't get anywhere, her body frozen as she could only see her mother's dying face.

Then, as if someone grabbed her from behind, she fell back, shrieking. But her hands clenched her throat, straining her voice. Feral looked into her eyes, the red gleam in her eyes, smiling with the same pleasure of death in her grin. Like Rose, Windy's chest experienced a dull pressure when Feral slid an arrow into her chest like a child stabbing sand with a stick.

Windy's body was slick with sweat, her cold body warming back up as her eyes desperately opened to life, fighting to see where she was. She must have fallen asleep earlier in the day after isolating herself in the leader's reserve. Windy pressed her hand against her chest, feeling not a hole, but a racing heart fighting to spring out of her ribcage.

She wiped the sweat from her face, shaking her head. She beat her head with her fist, struggling to forget the dream she had just experienced. Her nervous system wouldn't allow her to get out of bed, on edge of any impending danger around her.

As her eyes frantically searched the room, her body relaxed, understanding she wasn't in any danger.

She tossed her legs over the bed, standing up and leaving her once comfortable resting spot, leaving her weapon harness in the leader's reserve.

As if the spirits of the dead bodies rallied their home, the Community was bustling with work; most of the Community members, led by Brook, were preparing for the upcoming battle. Every day, Windy could hear her shouts from the Community as she chewed on the Peacekeepers. Even through the rough demands, the Community's peace was louder than any commanding voice, rallied by an invisible force that coursed through each of their veins.

As Windy gazed upon the training Peacekeepers, her body felt high. She knew something big was coming up; she just didn't know when. But deep down, she knew. This was it. If they won, they would save us all. But no matter how long it took to clear the Entropy curse, they would fight for years after if they needed to.

Windy bowed her head, as the Peacekeepers do in their earthly religion, and asked whatever god she was praying to for support. She needed anything and anybody to support their cause, as that would be their biggest spur.

Though the Community still reeked of the Entropy curse, everybody felt safe. Their safety is what ensured they all pushed their hardest toward freedom. They weren't threatened. They were a threat now.

As Windy strolled through the Community, her ears twitched nervously. So many people here were hurt, just like her, but they all seemed to move on with life, preparing for justice. How could they do it? Windy wrapped her heavy arms around her body, attempting to relieve herself from the dullness of jealousy creeping in her stomach.

She wanted to be okay. But she couldn't be so soon.

The longer she walked, the heavier her body became. Her eyes focused on nothing but the stone beneath her feet, focusing on only her footsteps. But wherever her feet were taking her, her eyes caught a glimpse of a light out of the darkness. A red light.

Windy's ears were glued against the side of her head as the whites of her eyes thickened their border around her brown irises. Her lips parted, revealing chattering teeth.

A divine, glowing red figure sat on its hind legs, its dark eyes focused on Windy as if it were expecting her.

Windy used all her strength to close her eyes to the darkness, her hands clawing at her head. "I'm going insane. I'm going insane."

But in front of her was a gentle chirp, followed by a cold sensation on her hand, as if someone placed a sheet of ice on her skin. When Windy looked up, the glowing red figure of Nodin stepped back, his ears erect and beak parted in happiness. His tail lifted into an arch, the feathers draping elegantly off the lengthy appendage.

"I'm going crazy. I'm going crazy!" Windy finally broke, her cries tearing through the echoing coliseum. She didn't realize it, but her face began to dampen with tears.

Windy dashed forward, running through the icy air. Her body began to heat up to its normal temperature the farther she got from the site of her vision.

But she wasn't alone behind her.

Not for long, that is.

Up ahead in the midst of her panicked sprinting, Windy could hear a raised voice. Hazel's raised voice. She sped up, wanting to catch up on the issue. Her feet slowed to a coordinated pace as she closed in on the two people.

"What? What does he mean he's not ready? What pushed him to send a Viper all the way down here to tell me that?" Hazel crushed the letter in her hand. "Is he not aware of how dire this situation is?"

The Viper swallowed a knot in his neck, putting his finger up matter-of-factly but hesitant. "No, no. He's aware. It's just that our Community has been in shambles for years and years. It takes the same amount of time to take a Community out of those shambles. He worked his hardest. Please, Miss Hazel. Understand our conditions."

As Windy watched the Viper beg for mercy, her ears twitched, thoughtful. The Viper didn't seem like they were still in poverty. He wore more kempt fabrics and looked cleaner, not like someone who couldn't take care of himself. Something was off in his statement, but Windy couldn't trust whether that was the case.

"Okay. Tell Heatwave that he's hurting himself more than he is others. We are going on without him, whether he likes it or not. Your leader needs to have a little more responsibility in his life, especially when it comes to civil disturbances like the Splinters."

Windy has never seen Hazel this upset.

"Yes, Miss Hazel. I will tell him that." The Viper ran out of the coliseum, leaving behind a troubled Hazel. Her fingers pinched the bridge of her nose, and her body heaved with a frustrated sigh.

"Hazel?" Windy stepped up. "Is everything alright?"

"No, Windy. Everything is not alright. Brook is telling me that the Peacekeepers are making good progress and should be ready to go in no time, but this Viper came along and told me that Heatwave does not even have his Community prepared. What allies we have."

Windy's heart dropped to her feet. "Oh."

"Yes. Indeed. If he is not ready, we will have to make our numbers work. Brook has it all under control, so if we were to leave in a few weeks' time, I'm sure we would be all set. But we need to catch the Community when they're least expecting it. If we wait too long, they'll think we accepted our fates, and they'll strike the Vipers next. I will check in with Brook to see if there's any status updates. But for now, Windy, please be prepared for anything. We might need to leave as we are. If that's the case, we need you to be in top condition."

Windy looked down, her mind contemplating their situation. "I can't promise you that my heart is fixed, but I'm ready to give our continent the freedom they all deserve. Whenever you give me the green flag, I'll be ready."

Hazel smiled, Windy's words taking a weight off her shoulders. "I cannot express my gratitude enough. Thank you, Windy. We are lucky you're still alive. Now, excuse me. I need to speak with Brook on some things." Hazel turned around, walking away with a sassy sway to her hips.

Windy pressed her hands to her mouth. Heatwave backed out of their offer. She couldn't believe a word the Viper said. She just couldn't. Why would he do that when he was so willing to help? They didn't have much time left, and this sealed it. The Community was recovering well from their attacks, but it was far too early to spring into battle after such devastation.

Too much.

Windy continued to roam the empty Community, her footsteps echoing through the barren floors of the inner coliseum. As Windy walked indoors, the sound of her footsteps was met by the patter of rain, creating a ruckus in the performance arena. Windy looked to the side, detouring to inspect the outside. She pinched the bridge of her nose, exhaling a painful squeak.

Not again. Please, not again.

Windy let the rain be white noise for her mind as she continued walking through the Community. She tuned in to the rain, relaxing her body and mind against the impending chaos that was about to greet them.

The commotion down in the performance arena quieted, Windy assuming that Brook had relocated the training Peacekeepers inside the coliseum. Brook would have made anything work. If she could make anything work, she could whip the Peacekeepers into fighting shape. Windy was sure of it. They all needed Brook to carry out her job one last time for everyone's sake.

Just as they needed Windy.

38

The Community fluctuated again. The sky was now dark with rain as it poured down on the Community once more. The water muddied the performance arena, making the terrain unusable for the training fighters. The weather has been nasty for days, which is surprising to many that it hasn't flooded yet.

Windy, Hazel, and Brook stood outside the coliseum's gateless opening, looking out at the rain.

"Well, this sucks." Brook spat out a raindrop that had fallen into her mouth. "This rain tastes disgusting! What is this? Acid rain?"

"Acid rain doesn't exist, Brook. We are too clean for such a myth to ever happen." Hazel's eyes focused on the darkened skies. "But you are right. It is unfortunate that our Community is suffering once more."

"This rain doesn't look natural. It never has in the first place." Windy stepped forward, cupping her hands to collect the water. She turned around, holding her hands toward them. "Look at this color.

It's kind of gray."

"Oh. Well, this more than sucks. This is not good." Brook's agitated eyes shot to Windy's hands.

Hazel exhaled, her breath shaky as she glared at Brook, her eyebrows looking like Windy's. "How are the Peacekeepers doing?"

"Well, ever since the rain started up again that day, we had to train inside the coliseum. But that only got so far when we ultimately needed more space. We obviously couldn't do it outside because we would trip on the mud and stab ourselves to death."

Hazel looked down. "Gather everyone this instant."

"What? But why?"

"Don't tell me you mean what I think you mean," Windy gasped.

"Gather everyone here this instant," Hazel repeated. "It is time."

It is time. There's no way! Windy stood staring down at Hazel, unable to ask if she meant what she declared. She shouldn't ask, though. The sudden, murky rain was too familiar, but with so little time to stock up, the idea of jumping into battle worried Windy. They were barely prepared after such an ambush by the Splinters, and their numbers were critically low.

How could they possibly get farther than here?

When the front entrance of the coliseum swarmed with survivors, Hazel, Windy, and Brook stood facing the Community, jittering in anxiety, anticipation, and hope. Goldilock sensed the excitement and fear among everyone, bleating at other deer, horses, bears, and cats whom Peacekeepers were mounted on.

"Peacekeepers," Hazel raised her hand, "today, we ask Mother Nature to embrace us with all the protection she can give us. May she send a hurricane just like this to drown our enemies. May she send in lightning to strike them down. Whatever she may send, let it be with destructive hands as we throw ourselves into the final game of life. If we win, we live. If we don't, we meet Mother earlier than we all wish."

The Community listened in silence, not cheering at her rally.

"On this gloomy yet hopeful morning, let us march to our enemies not with fear, but with anger in our hearts for those we lost, whether they be from our Community or others. Let us show those who plot to dictate our precious land of Quinta that we shall not bow down to a ruler such as Shambor, who is responsible for the terror inflicted upon our peaceful Communities.

"Let us show them our continent shall not be renamed the continent of Entropy, but remain to stand full of pride as the continent we call Quinta. Peacekeepers! Today, we march down the path of righteousness and cut down those who get in our way!" Hazel unsheathed her scimitar. "For all the inhabitants of Quinta, awake and asleep!"

The flurry of greens and browns raced through the forest and out of the destroyed camo of the Peacekeepers, their footsteps splashing through the mud. They would run. Run toward dangerous land. Run toward familiar land.

Their footsteps drove them to outrun devastation, with the hope of returning in peace. Quinta's fields raged with stampeding Peacekeepers, the sounds of footsteps stampeding through the earth.

As Windy ran through the crowd, her stomach boiled painfully, her nerves unlike any other. Sure, she had had her fair share of battles, but none like this. This one had two outcomes that had consequences everyone was aware of. But pictures of Windy's home and mother flooded her mind. That's who she was fighting for. To return home. She had been gone far too long.

The sun, though clouded by the dark sky, sat above their heads, desperately seeking to watch the fighters rescue it. The Peacekeeper army stood outside the Splinter Forest, peering into the darkness ahead. Hazel lifted her hand.

"Everyone who is feline cavalry, go ahead. Your animals have the best sight in the dark. We will follow you from behind. But do not enter the Community until you hear Goldilock."

When Hazel pointed her hand toward the forest, the Peacekeepers atop various feline animals ran ahead, their paws silently running through the brush. The Peacekeeper army followed.

There is no turning back. That was apparent to everyone as they ran through the forest. Peacekeepers on foot blended in with the forest, should a wandering Splinter find them. The Splinter Community appeared as any other Community, just as Windy first saw them. They were minding their own business, going about their day like normal Community members. But little did they know, an entire Community was preying on their downfalls, bodies impatient with adrenaline.

Then, out of the silence, a deer bleated, its cry echoing through the forest. And all of a sudden, Peacekeepers jumped out of the darkness, raiding the Community. Shrieks from Splinters, caught off guard, filled the Community, the pain dripping onto yet another Community. The Peacekeepers could see their surroundings once the Splinters began casting dark magic, the gleams acting as lights for them. Right from the start, the Peacekeepers gained the upper hand in the raid.

Popping out of the leader's reserve like moles, Shambor, Orion, Elise, and Haste emerged onto the battle scene, a different emotion on each person. Rage, devastation, distraught, and regret. "Do not let any of them leave alive! Cut every last one of them down deep into this ground! Especially that FOOL!" Shambor ordered his three advisors to spring into battle.

Now that the three more powerful Splinters had joined the fray, the Peacekeepers were put into a chokehold of risk.

"Protect Windy! They're after her!" Hazel called out, and not a moment later, Peacekeepers circled and defended the Skybird leader.

Through openings from the guards, Windy shot down Splinters at a distance, her archery proving herself to be a dangerous threat to the Community. As Windy took the role of sniper, a thought sprouted in her mind that couldn't go ignored. "Everyone! Keep an eye out for the Vipers. Those lazy snakes ought to have caught the message!"

The outnumbered Community continued cutting through the Splinters, hisses, bleats, neighs, and roars crackling through the air, aside from the whipping of dark magic. The Peacekeepers returned stronger than before, their element of surprise the most important factor in the battle.

As Windy fired each lethal arrow from her bow, she caught a glimpse of Orion out of the corner of her eye, her body instinctively turning around to swipe him. But as Windy and Orion briefly sparred against each other, Shambor's voice crackled through the battlefield.

"Orion! Leave her alone. Wait until she's in no state to fight!"

Without a word, Orion left the battlefield with Shambor, disappearing into the darkness. Once the Peacekeepers were free of the leader and advisor, they began catching up; their number of casualties was significantly lower than the Splinter's numbers. But in the midst of the sounds of death, gasps were made from both sides, a pause in combat rippling throughout the camp.

"Hey there, ladies! I was told you needed some help, so your knight clothed in fabric is here to help!" Heatwave's cocky voice broke the moment of silence; the Splinters fired up now that reinforcements had arrived for the Peacekeepers.

"Heatwave! Oh, you son of a boar!" Hazel angrily scolded Heatwave as she fought against a rabid Elise.

"Ah, what can I say? Stun your enemies long enough to cut them down!" Heatwave proclaimed as he snapped a stunned Splinter's neck like a twig.

"Hurry up and join us! We need all the help we can get!" Windy begged as she fought with the Peacekeeper guards.

Heatwave began ordering the Vipers into battle, the allied forces growing stronger with each drop of blood spilled on the forest floor. Even though both Communities suffered casualties, it wasn't enough to match the Splinter's losses. With their growing numbers, they could split up and cover more ground. Windy, leading no Community, ran off on her own, taking full responsibility for the risk she threw herself into.

But the Skybirds. Where are they? Are they gone for good?

As Windy dashed through the forest, a force tackled her from the side, leaving no room to see who her attacker was. On the ground, the same force pushed her down, a cold rod threatening to suffocate her throat. Only she knew that rod.

Feral.

Windy had to react fast. If she hesitated, Feral would know what she was going to do and avoid it. Her eyes darted to her quiver, where an arrow was teetering off the edge from the jump. She snatched the arrow, jabbing it into her back.

Feral screeched, removing herself from Windy as she flailed with the attack. Windy stood up, grabbing her flag to beat Feral as a method to stun her long enough to attack.

As Feral was regaining her composure, she couldn't fight back against Windy for long until an arrow shot past her, hitting Feral in her gut. She clutched her stomach, her feet stepping back. Now that Feral was occupied, Windy could check out who saved her.

But the people who saved her even saved her hope, which could extend to her life.

Skybirds stormed through the forest, some stopping to deal with Feral while the others raced ahead onto the battlefield. This wasn't a dream. Windy nearly being choked to death wasn't a dream. These were the real Skybirds, and they were alive.

But then, a Skybird gracefully mounted on a Winged Beast leaped in front of Windy, her eyes swelled with euphoria. "Windy!"

Windy inspected the duo, her mind rummaging through memories to remember who this Skybird could be.

And she knew her from so far back.

"Oakley, how are you alive?" Windy gasped, her voice stumbling over the waves of astonishment overwhelming her. Her friend from years and years ago now looked like the very warriors Windy admired as a child. She even carried herself with confidence as she handled Ruby, her love and knowledge of the native beasts paying off.

"Well, you see, Skybirds were always nomadic people. It was nothing more than a flight for our lives." Oakley shook her hand, undermining the terror the Community suffered.

"How could you be so calm?"

"Because I know now that our Community is reformed, we can save our brothers and sisters who have been torn from their families. Especially avenge those lost."

Windy's eyes fell to Ruby, memories of Nodin flashing across her overloaded mind. "Thank you. I never knew Skybirds were that flexible."

"Ah, it proved helpful in the end. Now come on. We need to stop this."

As much as Windy wanted to find Rose, she had to mix with her Community, at home with familiar faces once again, even if they weren't physically at home.

Pouring into the Community, the Quintan defenders were now fully stocked with their allies, the battle appearing to be a blowout. But blowouts weren't a thing in Splinter culture. They would fight until Shambor ordered them to retreat, or until they were all extinct in the hands of war.

As Windy raced across camp, Windy found Brook and

Heatwave's advisors both progressing on Elise, their figures worn from battle but not nearly fatigued with defeat. Windy jumped in, knocking Elise on her skull. The impact sent her head twisting to the side, her eyes struggling to find who could have done such an act on her. She jerked her throbbing head toward Windy, the sight of her alive and well encouraging her attacks.

"You! If it weren't for that nuisance Viper, you would have been dead!"

"So, you were the one who tried to kill me? Well, your luck will run out someday. Whether that be today or another day!" Windy declared as she stepped with Brook and the Viper.

"I won't leave this forest until I have your body drained of its blood in my arms!"

The intimidation hit Windy's nervous system, which suddenly told her that she was in danger, and she needed to flee. Her heart drummed against her chest, the impact sending a feeling of vertigo through her body. But through her vertigo, Brook and the Viper stepped in to continue fighting Elise, their efforts already tiring her out.

With the addition of Windy, Elise overwhelmed herself against the brute fighters. Her stress fueled her dark magic spell, her hands glowing as if she had plucked the sun from the dark sky.

"Step back!" shouted Windy as Elise's spell was charged, but she warned her allies too late, and they were all thrown back, their bodies feeling as if searing pricks of glass cut inside their body.

"We will meet again," Elise threatened as she turned around, retreating. As she ran into the void, Brook ran ahead, attempting to shoot her down, but to no avail. She threw her bow down, spitting her anger on the ground.

"You two. Keep fighting or fall back. Both are perfectly fine options, but the latter is recommended. We're already pushing the Splinters back so far," Windy quickly suggested to the two.

"No. We must not stop until the Communities are safe," Shah announced.

"I agree! Let's go, Shah!" Brook nudged Shah, and the two girls of completely different sizes left for another area of the battlefield.

So, now that Elise is off her list of priorities, Windy dashed through the forest to find Haste, the second of the siblings. As Windy ran through blades, clashing with dark magic from the groups of scattered fighters. Windy skimmed over each group of fighters, hoping Haste could be amongst one of them. Windy found herself traveling deeper into the forest, where signs of life were becoming less frequent.

Windy turned around, checking another area of the forest. Now that she was returning to the battlefield, groups of fighters returned into view. As Windy ran past the new groups, she continued to search for Haste, her nervous but determined eyes darting past each fighter.

Amongst a group of Skybirds stood one Skybird facing off against one Splinter, which seemed unusual, given the groups of fighters Windy had come across were clusters from each defending party.

Investigating closer, Windy noticed that one Splinter was Haste, and the lead Skybird was Rose. The guarding Skybirds, though armed and ready to defend her, were cheering as if they were experiencing a wrestling match. Rose's appearance was unchanged from when Windy last saw her, but now her eyes were full of dedicated life, her outward appearance unlike her inward ambitions.

Windy quickly closed in on the group, watching Rose and Haste battle each other with flying arrows and blinding spells. The sight of her mother alive and fighting in such a condition caused a deep wave of pride to flow throughout her entire body.

"Mom!" Windy called out, preparing herself to aid her mother against the Splinter.

Rose gasped, turning her head quickly to check if the voice behind her was her daughter. Windy stood beside Rose, glaring at Haste. "Step away from my mom!"

Upon hearing Windy's authoritative tone, Haste's eyes widened, stepping back as her body cowered. But through her fear, she stood up straight, sizing up the Skybird leader. "I have no choice but to stop you right here. For the sake of my Community, I must not let you breathe on this land!" Haste tried to sound intimidating, but it came off like a child playing pretend with their friends, and it made the group of Skybird fighters cringe, including Windy and Rose.

"Why is she talking like that?" Rose asked in a low voice, glancing at Windy.

"I don't know, but if she thinks she's hot stuff, then we need her to prove it. If she can't live up to what she thinks she is, then she will suffer the consequences of her actions."

Haste gasped, shaking her hands, stepping back. "No! No, no, no, no! I'm sorry! I'll go. I was forced to do this, and I'm loyal to my Community. If I didn't comply with Shambor, I would have died!

Please, just spare me!"

Windy lowered her flag, her once threatening demeanor now relaxed into guilt and sympathy. Rose noticed her sudden shift in attitude, astonished by her child's constant naivety.

"Windy! Have you not learned a thing? Do not trust this Splinter! She is tricking you like before!"

Windy pointed at Haste, her commanding tone returning. "Chase her out. If she dares attack any one of you, strike her down without hesitation! Mother, if she proves herself trustworthy, capture her with the Skybirds."

Upon Windy's demands, the group chased after Haste, who was fleeing for her life in a cowardly manner.

SPLINTER COMMUNITY

39

Windy navigated through the forest, leaving the Community fighters behind on the main grounds. She did not know the status of their efforts, but she couldn't think about that now.

Whatever was happening, she got no word of anybody retreating just yet. All she needed to worry about was facing her fears. She searched the forest, hunting down her victims. This feeling felt all too familiar to her, but Windy couldn't understand why. Her eyes scanned every spot in the darkness, her eyes adjusting in some instinctual manner that was unreal to Windy. It was as if the deeper she ventured into the forest, the stronger this primal instinct overwhelmed her.

She was a hunter, and her prey was the one who hunted down her heart.

Windy's feet slowed to a stop as her predatory gaze rested upon a figure in the distance, standing tall and not threatening. Her eyes focused in, and the unknown figure in the distance smiled, her red eyes supporting the cheeky smile plastered across her face.

Then, before Windy could react, Feral dashed off into the darkness, initiating a chase. Windy pounced after her, grunting animalistically. She reached for her mounted weapons on her back, pulling her bow over her head, grabbing an arrow, and swiftly demanded a flurry of arrows in Feral's direction.

Feral weaved in and out of the attacks, knowing she would do that. Finding the archery useless, Windy placed her bow across her body once more, now snatching her flag from her back, prepared for the anticipated fight that Windy sensed would soon be ahead.

But as Feral suddenly dove into the ground, Windy's feet slid against the bramble beneath her, clutching her flagpole as a method of comfort. The vision that lay before her eyes triggered every bad memory Windy could think of, ones she could never forget. In front of her stood Orion, grinning just as menacingly as Feral.

Feral then appeared from the ground, jumping in front of Orion. She turned to face Windy, her smug eyes overpowering her furrowed eyebrows. Orion wrapped his arms around Feral, their heads turning to meet each other's eyes, a gaze Windy once hoped to receive.

"Ah, my beautiful bird. My Skybird." Orion teased at the dark plumes in her hair, causing Feral to lean in closer to the Splinter. "How could I not love such a powerful woman like you? You're perfect like this." Orion turned his head to look at Windy. "Absolutely perfect."

Windy's nose wrinkled, her lips curling up in heartbroken rage. "Get out of my head!" she cried out, her voice nothing more than a roar.

"Ah, but how could I not?" Orion nuzzled Feral's forehead, speaking against her artificial skin. "I'm always right here."

"Enough with this! You can't trick me. I won't fall for a fake boy like you!" Windy threw her arm to the side.

"Oh, but don't you remember this spot? Right here?" Orion hugged Feral, raising the poisonous dagger he clung to in his hand, the knife making contact with Feral's back with a loud swoosh, Feral shrieking at the pain, disappearing.

Windy's body twitched with revenge and hate, her body itching to release its fury upon Orion. "You player! You're fake! You're dead to me!" She stepped toward him as if her prey had been backed into a corner and she was in total starvation. "I'm going to kill you. I'm going to kill you in the worst way possible. If your patience is this thin, come at me. Let me show you what a broken heart is capable of doing." Her voice was breathy, dripping with insanity. Orion was drying up what little sanity Windy had left with him.

Orion lunged at her, but Windy jumped beside him, sprinting to a tree. She climbed it, just as she had improved with her time at the Peacekeepers. While Orion followed after her, Windy was far swifter than before, leaping from tree to tree to flee from Orion. But before Orion could catch up to her, Windy ascended farther up a tree, hiding herself away from Orion.

In the treetops, Orion searched each tree, losing track of Windy. As his head shifted focus from one tree to the next, a whooshing noise flew behind Orion, and the next place he found himself was on the ground with an arrow pierced through the back of his neck, stunning his motor capabilities.

Windy sprang from the treetops, jumping from branch to branch until she could spring onto the ground. Kneeling beside his paralyzed body, her eyes flashed red as she snatched his dagger of poison, gripping it with both hands.

"YOU SPLINTER!"

She lifted the knife high above her head, sending it through his body with a bone-chilling crunch all the way through.

She dropped the murder weapon beside his dead body, peering into his lifeless eyes, her body panting as every negative thing that could exist in the words excreted from her system as breaths. But as everything flooded from her system, Windy's eyes calmed, realizing what she had done.

She gasped, her hands flying to her face, a wave of fear taking over her conscious mind. She sobbed, beginning to realize the irreversible mistake she had just committed.

I don't want to kill him, she thought. *But I am so angry with what I did. Whoever is listening to me, whoever could hear my thoughts. Whatever the Peacekeepers talk to. I'm sorry. I'm so sorry. I could have forgiven him and moved on, but he's dead. I can't apologize anymore. He might have been the enemy, but he had siblings who loved him. A life gone. A life I loved.*

Windy hugged herself, letting her tears fall just short of Orion's body. "I'm so sorry." Windy's grieving body lay on the ground, unwilling to move anytime soon. She wasn't done grieving. She couldn't be done. She was the real monster. She was serving no help to the cause.

"What a monster I am. I've been killing all these people when I should be figuring out this disease!"

But the longer she sat there, the longer Shambor was still on the run, the more the dominating plan for the Communities found room to brew into reality. His siblings. Shambor's minions could pull off Shambor's orders in an instant. A deadly instant.

Windy stood up, looking down at Orion's body. She closed her eyes, bowing her head before sprinting away from the deep forest. Her feet guided her toward the main Community with ease, knowing her way around the camp after growing so familiar with it.

Her dashes slowed into a walk as she looked around the camp, confused. Where were the Splinters? Has the battle finally been won? Windy walked over to Hazel, Brook, Shah, and Heatwave.

"Windy! You're back!" Hazel's face beamed, the anxiety that was once on her face fading away.

"Yeah. I had to take care of something," Windy said in a monotone voice.

"Well, glad you're alive and still pretty as always." Heatwave winked.

Windy didn't react.

But while the leaders and their assistants circled, a booming voice broke the silence, drawing the idle fighters nearby to look around and try to find its source.

"Splinters! Retreat, this fight is over! Consider this loss your worth in life!"

Like stray cats, Splinters dashed from all sides of the forest, running to one specific spot in the forest. Windy turned around, looking at everyone.

"Everyone! Don't chase them. Leave the forest. I will be right behind you."

"Are you sure it's safe?" Shah asked, her voice cautious.

"No. But I promise each and every one of you will get to know what freedom is once I return." Windy merged with the lines of retreating Splinters, blending in with their unbothered nature toward Windy.

The Splinters were running deep in the forest, each of them settling at one stopping point. But as Windy stood in the middle of the crowd, her tall form scanning for Shambor, the Splinters suddenly moved themselves away from Windy, creating a ring around her.

Before Windy could process their actions, Shambor seemed to fall from the sky, landing in front of Windy.

"Hello, Windy. We meet again. For the last time, that is."

Windy prepared her bow, an arrow neatly placed on the string. Her fingers found that she was running dangerously low on arrows, putting that information to the back of her mind. "For who, though?"

Shambor laughed. "Well, it won't have to be any of us if you could bow down in front of me, submitting yourself to my rule. The world would be a better place with the Splinters leading us all."

"The Communities are established with separate leaders for a reason. If we wanted it to be otherwise, we would have made the decision long ago."

"You know nothing, little Skybird. Times have changed; we are much different from when you were born. We can strip

Communities of their status if we wish, so if you don't comply, we will happily do the same."

"Not without putting up a fight." Windy aimed the arrow at Shambor, initiating the final battle between the two leaders.

"So be it!" Shambor unsheathed a sword from behind, which had been covered up by his cape. The sword gleamed green, similar to Orion's dagger.

Windy jerked her arm down, spontaneously firing the arrow at his leg while he wasn't expecting it. Shambor stifled his groan, using his sword to cut the wooden shaft off, leaving the arrowhead stuck in his leg like a bullet wound. Windy quickly replaced her bow with her flag, knowing they had to fight with similar weapons.

The Splinters forming the ring watched silently, their eyes darting between Windy and Shambor with equal despair.

The scratching sound of metal against metal claimed the silence as they sparred, arms holding weapons flailing as one tried to maim the other. Windy and Shambor fought like lions, their eyes focused on each other's and nothing else. After everything that had happened to Windy and the many people who had helped her over the years, she was truly ready to take on Shambor.

The skull on Windy's flag served as a wrecking ball, the hardened figure beating against Shambor, throwing his attacks off. Windy spun the flag around, using the sharp-edged skull to her advantage.

Agitated, Shambor swung his sword to slice the vine, but Windy's flagmanship skills gave her quick reflexes, using the weight of the skull to wrap around the sword, slamming her flag down to grab the hilt quicker. Windy jerked her arms back, reeling in the sword as if she were fishing. The blade of the sword dug into the ground with a soft thud, and Windy turned around to collect it.

While her back was turned, a brute force hit her from behind, causing her to fly back and roll against the ground. The attack made her ache, but she got up, picked up her dropped flag, and ran back toward Shambor. The two leaders raced each other for the sword that had been shifted farther back from the impact of the spell.

As they approached it, Windy's body adjusted itself, molding into formation to slide against the ground, picking up the sword and dealing a blow across his upper body.

"Fool!" Shambor shouted, turning toward Windy as she straightened her body from the slide. She ran after Shambor, leaping up and using her wrist to elegantly spin her flag, beating Shambor and slicing his back, mirroring her previous attack.

Enraged, Shambor raised his arm, looking down at Windy. "I will not let some fake Skybird tell me, a lifelong leader, what to do!" Shambor's hand summoned a dark spirit, the shape fading into existence. The figure's broad shoulders and burly arms shook the ground beneath it, its back hooves stomping. Its horned skull lowered, but it swung its head up and roared.

As the spirit looked down at Windy, she could tell the beast's skull looked all too familiar, and she knew what it was. She used the sword to slice the mysterious mask from her flag, examining the bundle of cold darkness in her hands. The only difference between the skull in her hands and the beast in front of her was that the beast's horns splayed out to the side and subtly curved inward.

The most chilling feature of the spirit was its luminous yellow markings—the same as Orion's. Even his hairstyle was the same. Windy gasped when she realized the game Shambor was playing.

This is Orion's Creature of Darkness.

Windy lifted the skull to her face, looking at the world through depression and sorrow. But as she peered through the skull's eyes, her body cramped, and she fell to the forest floor, the skull glued to her face. Her body shifted, bones cracking into place and muscles cramping as they grew. Once the transformation was complete, she arched her back, whimpering from the pain of her stab wound.

Orion growled in pleasure, his target now at the same level as he was. Shambor, however, stared at her transformation, dumbfounded. He snapped out of his daze, pointing at the Creature of Darkness. "Kill her once and for all! You failed once, but I am giving you a second chance!"

Orion galloped toward the Creature of Darkness, his head low. The Creature of Darkness also ducked her head, their heads clashing with what sounded to be a painful thud. But to them, their skulls were so thick that they served as a fighting weapon.

The beasts head-butted each other, swiping their horns across their shoulders. Their beaks clashed with one another, their fangs of shade meeting each other's flesh as they wounded one another. The Creature of Darkness reared up, roaring as she exposed her claws to scratch down on Orion. But Orion whipped around, kicking her in her chest.

She stumbled back, roaring in pain. She began bucking, her long legs reaching his body as he turned around, each kick hitting his body, cracking something inside little by little.

As the flurries of kicking, head-butting, biting, and scratching continued against the two bull spirits, the Creature of Darkness dominated Orion, dealing the most damage to his body.

Appalled, Orion threw his hand up, walking through a roaring Orion as he disappeared. Useless. Orion stormed toward the Creature of Darkness, his threat growing larger with each step he took.

The Creature of Darkness sat back, forcing the skull off her face. As the skull popped off, she gave it space above her vantablack face, her body shrinking back into Windy. Back in her original persona, Windy slipped her flag through the eyehole, mounting her flag back on her back.

Shambor stood face to face with Windy, his eyes promising death. "You," he hissed. "Worthless. If you wish to leave alive, I shall let you go. The only deal is you bowing in front of me."

Windy stared at him, refusing to comment or obey.

"Bow down. Or else your Community will be without any rules once again."

Windy continued to stay silent.

"Bow down! Or else the Communities you united will fall thanks to you!"

"I will never bow down to a dictator such as yourself," Windy snapped.

Shambor lunged forward, his sword wounding her leg. Windy bent over, grabbing her leg. Pain poured from her throat, deep from her chest. "Bow down to me!"

Windy straightened her posture, standing tall. "Shambor. This is useless. Your Community lost families and friends, their loved ones gone from this world. Is this truly the leader you want to be for your people?"

Shambor ignored her remarks, finding them threatening to his existence.

"Yes," Shambor growled before crashing to the ground, his hands causing a tremor within the area. A geyser consisting of dark magic threw their bodies into the air, Windy receiving the most impact. Shambor seemed to stand on the geyser, his sword lifting high above his body.

"DIE!" he screamed as he impaled her chest with his sword, slicing deep into her body.

Windy had no time to scream, the geyser disappearing from beneath her. Her dying body fell from high in the sky.

On the ground, a glowing red figure poked its head from the trees, looking around. It chirped, looking around at its surroundings. It's head shot to the sky, its body following soon after. The angelic figure was a Winged Beast, with a faint blue hue emanating from the glowing red.

Nodin.

As his strong wings pumped through the sky, his spirit flew through Windy's falling body like wind, her hair following the direction of his flying. The deep wound in her chest cleared up, leaving only a faint discoloration from its scar.

Always know that you are the best daughter I've ever had...
I hunger for a day when we can all live together in peace...
I'm not sure how we could do it, but I'll find a way for us...

She is the Daughter of the Wind...

Windy's weak eyelids regained strength, her eyes registering that she was falling through the sky just before she could slip into an eternal slumber for good. Her back hit something soft but hard at the same time. She looked underneath her, in such shock she couldn't exclaim.

Nodin caught her as she fell, gliding through the air.

Windy adjusted herself on his back, grabbing his spiritual mane, guiding him toward Shambor. "Fight!" Nodin darted toward Shambor, his ears pinning back as he snapped at the Splinter.

Shambor swiped his body to the side, barely dodging the Winged Beast's attack. He began sending flurries of dark magic their way, the poisonous spells bulleting toward them.

Nodin weaved between the spells, his reaction time on point. "Attack! Go!" Nodin barreled toward Shambor, Windy setting up her bow, aiming at Shambor. As Nodin flew past Shambor, Windy sniped Shambor in his collarbone, the force sending him back.

All traces of dark magic faded out of existence.

"Down! Down! Go! Hurry!" Windy patted Nodin's shoulder, the wind slapping her face, but it felt good. As Nodin chased the falling Shambor, she lined up the arrowhead to Shambor's vitals, closing her eyes once she found her sweet spot.

And then she loosed the arrow.

SKYBIRD COMMUNITY

40

Ow beautiful the mountains were. If there were a ranking for the prettiest Community, the Skybirds would come out at number one. At least, according to Windy's biased opinion. Meteors of red shot through the cerulean sky, Winged Beasts frolicking to be back home.

Windy stepped through the Skybird village, her steps filled with more pride than ever. Her flag waved in the wind, exposing the emblem that the Skybirds felt proud to call their own. It was as if wherever Windy walked, a breeze kissed her face, her purple-tipped hair flowing gracefully to the side.

Windy knocked on the door that enclosed her childhood, but was the same door that opened opportunity for herself and the Quinta continent. She opened the door with ease, unlocked for anybody to visit.

Windy smiled as she sat beside her mother, who was permanently affected by the chaos of the Entropy, giving her a hug bigger than herself. Windy didn't know her real parents, but Rose was all she could ask for.

"So, Mother." Windy sheepishly rubbed her neck. "There's a lot I need to tell you. Too much, in fact." Windy's voice was tinged with insecurity as she recalled her journey thus far, starting with her mother and ending with her mother. She didn't know all of the answers yet. She still had so many racing unsolved in her mind, even though their biggest threat was destroyed.

What are the Splinters?

Why are they so hostile?

Is there more to this Entropy I, or anyone, doesn't know about?

Though the Community had returned to its former beauty and grace, there was one small detail Windy failed to notice when she entered her home. The ceramic pot outside her home was corrupted of a grayish-blue fog; its flowers wilted, but their color was replaced by dark hues of green, blue, red, and purple, bled together infectiously.

It's not over yet...

 With a passion for helping others, **Dakota Kyle** is a new self-publisher in Richmond, Texas. She began writing at the age of thirteen as a coping mechanism against her father's passing from cancer. She is now an Honors College freshman at Houston Christian University, enrolled in a BFA Creative Writing program. She lives with her three cats and horse, runs a small business (DK3DCustoms), and is a competing barrel racer throughout Texas with a WPRA permit.

.